ALSO BY GERALD R. TONER

Holly Day's Café and Other Christmas Stories (1996)

Whittlesworth Comes to Christmas (1992)

Lipstick Like Lindsay's and Other Christmas Stories (1991)

THE CHRISTMAS TURKEYS

and Other Misadventures of the Season

GERALD R. TONER

BUTLER BOOKS
LOUISVILLE

ISBN 978-1-935497-27-1

Printed in Canada

Book design by Eric Butler
Cover design by Scott Stortz

Published by:

Butler Books
P.O. Box 7311
Louisville, KY 40207
(502) 897–9393
Fax (502) 897–9797
www.butlerbooks.com

TABLE OF CONTENTS

AUTHOR'S NOTE

Could nearly twenty-five years have passed since my first Christmas story was accepted for publication in *The Saturday Evening Post*? It could, indeed. Time does compress as we age and those years have whizzed by all too quickly.

My children have advanced from play lipstick and companions on road trips in the snow to young adults traveling and, at times, taking up residence in the most astounding corners of the globe. It is the modern parent's blessing and curse. All I can say is that if they have become citizens of the world, the world is a better place because of it. My wife, astoundingly, has steadily grown younger, excited about new hobbies, artistic expression and satisfying business forays. We have been fortunate to budget the time and resources to follow where often our children have led. I was never—as some postulated twenty years ago—ready or even desirous of going part-time on my professional calling as a civil trial lawyer. Neither did I stop writing.

While the law has fulfilled my professional yearning

since childhood, writing has provided an outlet for a guy of very limited artistic acumen. Writing has also provided both blessings and frustrations. Fortunately, the blessings have far exceeded the frustrations. To have been published in numerous national magazines without an agent or a literary résumé was miracle enough. To have followed with three cloth-bound books that saw national distribution and more than generous acclaim was a writer's dream. And finally, to have touched the lives of friends and strangers who have shared their kind words and their personal stories in letters, calls, exchanges on elevators and e-mails has assured me through the years that quality trumps quantity in most aspects of life.

The frustrations are those of anyone who writes. Several of the stories have been optioned for film only to flounder in the mystical industry that is Hollywood. Pelican Publishing—bless them for giving me a chance—refused to "pay to play" with chain stores who had purchased substantial quantities of each book at pre-season trade fairs, only to bury them away from the Christmas table because display to the public on front tables required additional funds. These are familiar refrains for any author. Yet these are minor complaints compared to the remarkable feat of being published and receiving appreciative input from readers around the country.

As the years passed and more stories flowed from the events of the Christmas season, I was prompted to re-evaluate the format and presentation of another collection. I wanted to clarify that these were never "children's stories" in the truest sense. (Would that I had such talent!) They were tales which addressed the peculiar and very special emotions that arise from the Christmas season, intended for family members from youth to seniors and all in between. So it seemed logical to present this collection in a format that would not confuse purchasers, while at the same time adding a little more adornment than a traditional, short story collection.

I went in search of an artist who would capture the flavor of the stories without presenting them as an illustrated children's volume. After numerous inquiries I was delighted to discover a talented young woman named Pascalle Ballard, referred by an old and dear friend, Beverly Bromley. Pascalle set about to create a black and white illustration for each of the stories that would be both whimsical and evocative. Her work truly sets the book apart and skillfully frames each story for the reader.

Writing is a satisfying, but laborious task; requiring (at least in my case) innumerable drafts to even come close to getting it "right." And "right" to the author may be "wrong" to the reader. I can only hope that this volume of "misadventures of the season" strikes a familiar and satisfying note to many of you. These are stories of and about our times, but with an author's prerogative, I have tempered the tough with the soft, the sour with the sweet. There are no grand and explosive miracles. There are some quiet epiphanies, often hard to explain as particularly special in their aftermath. Most of all, I hope readers will find a touchstone with their own seasonal misadventures and a familiarity with the conflicts of the characters.

CRIMES OF CHRISTMAS

When her parents named her Jane, their last name being Dough, they exhibited a rare burst of wit. Since Jane didn't share their humor, realizing as she did that their whimsy was at her expense, when she graduated from college and accepted the job at the law school, she changed her last name to Dougherty. So at moments like this, although there had been no moments precisely like this in her vanilla life, Jane was almost gleeful to give her now legal name, Jane Elizabeth Dougherty, to the authorities. This moment was unique because she sensed that she might be inching towards incarceration, and that was a totally new experience for Jane.

She had often wondered what the dingy, basement headquarters of the campus police would be like. Now she knew. Squeezed behind a vintage, World War II issue conference desk, dusky green and rimmed by a dull, brown brass beading, Jane sat upright in an equally drab folding chair. She knew she was under suspicion. And well she should be, since she was guilty.

Chief of Campus Police James Shue IV, with whom Jane had often shared communion over his "joke" name, had excused himself to take a phone call in the other room. What had been promised to take "just a moment" had turned into several. That gave Jane time to look around, to catalogue her surroundings, to organize its dimensions in her mind, and to create little, imaginary computer windows, one layered within the next, of the steps that would lead to her final arrest and conviction. Time was a commodity of which Jane was abundantly endowed. Time came with her station as the law school's head librarian and her status as a single woman. And too much time was one of the reasons that had led to her sorrowful, late life introduction to crime.

Even for a good-sized, but modestly endowed, state university, the offices of the campus police were spare. And the interview room into which she had been ushered was downright Spartan. Beige walls were adorned only by a few certificates verifying that Chief Shue was recognized by the state as a law enforcement officer. Brown blinds, stained by time, hung down from the single, rectangular window near the ceiling. Light, such as it was, crept in from a window well. The room had one door, one desk, two chairs. There were no lamps. Fluorescent tubes, fixed within an old metal grid, were centered within a checkerboard of yellowing, pressed-board, ceiling tiles. Not very high-tech, to say the least.

Jane leaned back as far as she could in her creaking, metal folding chair. Her long, spindly legs slid forward and her too knobby knees hit the table's leg. She extended her lean arms forward, using her thin fingers to maneuver her legs free. If only she had taken the piano lessons urged on her by her mother some thirty-five years before. Then her elongated frame, her less than modest bosom, high cheeks and prominent chin would have defined her as exquisite, elegant or even exotic diva of the keyboard, beautiful and mysterious. Since she played no instrument, other than the computer keyboard, she was nicknamed "Slim" by her colleagues, male and female alike.

The room's only other furnishing was a wall clock, which in the silence created by Chief Shue's departure, clicked away the seconds in its steady, quartz cadence, resounding almost as noticeably as pealing, Christmas bells. Ah yes, she thought, Christmas. Christmas and too much time. The two elements that had led her down this path and ultimately to this basement.

Actually her life of crime began at Thanksgiving. The Thanksgiving rush is not nearly as dramatic nor ostentatious nor crass as that surrounding Christmas, but it is there, just the same. People hurrying to bring closure to projects at work, desperate to say "that's done" about almost anything. Professors hurrying to prepare final lectures, law students hastening to catch up on casebook outlines, staff frazzled over the entire process. No one with enough time, let alone extra time. No time to take stock, to do something extra, to make some special effort. Jane, on the other hand, had plenty of time. And that reality is what started her thinking.

Jane knew that she possessed a talent never fully appreciated. As far back as grade school, Jane was imbued with the art of mimicry. She could copy a fairly complex watercolor, or even oil painting, before her peers were mastering horses and flowers and skies and trees. Even better, she could study another student's handwriting and with a stroke or two for practice, make it her own. Of course, the problem was that it wasn't her own.

So through the years she had done well in school, but never excelled. She could organize and catalogue and place into progression images, thoughts, words and collections of almost anything. But somehow, though it seemed to build inside of her like single drops of water behind a massive dam, originality continued to collect and yet never be released. Until this year.

It all started with a box of Christmas cards. Fifty to be precise. Jane purchased them the year before at a quarter of their original price. Beautiful, gold-pressed, Christmas cards featuring a shining star and a collection of exquisitely rendered men, women and children from around the world. Black and white, western and eastern, all reaching out to the star for warmth and light. The cards bore the simple statement: "One Light, one world." The weekend following Thanksgiving, after her Dough parents had repacked and returned to their second home in South Carolina, Jane sat down, as she did every year, to carefully pen her Christmas messages to friends and family. At the end of the morning she had exhausted her list, dispensed with care and thoughtfulness, from Joe Abbott to Linda

Yost. She had fifteen cards remaining and, as always, time to write many more.

Her excess inventory bothered her all day Sunday. Waste always bothered Jane. Yet the list was completed and Jane was a thorough and precise archivist, not given to either adding names or discarding cards. That Monday, watching Professor Donald Hall breeze through the library turnstyle, in a rush as always, eyes down, his mind fixed on some point moments or even hours in the future, a flash of fancy hit her. Hall needed more time. From observation and a keen mind for history, Jane knew that Hall had a family, a wife and two grown children living out-of-state. She knew their names from his online curriculum vitae, she knew their addresses, and she knew that he seldom spoke of wife or children. And she knew from brief snatches of conversation which he permitted when coming by her office to pick up a new publication or a volume obtained from another library that he yearned for them in a sort of hopeless limbo. Somehow, allowing his profession to possess him, he had simply grown estranged from their lives. Lack of words and expressions of love and simple time together had created a solid prison wall of separation between them.

Jane stared into the suffused, fluorescent lighting overhead and sighed. She could hear Chief Shue trying to end his conversation in the adjoining room. And she thought back to Professor Hall and the beginning of her Christmas crimes.

That Monday evening after Thanksgiving she composed three cards, carefully drafting her text, one to Hall's son and one to his daughter, and finally one to his wife. Each one bore a slightly different perspective, Jane fusing her mind into Hall's, enriching her message with the emotions she imagined he possessed somewhere deeply hidden within. In each she reiterated that he loved them, that he now realized he had allowed the years to dribble by without telling them, that he had been unwise in his expenditure of time, that he had been observant of his own needs and the needs of his students and colleagues at the expense of those whom he loved the most. And he asked their forgiveness. He also requested their confidence—secrecy in his message to them—and that they would simply accept his words and remember them in their hearts without revelation to another soul, even him. Jane's dam was leaking, even though she didn't recognize it at the time.

And though the words and expressions and handwriting were meant to be Professor Hall's, Jane deceived herself when she wrote them, thinking the emotions fueling them were solely his. The author is never completely divorced from her creation. Jane was a keen observer, a master forger, a Christmas chameleon of sorts, but in taking on another persona, she was revealing something of herself.

She held the cards for several days. Jane understood perfectly well the term "officious inter-meddler" and that it was not a phrase of endearment in the law. Though a part of her said "don't, his life isn't yours, you have no true perception of his conflicts, of the personal dynamics that make things work or not work in his family," there was the other side of Jane—the secret, edgy, gleeful side—that thrilled at the risk of finally dabbling in the forbidden. So she wrote them, sealed them, addressed them, and under the cover of darkness as she left the library one night, mailed them.

Jane noted the gray of dark becoming the dimness of dusk.

Shue was still talking on the phone. The room's only voice was the steady heartbeat of the quartz clock. As she thought back on it, there was a hiccup in time when she could have let it go at that. For a brief respite her first foray into crime satisfied her. In fact, she retreated, temporarily resolved that her nefarious transactions were at an end. And then came Peter.

Peter, the bookish third year student whom she had befriended two years before. Peter, with a mop of blond hair and a florid complexion born of carrying around an extra fifty pounds far too early in life. Peter, the old soul, who always dressed like a lawyer, carried an old accordion-style lawyer's briefcase and seemed possessed of some past, prior life as a lawyer. Peter, who hadn't quite made it on the Journal, had placed second alternate on the International Moot Court team and, she was certain, would make a superb lawyer in his current incarnation. In her nearly twenty years of watching students come and go, she knew the ones whose cloth was cut for the law. Peter was one of them. But he lacked some nexus, some small, last collision between his effort to gain employment and an employer's recognition of his talents. Every new hire wasn't a law journal or moot court or Order of the Coif type. Obviously, some students had to be in the bottom half of the class and most of those found jobs shortly after graduation. Peter's résumé was far more impressive. He was in the top quarter of his class. She knew because he had asked her to review his résumé in its first, handwritten draft, which was how she came to know so well Peter's almost too precise script, almost computer like repetition of "t's" and "s's" and various other letters that made one's handwriting distinctive.

Jane knew that another little communiqué with the hiring partner couldn't hurt. So she did what she had time to do and what Peter was too insecure to do. She wrote each of the hiring partners at each of the firms where Peter had been granted an "in" firm interview. Like everyone else, Peter knew that Jane had time to chat. So, in driblets of conversation now and then, after class and sometimes on the way to another interview, Peter confided his hopes and fears to Jane. And like nuts to a squirrel, Jane gathered up information and stashed it away for an appropriate use.

Dear Mr. ______:

Thank you for the opportunity to meet the many lawyers at ______ and to see your offices first-hand. I have spent my entire life preparing to be a lawyer. I feel that my education in the law has, at best, just begun. I would like to continue it with you. I can not pretend that I will give you as much as I will receive in return. But over the years, I can assure you that I will give you everything I have. And I would be proud to serve you and your clients and the law in a manner that would reflect well on my profession, my employer and myself. If I can do anything further to aid in your decision that I would be worthy of your employment, please call me. Again, it was a pleasure getting to know you and your firm and I hope our relationship has just begun.

Sincerely,
Peter McCain

And so, within the week that Professor Hall's Christmas cards were sent on their way, Jane finished Peter's cards and carefully deposited them in the same slot at the campus post office. The slightly guilty thrill she had felt one week before when she half resolved never, ever to do such an illegal and unsolicited act again—was now part of her dim past.

Jane Dougherty was hooked. Like the high from some terribly illicit drug, her emotions soared up and then roller-coastered down. And she needed more. Though she fully realized that she may or may not be setting events into motion that might help or hurt, bring joy or anger, much good or potential harm, Jane was convinced that doing nothing was unacceptable. She was also feeling a strangely delicious thrill that was both altruistic and selfish, selflessly generous and unabashedly narcissistic. And she couldn't help herself.

So she worked at the selection process with even more zeal, giving up evening hours reading old legal thrillers by Erle

Stanley Gardner and perched before the television watching *Law and Order* or *CSI* in their various configurations. On many pre-Christmas nights she consumed some of her seemingly endless, extra hours practically stalking her new victims. And the task, when she truly rolled up her sleeves and attacked it, was potentially endless. So many people failing so miserably—at least from Jane's perspective—in their communications and transactions with their fellow men and women. Mankind was a bottomless gold mine of missed opportunities and kind words not spoken.

The head of the university library systems was a prime example. Chuck Flood was only a year or two Jane's senior, widowed and hopelessly in love with Professor Megan England, who was now in her tenth year in the Department of English. Anyone with eyes could see he was crazy about her. The heads of the various university libraries would meet from nine a.m. to eleven a.m. every other Monday morning throughout the year. Flood would preside, allowing absolutely no interruptions, but always excusing himself when Professor England frequently appeared to spend Monday mornings in her dedicated carrel. Jane could almost predict the moment of her arrival and forecast Flood's excuse for taking a break. To anyone half observant—and Jane was far more than that—it was clear that he had a crush on her. Yet he was too shy to close the deal.

As Jane sat waiting for her Javert to get off the phone, her hands slid down to her hips in a "tough girl" pose. As if in one of the early fifties film noir series that she had religiously attended on Wednesday nights the year before, she could practically picture herself tapping down the end of a Lucky Strike and talking out of the corner of her mouth as she sucked in a white puff of smoke, "Yeah, I know 'shy' when I see 'shy,' Chief Shue. I lived most of my life 'shy.' But that was then and this is now, handsome." Of course, Jane only smoked when she drank too much which was almost never at all, but the fantasy was real. She was, after all, a keeper of books and recordings, and even law books had an element of fantasy about them.

Dear Megan:

As Christmas nears, I can't help but think of you—and the joy you bring to all around you. I am not the least of those. And while I may seem, at times, to be just a little formal and much too much the proper librarian, I want you to know how much you are appreciated. I confess that I am more than a little shy. And while I can't imagine that a beautiful and intelligent woman like yourself would find interest in dinner or even coffee or drinks with someone like me, I would be thrilled at the opportunity. If you would be interested, and you wouldn't mind initiating a word or two to let me know by suggesting a time you might be free and a place you might like to go, I think I could overcome my natural shyness and take things from there. If not, I'll take no offense, and simply close by wishing you a very, Merry Christmas.

Yours,
Chuck Flood

Jane struggled over this one. The challenge was greater, the stakes higher. She needed the card to sound precisely like Chuck Flood and she more than understood the restraint he would exercise in trying to express his attraction for her. He also needed to cover himself if Professor England was otherwise attached to someone significant. And Jane needed to prompt Professor England to break the ice. Moreover, Jane knew that this time she was playing cupid, interfering in affairs of the heart. While she knew he clearly had the desire, and obviously lacked the nerve, she was almost more afraid that Megan England would actually follow through than that she wouldn't. If she made the entry and he fumbled, Jane stood to do more harm than good. Yet it didn't stop her. She forged ahead, hoping for the best, almost giddy at the prospect that she would succeed.

Her criminal life was moving briskly forward and though she was prodigiously careful and methodical, she also realized that sooner or later her crimes would have consequences. She hoped, of course, the consequences would be for the good and she likewise hoped, whether consequences were good or bad, she wouldn't get caught.

Now, two weeks before Christmas, Jane's list was growing.

Her assistant had a grandmother in a nursing home. They had words some years before over a hairstyle or a piercing or a tattoo or all of the above and were now locked into a foolish silence. A card to her grandmother with the solicitation of forgiveness seemed more than appropriate. The head night custodian had a son in the army and while he worried about him all the time, he seemed at a loss for any means to tell his son what he felt. The challenge was in obtaining the custodian's handwriting, but Jane cleverly requested him to write out on a lined list his requested plan for cleaning the east, west and central carrels, creating the device that she would approach the students in each wing and request their cooperation in straightening up in advance. The note she ended up composing was simply stated in five-to-ten word sentences. He was proud of his son. He loved him. He knew he was acting out of love for country. He knew he was a good soldier. Simple things that he had shared with Jane during the evenings when she worked late.

Jane slowly brought her hands away from her hips and placed them palm down on the table in front of her. Chief Shue's phone call was ending and she could hear his footsteps approaching. James Shue was her undoing, her fatal error. The door knob turned.

Why couldn't she have left well enough alone? The others were amateurs. They would never trace their Christmas cards to her. They would never connect the dots with their fellow victims, never exchange bits and pieces of evidence until those pieces of the puzzle were transformed into a clearly-drawn jigsaw picture. Shue was a professional. Crime and solving crimes were his stock in trade. She should have never involved herself in his life.

Yet he was most irresistible. He was her age, divorced, driven, dedicated, handsome and masculine without the swagger and crass demeanor of a macho cop. He was

Chief of the University Police and as his title would imply, he was an officer of the law only in an academic setting, rather than in the mean streets of a major city. Like her, he was orderly, kept good records, possessed keen powers of observation and, while detached from much of what was going on around him, seemed quietly to yearn for more. And he had a need.

During his various visits to review security procedures and precautions addressed primarily to female law students coming and going from the library during the evening, while he was discussing muggings and thefts and even burglaries of valuable computers and other property, Chief Shue had revealed himself to Jane. His father, it turned out, had been a detective on the Chicago police force, a confidante of the first Mayor Richard Daley and a man who dealt only with felonious crimes. He intended for his son—James IV—to go to law school and become a public prosecutor. James would complete the steps that had always frustrated his father. He would put the criminals behind bars.

It didn't work out. James was bright enough. He did just fine in college. But a never fully diagnosed dyslexia had made the LSAT an insurmountable hurdle and James had chosen instead to follow the path of law enforcement. That was his father's first, great disappointment. The second was James's choice of employers. He could have easily returned to Chicago or Indianapolis or any good-sized, mid-western city to work on their police force. That would have been honorable in his father's estimation. Instead, he chose the life of a campus cop, chasing down petty thieves and the occasional rapist, executing plans to thwart mass murderers and terrorists, all the while knowing that if a big case ever arose, the state police or FBI would be called to the scene immediately.

Into this man's history Jane had intruded. Her card from him was to his father. Simply stated, as straightforward as James presented to her, his message was one of Christmas mediation.

> Dad, far too much time has passed since last we wrote. Life here is good. Not exciting, nor on the edge, nor liable to make the news on CNN. But it is stimulating and good. I am making a difference. Most of all I simply wanted you to know how much of a difference you have made. I don't mean to the windy city (Jane had heard him refer to Chicago by its well-known nickname), but to me, your son. I've always wanted to follow in your footsteps, to live by a code of behavior that puts means above ends, and holds right over might. And while your plans for me may not have conformed in all ways to the path I have taken, I believe that the way in which I have pursued my life has always been practiced by the principles you taught. I hope we'll have time together this Christmas. And while I won't suggest it again, I'll wait for your call. If I hear from you, I'l1 make the time work out.
>
> Love and Merry Christmas,
> James

Jane knew it was consistent with James's feelings. He had expressed them in bits and pieces during their late night visits at the reference desk or when he had escorted her to her car three blocks from the library. But she also knew that the rift between father and son was deep. She wasn't sure if James would have ever swallowed his pride, and the words exchanged in a heated past. James was stubborn, as was his father. And for one to write or call the other was a stretch. Now, on reflection, in the basement interview room of the university police, she realized it was probably too much of a stretch.

"I'm sorry for the interruption." Chief Shue entered the cramped confines of the conference room and rested his lean frame against the wall facing Jane.

"No problem," Jane smiled, "I've got lots of time."

"Yes," Shue paused, "I know."

Jane smiled again, though her hands and feet were chilling over as her blood rushed to her face. She would wait for his accusation before making any formal confessions.

"So," he continued, "you're probably wondering why I asked you to come over this afternoon."

"A little. Yes."

"Well, I've come across a little—well—situation here on campus."

"Situation?"

"Yes, well it seems there have been some unusual," he paused to choose the correct word, "communications being exchanged."

"How so?" she affected nonchalance, even as the chill in

her extremities traveled across her shoulders.

"I thought you might be able to help me out, Jane. Could you?"

"I'm not sure, until you tell me more."

"For a straightforward, no-nonsense librarian—and a law librarian at that—you're making me work at this pretty hard."

"Work at what, James?"

Chief Shue looked down at his spit-polished shoes, then slipped his thumbs into his standard issue, patent leather gun belt. "Well, it would seem that someone has been forging Christmas cards, of all things. They've been deposited at the campus post office and sent to various folks around the world."

"How did you determine that?" She tried to smile but her attempt came off as a twitch.

"Well, it wasn't so hard really. Professor Hall approached me a week or so ago. At first he was just curious whether there had been any reports of unusual postings of Christmas cards. I told him no. He would have left it at that, but I delved a little further. That's my business, you know. I told him that as long as he had brought it up, he at least owed me an explanation."

"And did he explain?" If she was about to be arrested, Jane wanted first to determine the effect of her crimes.

"He did. Seems he got letters a few days apart from his son and daughter out-of-town. You probably didn't know that—that he has children living out-of-town."

"Actually, he may have mentioned it to me in passing."

"Well, anyway, then one morning his wife said something to him. She had gotten a card from him as well. I forgot to mention that Christmas cards were what his children's letters were about as well."

"Well, what did they say?" Again, Jane wanted to know if her crime had resulted in harm or healing.

"Can't you imagine?"

"Well, no, I can't. Say, James, you're being awfully coy," Jane felt her underarms going tactlessly clammy with perspiration.

"I suppose I am. Then there was your third-year student friend, Peter McCain."

"Nice young man."

"Oh, yes. Peter talks to me sometimes just as he does you."

"And?"

"Seems Peter received two job offers—both from senior partners in firms downtown, both thanking him for his Christmas cards. Cards Peter told me he never sent. Almost like the cards Professor Hall's family received."

"I'm so happy for Peter." For the first time since sitting down, Jane felt joy run through her like a soothing drug. Whatever happened to her next would matter far less. "He deserves some choices in life."

"And yet I wonder, Jane, whether his life required tweaking from an inter-meddler? Whether that was even right—let alone good for Peter in the long run." Chief James Shue IV had used the very word that had haunted Jane two weeks before.

"Sometimes a little tweak from an outside source is a good thing."

"I'll bet you do believe that, Jane." Chief Shue straightened up. "So I became curious. And my curiosity prompted me to review security videos from the past few weeks." Jane sat upright. "You know, a person can hardly breathe these days without being caught on film."

"And what did you catch on video, Chief Shue?"

Chief Shue smiled. "I caught you, of course. Right down to the card you sent this past week. The one where you forged my handwriting and signature."

Jane's lips went dry. She licked them, but her tongue was just as arid. Her eyes fell briefly to the table, then rose and leveled on Chief Shue.

"The mails are supposed to be slow at Christmas."

"Guess you got lucky, Jane. Your cards all got through."

"I guess so," Jane's confession was so oblique, so lacking in the drama she had foreseen that it disappointed more than shocked her.

"Innocent enough—interfering in the lives of others. Of course, we hear more about it these days in connection with the internet. Phony chat rooms and 'my space' and all that. It's a federal crime you know. Or, at least, you should know, given that you're a law librarian."

"I suppose you're right, James. But I'm not sorry. Not sorry one bit," she started tearing up. "Day after day, night after night, I watch people who don't have the time or won't take the time or don't have that little ounce of whatever is needed to do the right thing. And suddenly I realized that I had the time . . . "

"And you could help decide their fate for them?"

"I was just doing what I knew they wanted to do . . . but couldn't or wouldn't do."

"Playing God?"

"No. No, I didn't mean to do that."

Chief Shue finally pulled up another, dented folding chair and sat down across from Jane.

"There were probably more, weren't there? Others whose cards I saw you dropping into the mail?"

Jane nodded. She didn't have many tears. She was too old and too dry for too many tears. But she brushed away the few that she had.

"Since you've thrust yourself into my life as well, you know that I've always tried to emulate my father. I've always wondered in difficult situations what he would do."

"Yes."

"And I assumed, when I asked you to come over here this afternoon, that if it were my father solving this crime, he would question his suspect, tease them until he had them, spring his trap, and effect a confession. Charges, indictment, prosecution and sentencing would all be a snap from there."

"So," Jane took a deep breath, "let's get on with it. I suppose I should call a lawyer. At least I know a few."

"Well," Chief Shue's gaze was unblinking, "I suppose you could call a lawyer, though I really don't mean to attempt anything criminal or illegal—at least that's not my intent."

"Now, I don't understand."

"When I called you this afternoon I was really concerned about being consistent, about not doing something my father wouldn't do. I've done some things he wouldn't do as you well know, but not many. But I was ready to do what I had planned, consistent or not with his way of doing things."

"I'm afraid you're losing me, James. Could I just call a lawyer and get this over with?"

"Then my father called. That was him on the phone out there."

Jane sighed. "He got the card?"

"Oh he got it. He asked who wrote it."

"Oh . . . "

"Said that I couldn't possibly put all of that down in so few words—and so eloquently stated. He wondered if I had hired a ghost writer, or a girlfriend." Shue shook his head. "So I told him about your crimes. And how I found out about them. And how you were in the next room. And you know, the really eerie thing was that he was thinking the same thing as me."

"Which was?"

"That it was so ironic—it being Christmas and all—that the usual Christmas story is about some Scrooge who is held to account for failing to do good things during his life. And here you were, needing to be held to account under the law for trying to do good things during your life. Life is weird."

"But what I did was wrong. It was a crime."

"Oh yes, it was a crime. But my father and I agreed it wasn't wrong. And that's what surprised me. Because I knew that it wasn't wrong even before he called. And when he called—which was a damned big surprise, considering that we've hardly spoken in five years or more—I never figured he would agree with me on that. But he did. Funny," Chief Shue tweaked his nose, some image fleetingly interrupting his train of thought, "that he thought I should deprive you of your primary weapon."

"Weapon?"

"Too much time. We agreed that the punishment should fit the crime. That disarming the criminal might be far more effective than indicting them. So—since you obviously have too much time—I was wondering if I could rob you of some of it. And under those circumstances, if you think you might need a lawyer before you answer—then please feel free. But my deal is this—my offer for you to cop a plea if you will—could you join me for dinner?"

Jane was not prepared for this, nor was she prepared for what followed. Even in crime Jane was neat and orderly, logical and studied. James Shue's message was none of the above.

"You want to go out to dinner with me?" she asked.

"Oh, I've thought about it many times. But to tell you the truth—and I guess this is the afternoon for truth-telling Jane—I didn't know what we'd talk about. I mean, you're a beautiful woman, Jane. I guess you're about the prettiest woman on this campus. And there are a few. But pretty's not everything. I mean, there's got to be some spark there too. And Lord, I feel presumptuous, because I'm neither pretty nor the sparkiest guy on campus. But until this last day or two, you were hiding that spark pretty well. But now—well—you're a pretty hot handful if you know what I mean. And I wouldn't blame you if you turned me down cold."

"But what I did *was* a crime. And what if I say 'no' to your invitation?"

"Well, I guess we all commit crimes every day, Jane. And I would appreciate it if you retired your Christmas cards while you're ahead. But you've done so much good—for Hall, for Peter, for whomever else you messed with, and for me—that I'm not going to be the heel that turns you in. I mean, you've got to see the forest for the trees as they say, and Dad and I agree there are times when you simply throw your evidence into the old circular file. As for dinner, I was just being cute about the plea bargain stuff. I mean, I didn't mean to harass you or anything. You're free to get up and walk out and that will be it. I'll wish you a Merry Christmas—just no more cards!"

Jane laughed, truly laughed from deep down in her gut for the first time—the thought danced inside of her brain—since she had changed her name to Dougherty. "You are a tough, brilliant, very pretty detective, Chief Shue. And I would be more than pleased to accept your kind invitation for dinner." Her laughter melted into a smile matching his own. And in the brief flash of time that it took Jane, very un-Scrooge like, to look into the future of a Christmas yet to come, she foresaw laughing more and cataloguing less. And that, she thought, made her brief life of crime very worthwhile indeed.

THE CHRISTMAS TURKEYS

Larry and I were best friends—had been since college. Larry's family had a little money; mine had a little less. Larry was the better scholar; I was the slightly better athlete. Larry was tall and slim, like an angular professor; I wear the expanding girth of a nose guard. After college we went to law school, roomed with each other, married girls who were also best friends and associated with different law firms in the same city. Most importantly, we joined the *same* church. We could have joined different churches. Larry grew up Episcopalian and I grew up kind of Baptist. Either would have served the purpose of prayer, but the Presbyterian Church provided another outlet entirely.

You see, besides being best friends, we did our best to be good husbands and fathers—especially the father part. And the more we fathered and husbanded the less we saw of each other. That's where the good works of the Presbyterian Church came into play. Every year we were the first to volunteer for the annual Christmas turkey and food stuffs giveaway. We had only two ironclad requirements. First, we got the Germantown neighborhood and second, we got it together. Now I hate to disappoint anyone reading this epic who is expecting something uplifting at this point, but the reason was a practical one. Germantown had more bars than any of the other eligible giveaway neighborhoods and visiting one or two of these local establishments would be no fun whatsoever if Larry and I couldn't do it together. The Reverend Frederick Alexander Chastain knew this, of course, and tried in various ways to curtail our excursions into Christian fellowship.

Larry had somehow gotten elected to a lengthy term on the Session of the church, and one of his most difficult tasks each year was to get around Reverend Chastain's best efforts to separate us. This was particularly difficult because the Germantown neighborhood was a hotly contested piece of real estate both in and out of the church. Outside the church there were the Maple Street Baptists. Reverend Chastain had attempted to forge a social caring alliance with the Baptists over the turkey baskets. After one year, the alliance had disintegrated. We favored Butterball, the Baptist's Tyson; some of our ladies thought Mandarin oranges would be a nice touch, which didn't square with the Baptist ladies who were in favor of less frilly items like canned green beans and corn. And so on. So they took to dividing up the neighborhoods like two cold war powers. Larry's job—and he did it admirably—was to make sure that, at any cost, Germantown remained safe and secure in the Presbyterian camp.

Inside the church, Reverend Chastain was always trying to separate us on turkey basket night. We knew this because the church secretary, Esther Mobley, was our mole. Reverend Chastain never suspected. He would give the assignment list to Esther, careful to make sure that Larry and I were paired with someone really dull. Then Larry would drop by and see Esther, bring her a box of candies and maybe a little fall flower arrangement, and presto chango—we were back together again.

"Did you get the neighborhood?" I asked. Larry was getting out of his car and I, mine, as we walked towards the church.

Larry winked. I grinned. The fix was in. "It was tougher this year," Larry added. "Fred's suspicious. I think he's on to us."

"How did he find out?" My voice grew hush as we stopped for a second on the front steps of the church.

"I think he saw Esther's flower arrangement the other afternoon and then he caught the two of us laughing right before a Session meeting."

"Well, that was dumb," I scolded, "because the first thing you learn as a Presbyterian is that committee meetings of any sort are very serious and you never laugh going into them!"

"Okay. Okay. But I think it's still a go."

"Well, we'll see." Then I winked, as he had moments earlier, so Larry would know I was just kidding about any doubt concerning his ability to rig the turkey giveaway.

Inside the Fellowship Hall, everything was strictly business. Like all Presbyterian events, the Christmas Turkey Giveaway was meant to be a serious and socially redeeming event, open to all in need and completely non-denominational. Details had been reviewed and revised a dozen times in committees and sub-committees. Each pairing of turkey givers was intended to constitute a sub-committee of the sub-committee.

"Now here are the lists." Fred Chastain stood among the small conclave of volunteers. "Jim and Betty, Bill and Sally, Ann and Stewart . . . " he paused, "Larry and Barry . . . "

Larry nudged me as if the pairing came as a great and unexpected surprise. I nudged him back and shrugged my shoulders. We chuckled and glanced around at the other couplings. I reached out to accept the list of names and addresses. Reverend Chastain seemed to hold onto our list for an extra moment or two as he said very pointedly: " . . . and above all, please remember that this is a Hopeful Presbyterian Church event. We are sharing what belongs to all of us by God's grace . . . we are representatives of Hopeful." His eyes bore a hole right into me. "Not Santa Claus and his Helper."

We made our exit before Reverend Chastain could figure out a way to undo Esther's deception and rescind our assignment.

"I think this is it for the Giveaway," Larry groused, as he packed the last of twenty-five turkey baskets into the back of my van. "After this year, caput! I know it."

"You mean the whole show or just us?" I brought the back door down with a muted thud.

"Both." Larry climbed into the passenger's seat. "The Giveaway barely passed Session this go-around. About a third of the members think its patronizing and almost as many think it infringes on the receiving families' rights to choose a vegetarian lifestyle. If those two factions get their act together, the turkey deal's off."

"They could always trade the turkeys for beer and cigarettes," I chortled. I would never say that in public.

"Well, you're not far off . . . I think its going to be a straight-out check for twenty-five bucks next year . . . mailed the week before Christmas . . . spend it as you like!"

"No," I exclaimed, though my outrage was mostly selfish.

"I wouldn't kid you," Larry flipped on his flashlight to examine the addresses. I made the first turn into the neighborhood. Neither sectarian squabbles nor politically correct parishioners would dissuade Larry and me from our appointed rounds. The sooner we distributed the birds, the sooner we hit the local pubs.

"What's the first address?" I asked, eagle eyes trained on traffic lights and street signs.

"One Hundred Five Swan Street." Larry squinted in the darkness, holding the list closer to his increasingly myopic eyes.

"Okay, turning left on Swan . . . " I completed the turn, "hey, will you look at that!"

I slowed reverentially at the sight of a little white-and-green-trimmed shotgun-style house, outlined in white mini-lights. One particular cluster hung like icicles over the front door.

"They went to a lot of trouble to make it look like that!" Larry exclaimed.

I seconded the compliment and pulled to a stop by the curb next to the house. "That doesn't happen to be one hundred and five?" I asked with an expectant grin.

Larry wiped the moisture from his breath away from the passenger's window and peered right and left for a number. "Nope," he finally saw it, "this is one hundred and one. Too bad, we could've told 'em their place looked nice."

"Oh well."

We reaffirmed our feelings for bright, cheery one hundred and one even as I pulled the van up a few feet to one hundred and five. I turned off the engine, reached around and grabbed a turkey basket. Larry slipped from the passenger side of the van and ambled to the front steps of one hundred and five while I caught up with him.

Larry knocked on the door and we waited in silence. Larry looked at me and I shrugged. We knocked again. Somewhere inside we could hear a cough, then a woman's voice.

"That you, Larry?"

Larry's mouth dropped and he turned to me as if he'd been caught in a scene from a soap opera. "I swear, Barry, I don't know anybody here!"

"Well someone behind that door knows you!" I smiled slyly. "Wait until Elaine hears about this."

"Larry? That you? Who's out there? I'm calling the cops."

"No . . . no . . . " Larry panicked, "it's me. I swear. Don't call the cops."

The door unlatched and opened a few inches. A woman in her thirties peered out the slit at Larry, then me.

"You aren't Larry. What do you want? I gotta gun . . . and it's cocked and aimed right at your . . . "

"Now listen, lady, my name is Larry. Maybe not your Larry. In fact, I know I'm not your Larry. But I'm Larry. And this is Barry. We're from Hopeful Presbyterian Church. We've got a turkey and some other food for you and your . . . " he glanced down at his list, " . . . your kids, Lucy and Bill."

"I don't care much for turkey." She opened the door and we caught a whiff of stale tobacco radiating from her half-opened bathrobe. "And the kids are down at Protective Services. Took 'em from me just like that!" Her face relaxed slightly. "But Larry likes turkey fine, so okay." She opened the door, grabbed the handle of the basket and pulled it from my hand. She slid it inside, yanked the door shut and left Larry and me on the dark front stoop.

"Well, Merry Christmas to you too, lady!" I addressed the paint chipped door.

"Okay," Larry said, "one down, twenty-four more to go. Next one's . . . ," he searched our list, " . . . in the next block."

So we went through the same process in the next block.

The door opened all the way this time. Things were looking up. The man's expression was chilly, the air rushing past him hot. Larry and my thoughts were identical: utilities must be included with the rent.

"Well, what is it?" the man in the T-shirt asked.

"We're looking for Juliet Johnson?" Larry searched his list for a man's name but found only Juliet. He turned to me with a "we goofed again" grin just as the man turned around.

"Juliet!" the man screamed towards the back of the house. "Two guys out here want something."

"Well, we don't exactly want anything," I laughed, trying to lighten the man up a little.

"I don't know what they're selling," the man continued, oblivious to my good cheer.

"We'd like to provide your family a little something to make the Christmas season . . . " I tried to get our standard greeting out and failed a second time.

"It's another turkey," the man yelled towards the back of the house. "You can come in," he stepped aside, "she's in the bedroom."

His tone softened slightly. Larry winked at me. We were really making progress now. We walked into the living room. One look around and our thoughts ran in tandem. No carpet but a 32" television. The couch was pock-marked with a potpourri of stains and burns but the VCR and stereo looked fairly new. There were no pictures on the walls but in every corner of the room a clutter of toys lay mangled together.

Juliet appeared. "Yeah?"

"I'm Larry. This is Barry." I nodded. "And we'd like to . . . "

"You from the church?" she cut Larry off in mid-sentence.

"Yes, we are. We would like you to have . . . "

"Okay, fine. But the kids are at their father's and T.J. here . . . you've met T.J.? No? Well, this here is T.J. and he already got a turkey from the Maple Street people this afternoon, but thanks, we'll freeze it or . . . "

"Now wait a minute," I interrupted this time. "If you got a turkey already, then maybe we can find someone else . . . "

"Now that's my turkey isn't it? Her voice took on an edge. "What do you think, T.J.?" T.J. was frowning again. "'Cause if its not, what the hell are you doing here? And if it is, then you better put it down, 'cause its mine."

Here was a street fighter the likes of which we were not about to cross. Larry quietly put the basket down on the floor and we both backed out the door smiling.

We were in the car before T.J. could add his own political commentary. I flipped the door lock switch, gunned the engine and tore out from the curb.

"Okay," I spoke first, staring straight ahead, "they're right."

"Who's right?"

"The anti-turkey, pro-cash in an envelope crowd. If folks want a carton of Marlboros and a cold six of PBR who are we to cram turkey down their throats?"

"Not so hasty," Larry fumbled with his flashlight. "Sooner or later we're going to hit a winner."

"Who says?"

"Its got to get better."

"What if we just saw 'better' and at the next place we get shot?"

"Are we agreed, at least, that this is no fun?"

"Agreed," I said.

"Might I suggest," Larry turned off the flashlight, "that we ponder the situation over a nice cold brewsky sitting in a nice warm bar—of which there is one on every corner."

I glanced around. He was right. "Excellent idea, old buddy. How about this fine establishment, right over there?" I pointed to a place across the street and half a block into Germantown. The Schnitzel Cafe.

"Fine with me, as long as we don't forget Rudolph's Bar a couple of blocks down."

"That's not a problem, Larry, my friend. Under the circumstances of our recent, narrow escape I believe we should sprinkle a few of our dollars in several establishments."

We sat with our coats undone, sipping from our bottles of regular Budweiser. The local patrons were glaring at us just enough to let us know that we were guests, not regulars. Larry sat for what seemed like a long time staring out the front window.

"What are you looking at?" I asked.

"The house across the street." Larry took a sip from the long neck bottle and finished his first beer. He motioned to the bartender for another. "It's a little like that one we saw a few blocks back—the one with all the lights—only better."

"Is it on the list?" I was nursing my first beer since I was the driver.

"I don't know, but I was just thinking, gee, I hope it is, 'cause I'll bet those folks would really appreciate a turkey basket."

Larry pulled the list out and held it up to the neon light of an old Oertel's '92 sign that hung by the mirror over the bar.

"Let's see," Larry was speaking to himself, "that would be . . . uh . . . two twenty something and we've got nothing on the list in the two twenties."

"You guys need some help?" One of the neighborhood steadies left his station at the bar and slid towards us.

"We were wondering about the place with the red and white Christmas lights across the street," I said.

"Yeah, we're delivering Christmas turkeys for some folks in the neighborhood. And we wondered where our next house was," Larry added.

If the regular suspected he was part of a needy neighborhood he didn't let on. His face was perfect poker.

"Well, the O'Laughlins live across the street. They've lived there since the neighborhood was half Irish. He's retired from the foundry down the way. 'Course it went bust in the eighties, but he's on social security." The regular motioned to the bartender and he joined us. "These guys are asking about the O'Laughlins."

"Yeah," the bartender chimed in, "they're good folks. You guys with the television station or something?"

"Well, not exactly," Larry fumbled, "we're with a church. It's sort of a tradition to help out some of the needier folks at Christmas."

"Well, the O'Laughlins deserve a break all right," the bartender avoided the word "needy."

"Gee, I mean, that's too bad," Larry empathized, "they're not on the list. Looks like our next stop is the Fowlers up in the two eighties."

"Jesus Christ!" the bartender exclaimed, "they're a worthless lot."

I looked down and shook my head. I knew what Larry was thinking. Larry took a sip from his fresh bottle. He didn't want to argue but he was suddenly pressed to defend the list he held crumpled in his hand.

"Well, I'm sure Reverend Chastain wouldn't have included the Fowlers unless . . . "

"Unless they conned whoever gave him the list," the regular seconded the bartender's disgust. "The Fowlers are pretty slick. And they know all the 'ins' and 'outs.'"

"Well, that seems a little harsh at Christmas." I determined not to let Larry take the full brunt by himself.

"A spade's a spade," the bartender grunted.

"Well, to each his own opinion." The last thing Larry wanted was a brawl over church business.

"Sorry, but it's true," the bartender reached under the bar and grabbed up two fresh bottles of Bud. "These are on the house."

I had been nursing my beer, but with the proprietor's generosity I could hardly refuse. Larry and I tapped our old bottles together and finished what little was left. We lifted the new longnecks and toasted the bartender.

"Maybe you're right—maybe not—but would you mind

taking a look at the rest of the names on the list?" Larry inquired.

The bartender got some reading glasses from his pocket and started scanning the list. The regular leaned over to see and they studied the list together. "The Williams . . . black family down the way . . . great folks, having a tough year. Let's see, the Prichetts. Straight from the hills. They're okay too. The Halls . . . " both the bartender and the regular started laughing and poking each other. " . . . they'd cheat you blind. Deadbeats, every one of them." He went on ticking off about half of the names on the list. The regular picked up on a few the bartender couldn't place and then they both looked at us with a "well, now you got our two cents worth, what are ya' going to do about it" look in their eyes.

Larry looked at me. By now the cold beer had begun to warm our insides and lighten our thinking. Larry didn't have to say a word. I knew exactly what the question was.

"I don't know," I began. "How can we decide who's needy or not, who's worthy and who's milking the system?"

"It was a lot easier just following the list," Larry added. "We didn't have to think!"

"But if we follow the list, we're going to give turkeys to some people who probably don't deserve them and leave out some folks who really need them."

Larry turned his shoulder away from the bartender. Being a man sensitive to subtle nuances, he went back to washing beer mugs. Larry lowered his voice. "Who the hell are *we* to decide?"

"Somebody's got to," I rejoined.

"Somebody already has! And that somebody's Reverend Chastain. He's no dummy you know! Maybe these sleazy types are in need of a little redemption. Maybe he's already figured that out. It's all part of the big picture which we don't understand."

"Now you're getting philosophical on me." I took a long sip of beer. "What about the O'Laughlins? They're not on the list!" I punctuated my thoughts with another gulp of Budweiser.

"Maybe they're on someone else's list."

"Not likely. You know we're the last church except Maple Street that gives out turkeys and baskets and stuff."

Larry held the list between the tips of his fingers as if it might explode. He eased it down gently on the bar and it stuck in a wet spot left by our bottles.

"Okay, Barry, my boy, what do we do?"

I closed one eye, carefully considering my response. What indeed, I thought. Contemplation required further sustenance.

"Two bags of beer nuts please," I said to the bartender. He smiled, whisked two bags from the clips that held them hanging behind the bar and returned to a weighty discussion of the early basketball season with the regular.

"Larry," I finally began after deep contemplation of the situation at hand, "what we have here is a crisis of spirit. Christmas spirit."

"I quite agree," Larry said. "I suppose we should follow our orders. We're only twenty-three baskets until the end."

"Well," I thought out loud as I sipped my beer, "our orders are to follow the list. Now, if someone—say our friends here—were to change the list, then we could still follow our orders by being faithful to the list. The only difference would be that it would be a slightly altered list. Only slightly, mind you."

"Yeah, but the ones who didn't get a turkey would be calling the church tomorrow."

"Not necessarily," I interrupted, "our first two customers weren't exactly waiting for us with baited breath."

"You got a point there. You do indeed, Barry, old boy, old buddy, old pal . . . "

"You're right I do. And if they did call, then someone else could come out with some more baskets. Why, we could give enough to the turkey fund to make sure that it didn't cost the church another penny!"

"Right!" Larry exclaimed. "I mean it's not a perfect world and we're not perfect men and it's not a perfect solution . . . but I'd drink to it all the same."

"As would I." I seconded Larry with a sudden gush of tearful emotion.

"Then I say we do it!" Larry brought the bottom of his bottle down on the bar like a gavel.

The bartender and the regular turned around. Other patrons had thus signaled fights, prompting a visit from the police.

"We're not fighting . . . " Larry assured him. "In fact, we need your help."

"Yes," I slurred ever so slightly the single spoken word,

"we need you to, uh, make some alterations in this list here." I pointed to the paper lying innocently on the bar.

"I think," Larry added, "my friend and I will walk over to the pool table for a moment. We will watch some of these skillful lads and have maybe one more?" he looked to me for approval.

"One more . . . ," I approved.

"Beer. When we come back we would be most appreciative if our humble list were, shall we say, enhanced."

"Yes, I would say enhanced," I agreed good-naturedly.

"Some names off. Some names on. And then, if you could, or would, like to join us on our mission . . . though I know, of course, you're working . . . "

The bartender called back into the kitchen. "Ruby, can you take over the bar for about thirty minutes?"

A strong, harsh voice affirmed that she could.

"I'd be glad to join you."

"Could I come along?" the regular asked.

"Well, of course," I said, a sudden wave of Christian fellowship overcoming me.

"We'd be delighted," Larry added. "Now, we'll just take a stroll." He motioned to me and we slipped away from the bar and wandered towards the game room. Life continued at the Schnitzel Cafe. Pool was played at a table distinguished by its indistinguishable grain. Cigarette burns and the rings left by beer bottles were its only decorations. Two long-haired, muscular guys in their twenties played eight ball. They nodded at us and continued their game. A group of mostly men and two or three women in overly tight jeans gathered in a corner around the light of a wide-screen television.

"Are you sure we're doing the right thing?" Larry leaned towards me in a whisper.

"No," I answered, "but to err is human . . . and to . . . " I forgot the rest, "anyway, all I know is that I would've gotten pretty depressed if the rest of our stops were like the first two."

We glanced back at the bar. Our new allies were hard at work. "I guess we're committed." Larry slapped me on the back.

"Right."

I drove carefully. The bartender sat next to me, his leather jacket zipped halfway up. Larry and the regular sat in the van's second seat, turkey baskets piled up around and on them.

"Okay, this place is on your list." The bartender pointed out a brightly lit bungalow to the right.

I pulled over and with a minimum of stumbling over half-spilled turkey baskets, Larry and the regular joined us on the front walk.

"These are proud folks," the bartender cautioned, "you can't go telling them you're from some church."

"But we are!" My voice was raised a decibel by the Budweiser and the bartender shushed me.

"Okay, when I was a kid we used to do something like this . . . only it was mainly Christmas caroling."

"I can't sing," Larry pleaded.

"They won't know the difference," the regular consoled. "The husband's tone deaf. I know him."

We were at the door, and before Larry and I could protest any more, the bartender pounded on the door and started singing. "Jingle bells . . . jingle bells . . . jingle all the way . . . "

"That's not a . . . " I started to complain, but the regular jabbed me in the ribs and I joined in. We were a poor choir and nowhere close to a barbershop quartet, but the door opened and our audience didn't seem to notice. The neighborhood hadn't seen carolers since the bartender was a kid some thirty years before. Any caroling—even pitiful caroling—was a welcome change of pace.

The man and woman were probably in their forties. They looked older. Their kids ranged from a baby to a girl who was still wearing her K-Mart jacket from a night's work. We had no way of knowing if the younger kids were the couple's children or grandchildren but that didn't matter. The group was a hodgepodge, but they were all smiling, though I tend to believe they were laughing a little at the four of us. All the same, when we were through singing the first verse twice, since none of us knew two verses of any song, we got a big hand of applause.

Larry and I held the basket up. "Merry Christmas!" was all we could think to say. But that was enough. Thanks and invitations to come in for a bite to eat flew right and left. The bartender and the regular took it all in stride. But not Larry and me. We found ourselves blushing and breathing faster and stumbling over our words. And no matter what you're thinking, it wasn't the beer that made us so awkward. It was the spirit of Christmas suddenly undressing us in the presence of unexpected company. We shouldn't have been caught so off-guard. After all, it was why we had gone into the night in the first place. But I don't think we realized that until just then, when the old Christmas spirit jumped up and smacked us right between the eyes.

We declined their offers. There were more houses to visit, more people to serenade. The other stops went by in a flash. Turkey baskets seemed to flow from the van like toys from Santa's sleigh. Widows, old couples, young couples with too many kids, all kinds received their bounty from a list revised slightly by our consults from the Schnitzel Cafe. When we exhausted the list there were still four baskets left.

"I say we give one each for the best lights!" Larry moved our committee to a decision and we all agreed. I was given first choice and I suggested the O'Laughlins. Unanimity. I drove back towards the Schnitzel Cafe.

Again we hit them with a Christmas carol first. When they appeared at the front door, Larry's creative juices started flowing.

"We're the neighborhood festivities committee and your house has been selected as a finalist!"

Silence. "I never won anything before!" old man O'Laughlin finally exclaimed.

"Well, there's a first time for everything." The bartender smiled at Larry and me. I wondered if he was also thinking of our unexpected appearance at the Schnitzel Cafe. I never asked.

The bartender chose the next house and the regular the third. We found ourselves parked back at the Schnitzel, one basket remaining. We puzzled over it for some time, staring at each other between long silence and an occasional belch. Larry finally leaned forward. He pulled his wallet from his pocket and motioned for me to do the same.

"My friends," he said, "you've made the evening easier, and a lot cheerier than before we crossed your threshold. I'm putting twenty bucks in this last basket and my friend Barry is as well." He winked at me. I overcame my initial shock and anteed up, following Larry wherever he was headed. "Now I'd appreciate it if you'd take this little deposit, along with the turkey, cook up something along with it and invite all the worthless types you took off the list for some kind of dinner—sometime between now and Christmas."

The regular started to protest but the bartender cut him off with a loud burst of laughter. He drew a breath and exhaled. "It's our neighborhood, isn't it?"

"It's our neighborhood too," Larry added, "and that's why we'd like to share a little bit with everyone."

The bartender smiled. "I understand. You don't need to say another word. There's only one condition."

"Which is?" I asked.

"That when I throw this little feast, you two come back and join us—if only for a little while."

"Deal," Larry showed a thumbs-up.

"Deal," I added.

"Done," said the bartender. "Now, would you come in and have one more on the house . . . "

"I don't think so . . . " I started. My driver's license hung in the balance.

" . . . coffee, that is," the bartender completed his invitation.

"Invitation accepted," I quickly reversed.

We drove home in my empty van, the radio turned up to Christmas carols sung on key. We didn't speak much. We were in trouble and we knew it. Home too late to kiss the kids goodnight, unprepared to answer Reverend Chastain's inevitable cross-examination, too inarticulate to explain to our wives an experience they hadn't shared with us. We were in trouble, alright, but smiling every block of the way home. We were best friends and knew without dissecting the evening that our mission had been a success.

THE LAST CHAPTER

I might as well tell you the truth. I took the nursing home job for money. Money and a chance to make my résumé look better. I needed the money for a ski trip my buddies were planning between Christmas and New Year's. I needed a better résumé in case I ended up applying to a smaller, private college. I know that sounds a little mercenary, but everyone was doing it. Those colleges love community service. Lettering in football and baseball were all well and good, but a little community service would be the icing on the cake.

When I met him, he was ninety-something. He seemed even older than that sitting by the Christmas tree in the main living room of the nursing home, all shrunken down into his plaid blankets. He kept staring at the tree as if it was going to talk to him. It wasn't much of a tree at that. I had helped the regular attendants decorate it right after dinner. It was my first official task on my first official night.

"It's time for bed, Mr. Sauer," I reached for the back of his wheelchair.

"Get your hands off me," he snapped. Mr. Enwright had told me that the old men in general were tougher than the old women and that old man Sauer was impossible. He also warned me to remain in control. "Don't let him boss *you* around or the game's lost." I think Mr. Enwright saw himself as half warden, half zoo-keeper. Not very flattering to him or the residents, but that's the way it was. He wasn't the kind of guy I would want caring for my grandparent, but then all of mine are dead.

"Ten o'clock is lights out." I thought if I reminded Mr. Sauer of the rules, he might go peacefully.

"It's almost Christmas, son." He tried to smile but I could tell he was conning me. "Take a little mercy on an old man."

"You know the rules, Mr. Sauer."

"Damn the rules." He dropped the give-mercy-to-an-old man facade. "Say, you don't happen to have a cigarette do you?"

"I don't smoke . . . and you know that's against the rules too."

"You can't do anything in this place," his voice dropped. "I just want to sit for a minute."

"Okay. One minute. Starting now."

He looked at the tree, then back at me, winced and looked back at the tree again. I remembered what Mr. Enwright had said about the rules. "They'll break 'em all. They're like children. Be kind, but firm, and if they become difficult, call for help."

"Your minute's up, sir."

"I know that." Mr. Sauer turned back to me. "You called me sir."

"Yes, sir, curfew."

He smiled, though in the lights of the tree I could see that his eyes weren't smiling at all. Mr. Enwright had warned about the trouble-makers too. They get all mixed up about where and who they are and they can fight with the strength of a young kid.

"Why don't you just go upstairs quietly?" I thought I would try one last time.

"You're new, aren't you?"

"New?"

"Here. At the home."

"It's my first day."

"You act like it."

"I'm part-time through Christmas."

"Things happen at Christmas," he said. His right eyelid seemed to lower, as if he was winking at me, but not on purpose.

"I'm only working here until Christmas day."

"Well, I don't plan on staying long either. Have a seat."

I started to sit down, then realized he was conning me again, just like Mr. Enwright had warned. I started to get up, but he waved his hand for me to sit down and I obeyed.

"I could tell you weren't a regular. The regulars never call me 'sir.' They call me 'pops' or 'old buddy' or 'old timer' or 'Mr. Sauer' or even 'Marshall' . . . I think I hate it most when they call me by my first name. You ever go downtown?"

I wondered what he was driving at. "Sure. Sometimes. Not much, but sometimes. My dad's office is downtown."

"Where?" His voice was a hungry growl.

"He's in the Kaelin Building."

"Ah . . . " the urgency of his tone melted into satisfaction, like the sound I've heard from some men puffing on a good cigar.

"Now, I think we'd better go up . . . "

"Across from the Kaelin Building . . . " he interrupted me, "right where that big glass box of a building is . . . "

"The power company building."

"Right. Where the power company building now stands, the Sauer Building used to be. It was the Kaelin's twin. My father and old man Kaelin were best friends. One night they were at the Thackeray Club and over too much brandy they made a deal to build the first two skyscrapers in the city. Twins. Swore they'd stand together on those sites forever."

"So did you sell it?" All I could remember was that the preservationists wanted to save the building but couldn't.

"I didn't. My nit-wit grandson did. Didn't even bother coming back from West Palm to close the deal. And I was the fool for ever giving him a power of attorney in the first place."

It was hard to imagine this funky old man ever having the power or the money to own a building. It was almost as hard to imagine him working downtown. He must have read my mind.

"I wasn't always like this. I was a pretty handsome fellow and, when I was fifty, every woman I knew—including my wife—thought I looked thirty." He laughed. "Of course, they could have been lying, but I don't think so. I was chairman of the biggest bank in the state, I owned a race horse, a cottage in Maine and I was on the boards of most of the companies that amounted to anything around here."

"You?"

"You don't have to sound so damned surprised. Makes me feel worse than I already do."

"Sorry."

"Don't be. I don't need anybody's sorries. I had a good life. I got done most of what I wanted to get done. And I spread it around. Maybe too much. You ever go to the orchestra?"

"Sure."

"Sure . . . easy to say, isn't it? Well, I started the orchestra just before the War. And the opera. And the children's hospital. And the Light House Shelter—we had our skid row types back then too. And . . . and . . . " he waved his hand as if in disgust. "Never mind. Take me to bed."

"I remember now. I saw your picture at the Center for the Arts."

"It's a wonder they don't have 'In Memoriam' beneath it. I didn't even get invited to the dedication last year. Someone told me they didn't know where to find me."

"I think that was almost five years ago, Mr. Sauer. I remember because . . . "

"Take me to my cell. You've got orders to follow, don't you? You're under Always Right's thumb, aren't you? Now get me to bed."

When my shift ended after midnight, I went home thinking about Mr. Sauer. Why wasn't he in a nursing home in Florida? Why was he in a nursing home at all? A guy like that could afford a private nurse. Where were his kids or grandkids? How could someone like Mr. Sauer end up at the mercy of someone like me? Worse still, at the mercy of the regulars who worked at the nursing home? I would have gone to sleep inventing answers, except I had plenty to keep me wondering about things a little closer to home.

Nobody seemed happy this Christmas. My older sister was engaged to a guy no one liked. Mom and Dad were arguing more than usual. Maybe it was about my sister. She wasn't even sure she'd be home for Christmas. If she came home, it was going to be when I was off skiing. Maybe they were upset about my ski trip. Not that they thought I'd do something dumb or get in trouble or whatever. It was just that I was getting older, I was the youngest, and in awhile I'd be off to college the way Sue Ellen had left five years before. They had been pretty sad the Christmases of her junior and senior years too, but I had been there to remind them that the nest wasn't quite empty. It was times like that that I wished I had a little sister or brother.

As I started to drift off to sleep, my last thoughts were of Annie. If the rest of the family had their worries, she was mine. She was a year older than me and already away at college. We'd dated during the spring of my sophomore year and then all through the summer. When she left for college she'd told me she would write and call. For awhile she did both. Back in October she'd made a date to join me for the ski trip. Then things changed. First her letters stopped, then her calls. Then she cancelled out of the ski trip and my love life crashed and burned. I would be going on the trip without her.

The next day I went to work wondering if I would even see Mr. Sauer. I figured I would but something told me I wouldn't. There weren't that many senior men at the nursing home and they sure didn't check out for the holidays, but I just had a funny feeling. The day before I hadn't noticed him until it was time for lights out.

As it turned out, I was almost right. I didn't see him that afternoon. He must have skipped dinner or taken it in his room. And I didn't see him early that evening. I was beginning to feel as if I'd said something wrong the night before and that he didn't want to see me. But when it came time for them all to be in bed, there he was, sitting off to the side of the Christmas tree, over by the big leaded glass windows that make the place look like an old English manor home.

"I thought I'd missed you, Mr. Sauer. Where have you

been keeping yourself?" He kept staring at the tree. "Been hanging out at the local bars?"

"You think you're pretty funny don't you, Peter?" His words seemed to cut right into me. Plus, he used my name. I hadn't told him my name the night before. He must have asked one of the other attendants.

"I'm sorry. I was just trying to be friendly."

"He didn't come again today."

"Who's that?"

"Dickie, the little shit."

He said it with such vehemence that I didn't know what to say. You never expect old people to use four letter words. Especially at a nursing home.

"Dickie?" I finally walked over to him.

"My grandson. He's my official sponsor at the club here."

"He was going to visit?"

"He's in town. He never said he'd come by. I just thought he might."

"Does he come to town often?"

"Not often. Once or twice a year."

"Is he your only grandchild?"

"I have a granddaughter. I don't see her. She lives in California . . . around Monterey or someplace. She's almost your age by now. Her mother married one of the Kaelin boys. She died when my granddaughter was little." He looked up at me and for the first time I noticed a genuine softness in his eyes. "She was my youngest. She loved me. She would have never done this to me."

"Maybe your granddaughter will . . . "

"Her father remarried. She never got to know me."

"How long have you been here at the home, Mr. Sauer?"

He didn't answer at first. For the first time since he'd spoken to me he seemed less than all there. "My grandson moved me in here . . . " his eyes darted around. "Five years ago . . . no, ten. What year is this?"

"Two thousand nine."

He looked down as if I was going to or had just slapped him. His voice seemed weak, as if it was hard for him to take a breath. "More than twelve years ago. Longer than the time from when a kid starts to school until he graduates." He looked directly into my eyes. "Twelve years seems like a long time to you, doesn't it?"

"Yeah, sure, I mean absolutely," I fumbled. "Why didn't you get an apartment?"

"I tried. Right after my wife died. Didn't work. Damned arthritis kept me from getting around."

"And Dickie's father or mother . . . your . . . ?"

"Dickie's father was my son. Drank himself to death. Dickie was a grown man when he died, but I think he blamed me for it."

"How come?"

Mr. Sauer looked at me and smiled, sort of like I'd just said something really remarkable. I'm not sure anyone had ever asked him that question.

"Because I loved Richard too late in life. I wasn't home. Remember, I was busy making banks and operas and cities.

So my son grew up having plenty of money and fun and not much else."

"Have you and Dickie ever tried to make up?"

"We tried . . . and failed. We fought over business. We fought over his wife. I left most of what I owned to his father, so Dickie inherited it. He made a mess of it in a fraction of the time it took my father and me to make it."

"Couldn't you have retired somewhere else than here?" It was none of my business, but he wanted to talk and I was curious. I figured Mr. Sauer was too bright to be in a retirement home with so many far away stares and empty smiles.

"I've got nowhere else," he shrugged his shrunken shoulders. "It's all gone. I lived too damned long. A parent's nightmare is to outlive their children. I outlived them both and look where it got me." He laughed. "Soon enough, though. Soon enough."

He rambled on for what seemed like a few minutes, but it turned out to be almost an hour. He spoke less about business and what he had done and more about his family. His son was born when Mr. Sauer was in his late twenties. As Mr. Sauer put it, he turned around and the little boy with the chubby face was a grown man with a fat face and a drinking problem—Mr. Sauer's problem. His daughter was born when he was in his forties. She really had been the bright spot. He must have learned something from raising, or not raising, his son. After his wife died, his daughter kept him going. Then she was killed in some car accident while she was living out in California.

He tried to set things straight with his son and save him at the same time. Neither plan worked. His son died after Mr. Sauer's daughter. It had something to do with his drinking. Mr. Sauer wasn't too eager to share the details. And that led him to talk about Dickie. Dickie must have blamed Mr. Sauer for his father's death, because it was after his father's death that Dickie had Mr. Sauer placed in the home.

I let him talk until he was tired. The night before, I had been a good nursing home cop. This night I was lousy. I let him go on and on. He needed to talk and, to tell you the truth, he was a pretty good story teller. Every once in a while I chimed in with a few pearls of wisdom, but mostly he was a one man show. Eventually his voice lost its strength and there were longer silences.

Neither of us said anything for what seemed like a long time. We had gone way over the curfew. When he finally looked away from the tree and towards me, he was ready to go. "Take me upstairs, will you?"

"Sure. Sure, I will, but if you want to sit down here for a little while longer, I'll take the heat."

"Thanks, Peter," his tone was truly kind, "but I really need to get some rest."

I pushed him towards the elevator and took him up to his room. The other rooms were dark, their doors shut. When we got to the open door of his bedroom he held up his hand as I started to wheel him inside.

"Thanks, but I don't need any more help right now."

"Okay." I wanted to tell him that I appreciated his telling me about his family, but I wasn't sure what to say.

"Thanks for your ear." He seemed to read my thoughts. "See you tomorrow."

As I left the nursing home that night, I walked around to the back of the building to see if I could see his room. It was past midnight but there was a faint light coming from one of the windows. He must not have been all that sleepy, just ready to be alone. I watched for a few minutes, but his light didn't go out. Then I went home.

Days at Christmas come at you like ocean waves when you're a little kid. They start sort of slowly, almost gentle, then they pick up steam and, before you know it, you're buried up to your nose. You're off shopping, then wrapping, going to parties, special school concerts, decorating the tree and the house. We were all caught up in it. Mom, Dad, and me. As if we were all putting our head down into the waves and hoping we'd still be standing when they passed. Around two days before Christmas, everyone started losing their balance.

"Why do you need to leave the day after Christmas?" My mother's question was really an accusation.

"Because that's how we planned it." I tried to be calm but my voice cracked anyway.

"Well, your sister may get here by then," my father chimed in. He was by the sink drying the dishes, trying half-heartedly to be neutral.

"And she might not!" I paced the kitchen, picking up

speed. "If she's not coming home for Christmas, she might not be home the day after Christmas or the day after that."

"I just think it's bad timing." My mother looked as if she might cry. I hated it when she did that.

"You'll have plenty of years to go on ski trips," my father added.

"Not with these guys. We're all graduating next year. Who knows where we'll be then."

"Who knows where we'll all be next year?" My Mom was crying. First the look, then the morbid hint of uncertain life, then the tears. I hated when Mom did that too. Conversation was over. Things could only deteriorate from here on. Dad would get upset and Mom would lose it completely.

I felt trapped and alone. For the past week, I had dreaded spending my free time at the nursing home. Now I wished I were there. Anywhere but home. I needed to get away. I didn't say another word. I got my coat on, grabbed my ball cap and left. I didn't know where I'd go and I didn't know when I'd come back. Not all night, but at least for a couple of hours. Long enough to think.

The night was clear and getting colder as the last clouds from the afternoon blew out to the east. The moon was full and so clear you could see craters and shadows as if it was a photograph. It was a good night for wandering.

What was really bugging them? They had okayed the ski trip two weeks before. They knew that was one of the reasons I took the job at the nursing home. I hadn't surprised them with it. I hadn't told them I was going, I had asked them. And they said it would be okay.

Every house I walked by seemed happier, warmer, more peaceful than my own. Light sprinkled every evergreen and holly. Santa Claus sleighs and manger scenes dotted every block. Peace on earth, good will towards men. But not at my house. Deep down I knew it wasn't anything I'd done. It was my sister. But Mom and Dad sure weren't making any allies by jumping my case.

I weaved in and out of the side streets of my neighborhood, walking the main roads for awhile, then drifting through the alleys. I was just walking it off, but the more I walked, the lonelier I felt. The further I got from home the more I wished I was back there. That's when I turned around and started back.

I was getting closer to home when I made a turn or two and found myself standing on the corner outside of the Bingham Home for Men and Women. It sounds funny, but I'd gotten used to the place in the couple of weeks I'd worked there. Its drabness, its Lysol smell, even Mr. Sauer seemed better than fighting with my parents.

In a backwards sort of way, Mr. Sauer and I had become friends. It started that first night just talking about who he was and who he'd been, his family history and the pain that brought with it. During the nights and occasional days that followed, we had covered politics and local history, the changes in the city and the state. We had even talked sports, except Mr. Sauer didn't seem to know what had been happening for the past twenty years or so. He wasn't always pleasant and sometimes he seemed to forget I was around, but I always knew he enjoyed the company.

For awhile I stood out on the street peering inside, feeling like some burglar about to grab what I could and run. A funny thought ran through my mind. What I was really there to steal wasn't a thing. It was something else, a thought, a vision, a sense of something. I wasn't sure. But there he sat, pulled over near the side of the Christmas tree, hunched down in his wheelchair, visible through the window but hidden from anyone in the room. He was staring upwards, at the top of the tree, as if something special was about to happen. I could see him, but he couldn't see me. At least he wasn't looking at me.

I stood outside for maybe ten minutes, then turned to go back home. It would be silly to go inside. It was my night off. Nursing homes aren't exactly social hot spots. And I really didn't know the staff that well. But I went in anyway. The woman at the front desk said hello and I made up an excuse about leaving my scarf the night before. Then I walked into the great room. This time, even though I knew exactly where he was, he saw me before I saw him.

"Thought this was your night off," he said.

"It is. I forgot something."

"Must have been important."

"Hmm?"

"Important . . . to come back to this place on your night off."

"Right, yeah," I couldn't think of anything else to say but, "I left my scarf."

"Scarf?" I could tell by his tone he wasn't buying that. "Sure," he continued, "that's a good reason to come back."

"Okay, well, it doesn't look like it's around here, so I better get going."

"Sit down and stay awhile." As he spoke, he wheeled closer to me. "Tell me what's new outside the Big House."

I had to laugh. He was imitating one of those gangsters from an old movie. It was the first time he'd ever made a joke.

"Not much. Family hassles."

"Ohhh . . . ," he drew the consonant out and nodded his head, "my specialty."

"My Mom's all bent out of shape because I'm going skiing after Christmas."

"Wants you home with her?"

"I guess. But she already knew about it. And Mom and Dad both said it was okay."

"Well, go then! To hell with 'em." He flipped his hand in dismissal. I didn't know what to think. That's what I wanted to hear, but now that I'd heard it I didn't feel reassured. It sure sounded strange coming from Mr. Sauer.

"Well, I think they're really bothered about my sister being away for Christmas."

"That's their problem. You've got to lead your own life. You don't owe them." He paused, looking me in the eye. What was he saying? Did he figure that because his own son had stopped loving him, every kid had the same right?

"But you're wrong, Mr. Sauer. I do owe them . . . sort of.

They're my parents. I love them. I just don't want them to tell me what to do."

"Well," he paused again, nodding slowly, "if that's what you're saying, then that's a little different."

"Yeah, it is. I mean, I want to go, but . . . " I didn't know whether to share any details about Annie with him. "But not as much since Annie cancelled out."

"Who the hell is Annie?"

"Well, she was a girl I was dating. She was going on the ski trip, but that's a long story. She's got other plans."

"She dumped you, eh?" Coming from him it sounded crusty, but not cruel.

"Well, I guess."

"And that makes you the odd man out?"

"Sort of."

"You'll carry extra bags and run out for dinner and make arrangements and so forth?"

"Yeah." He didn't make it sound like much fun, "but I still have to go."

"Have to go?" he squinched his face as if someone had just given him a lemon to suck on. "Now I'm confused again. Your parents can't make you *not* go and your friends can't *make* you go. So who's making you go?"

"Well, no one."

"Oh," is all he said. The subject was closed. "So, Peter, you have big plans for tomorrow night?" Sometimes he didn't know one night from another, but Christmas Eve was different.

"Well, I'm working until ten. Mr. Enwright said I could leave an hour early."

"Always Right's a big-hearted fellow."

"So I'll be here at the party until then. After ten, I'm going to Christmas Eve service with Mom and Dad."

"The party?"

"The Christmas Eve party here at the Bingham Home."

"Oh yeah. Right. The party."

"So, I'll see you here?"

"Nope. Old Dickie's coming by. We'll probably head down to the Thackeray Club. Big dinner. All the old boys will be there. Gives them a chance to check out who's still around. You know how that is."

I must have stared at him for awhile. I've got to admit that I hadn't expected Dickie to do anything that thoughtful in a thousand years. Maybe he wasn't such a shit after all. The only bad part was that Christmas was *my* last night at the Bingham Home. I didn't know whether to say something or not. I didn't want it to sound as if it mattered, but I wasn't sure.

"Well, listen, Peter," he finally spoke, "I'm getting a little tired. You don't mind if I turn in?"

"No. No. I don't mind." I hesitated, "I guess this is going to be goodbye. I mean, tomorrow's my last day and all. I'll be home Christmas and then off skiing."

"Right. Well, it's been good getting to know you, Peter. If you could just give me a hand upstairs, it's curfew time. You remember the rules?"

"Right!" I laughed. Our two weeks getting to know each other suddenly seemed like two years. I helped him to his room, got him to the edge of his bed and left.

When I got home it was as if nothing had happened. Dad was reading. Mom was going through Christmas cards. They both said hello when I came in, but they didn't ask where I'd been or what I'd done. I was glad I'd taken a long walk and I guess they were too.

The next morning I got up early. As usual, there were still some Christmas details I hadn't covered. A few stocking stuffers, some last-minute plans for the trip, and then there was Mr. Sauer. I wanted to leave something for him under the tree. He'd spent enough time staring at it. Maybe he'd get it Christmas morning or even when Dickie brought him back to the nursing home on Christmas Eve. So I started looking. Shirts, ties, wallets. He didn't need that stuff. He didn't wear after-shave. Cuff links and tie bars were of no use. I must have spent an hour at the malls without seeing anything. Then I was going by the Museum Store when something caught my eye. They carried items from the museum downtown as well as from Chicago, the National Gallery, the Metropolitan and so forth.

There it was. The once and never-again Sauer Building. First skyscraper in our city. "Exemplary of the art deco styles common in the 1920s and early 1930s," said the little flyer that came with it. Christmas past, I thought.

It wasn't cheap, but then I'd picked up a little extra cash working.

Thinking of Christmas past made me wonder about Christmas present. In Mr. Sauer's case, I wasn't too sure about Christmas future. This was about his last chapter in life, even if I didn't want to think about it. So I looked for one more thing at the Museum Store. And then I saw it. It wasn't big, but it didn't need to be. I would add a few things to it—which I did after a few phone calls and some time on the internet—but I hoped it would work.

The party started on time. We actually did a pretty nifty job at decorations. Mr. Enwright sent me into the attic to grab some silver and red balls and I found two or three boxes full of ornaments and greenery. I brought them all down and the staff and seniors seemed to get a big kick out of adding to what was already in the Great Room. All of the seniors, that is, except Mr. Sauer. Old Dickie must have come by early. I really couldn't blame him. Even with the added decorations to the Bingham Home, life had to be more lively at the Thackeray Club.

One of the staff played piano and we sang all of the Christmas carols and songs in three different music books. Some of the old folks joined in, but most just listened. They enjoyed it and so did I. I don't think Mr. Sauer would have enjoyed it, though. He would have sat by the tree and thought of sad times he hadn't even begun to tell me about.

I had been hoping to catch him before he left. I wanted to give him his presents first-hand, instead of putting them under the tree, but then things are never perfect—especially at Christmas. I slipped his presents under the tree with a big tag that clearly said it was for "Marshall Sauer." The party wound down around nine forty and I was out the door and on time to meet Mom and Dad at ten.

I left the Bingham Home thinking about Mom and Dad. The day had passed. I'd seen them coming and going and neither of them had said another word about the ski trip. Maybe it was Mom's way of letting me know it was okay. Or maybe she just didn't want to get upset again on Christmas Eve. I don't know.

As I was running for the car, something made me stop. To this day I don't know what it was. A change in the way the wind was blowing. The flicker of a street light. A car's headlights glimmering off the branches of the trees. I turned and looked up to the row of rooms along the side of the home, up to the window where his lights had burned beyond curfew two weeks before. His lights were on. The lights were never on when residents were out.

I turned and ran back inside. Mr. Enwright was picking up paper plates and plastic cups in the Great Room.

"Forget something, Peter?"

"Did Mr. Sauer's grandson pick him up today?"

"Dick Sauer?"

"Yeah."

"I don't think I've seen Dick Sauer in three or four years.

He had the old man's will revised awhile back and was by to get it executed, but that's it."

I started up the steps.

"Peter," Mr. Enwright called after me, "it's curfew time. They're all in bed . . . ." His words trailed off as I turned the landing to the second floor. I got to his room and knocked too loudly to be polite. There was no answer. I knocked again. Still no answer. The rooms weren't locked, or lockable, but there was a courtesy rule that you didn't disturb the seniors if they didn't want to be disturbed. I didn't care. I threw open the door. Mr. Sauer was sitting in his chair, fully dressed, staring down at a book I could tell he wasn't reading.

"You lied to me."

"Dickie couldn't make it," he said matter-of-factly.

"That's a lie too. Dickie was never going to make it."

"So?" he said. "That's my business."

"Oh yeah!" I was so angry I couldn't think of anything else to say. "I don't think so!"

"Then whose business is it?"

"Mine," I blurted. "You made it my business when you told me about Dickie and your family and your life."

He thought for a second. "Perhaps you're right." And with that admission he ended my anger as if he'd poured it out of a bottle onto the floor.

I looked at my watch. It was ten-fifteen. "Come on," I said. "We're going to church."

"No," he tightened up and drew away from me.

"Yes." I said. "I'll help you into the car. We can take

your wheelchair. You'll be up past your bedtime but you usually are anyway."

"No," he repeated. "I can't," he fumbled his words. Mr. Enwright appeared at the door, huffing and puffing. Mr. Sauer turned to him. "Tell him, Enwright. It's against the rules."

Mr. Enwright was red in the face, trying to catch his breath. He looked at Mr. Sauer, then at me. I was ready for the inevitable recitation of The Bingham Home Rules and Regulations.

"Damn the rules, Marshall," Enwright sputtered. "If this boy wants to take you to church, you're going. It'll do you good. Now get a warm coat on. It's cold out there." Enwright straightened up and turned to go. "Don't let him keep you out past," he hesitated, "four a.m., Peter. Old Sauer's a handful." Then Mr. Always Right left.

After that, Mr. Sauer didn't fight me. In fact, he acted as if we'd had a date for weeks. Maybe we had. We went to church without a hitch. No one stared or looked at us funny. Mom and Dad accepted Mr. Sauer as if he was one of the family.

And when the service was over and before everyone left, my dad took over where I would have never thought to. He caught one of the old guys—younger than Mr. Sauer, but still pretty old—and introduced Mr. Sauer to him. Well, it turned out they knew each other from way back. Not well, but enough. That led to another introduction and then another and another and before you knew it, you'd think old Sauer was at the Thackeray Club knocking down "highballs." And so it went. In the middle of it all, Mr. Sauer turned to me, smiled that half-sarcastic smile of his and winked.

So there it was, the last chapter. Well, sort of, but a long last chapter and one that didn't end for some time to come. We got in so late that my presents didn't get opened until the next morning, after Christmas breakfast. And as Mr. Sauer told me the day after Christmas—since I canned the ski trip, I had plenty of time to visit friends—he had just put his replica of the Sauer Building on his bedstand and was starting to examine the inscription on the leather-bound address book I had added for good measure when the most astounding thing happened.

"Peter," he told me, "you wouldn't believe it. I was just reading your directive to 'fill this address book up with new friends!' when my phone rang. Hell, it never rings! Not even on Christmas. You're not going to believe it, but out of the blue, my granddaughter in California called. She thought I was long dead. Turns out she goes to college up at Northwestern. On her way back from the West Coast, after New Year's, she's dropping by to see me. Can you believe that," he said, winking at me again, "out of the blue."

Not exactly out of the blue, I thought. My time on the internet had worked. "Did she sound like she was . . . " I was going to say "upset," but Mr. Sauer raised his hand and stopped me.

"She sounded very bright . . . very attractive . . . just like her mother. And she sounded very eager to meet my friend at the Thackeray Club who called her the other day . . . to tell her about me." He paused and placed his hand lightly on mine. "Now I wonder which of my many, old friends that could have been?"

THE OPEN HOUSE

Cobb's house was the abomination of the block. Actually, it was the abomination of the neighborhood. In the preservation-conscious Victorian Village—or simply the Village as it came to be known—his was the one house everyone wanted to tear down. That opinion had been universally held, long before our Christmas Open House or even our move into the neighborhood. Our only shame in life was having Cobb as a neighbor.

That's why I hoped Jerry Lyndon and his wife would focus on our house and not Cobb's as they searched for a place to park. Jerry is our association president. He put Katie up to hosting the Open House. And he promised the party would all work out in the end. I just didn't want it to begin with some wisecrack about Cobb's hovel. I watched them struggling to maneuver a Ford Expedition into a space better intended for an old Volkswagen bug, feeling my armpits grow clammy. How the other hundred or so guests were going to find a place on or near our block was their problem.

"Merry Christmas, Joel," Jerry called out to me from across the street, but he was staring at Cobb's house. Lynn clutched his arm. The dusting of snow that had started just an hour before had turned my brick front walk into a luge course fit for the Winter Olympics. I watched them slipping and sliding towards me, hoping Katie wasn't inside watching. One of my assignments had been to warranty the bricks safe and passable for all humans. Jerry and Lynn were about forty and they were taking baby steps. If they were having problems the older guests would be flying into the yard right and left.

"Merry Christmas, Jerry. Merry Christmas, Lynn. Hope you make it to the door!"

Jerry laughed. Lynn's eyes were locked on her toes. Jerry was still staring back at Cobb's place. "Your house looks great," Jerry said, extending his arms in exclamation, just missing Lynn. She ducked. I guessed it wasn't the first time she had to avoid Jerry's politically-charged exuberance. "Too bad everyone in the neighborhood can't get with the program." Jerry swung his thumb back towards Cobb's house across the street. With that he and Lynn jerked violently forward then backwards as they hit a slick spot. Great. Not two minutes into the Open House and Cobb's house had not only been hung around my neck like the proverbial Albatross, but, as an attractive nuisance, it had caused my most honored guests to careen towards a swan dive on my front walk.

They tiptoed the rest of the way to my door in silence. My gaze drifted beyond them to Cobb's place again. What could

I say? Jerry was right. The house was a 120-year-old, three-story Queen Anne "cottage." Like a bloated gingerbread house, faded brick and crumbling wooden fish scale covered parts of the second and third floors. That's where Martha Stewart ended and the Norman Bates' look took over. The front and side porches leaned away from the rest of the house and the box gutters looked as if they were about to fall off from sheer weariness. They no longer channeled rainwater, verified by the water-stained front of the house. The slate roof was twenty years past its life and periodically, like discarded teeth, it spit old panels into the front and side yards. Nice impression to give any passer-by.

Worse still, Cobb was a reflection of his house. Most of the time he never left it. When he did, he sported an old coat and hat, baggy trousers Goodwill would have rejected, and a tattered, frayed dress shirt. He always seemed to have a three-day beard and his hair was thin and long-ish, sticking out at angles from his hat. He seldom spoke, looking down or away. It would be fair to say that house and owner were a match for each other.

Jerry and Lynn went on in—our first guests—and I had a moment before the next couples unintentionally skated up the walk to admire our own house and contrast it to Cobb's hovel. We had tuck-pointed our brick, repainted the trim, replaced broken or missing slate, refinished the front doors and added leaded glass—potentially spending our children's college tuition but proud to boast an award-winning exterior in exchange for a second mortgage that exceeded our first. Inside, we had restored a tenement style four-plex into its original configuration of over a hundred years before. We had torn out walls, rewired every socket, re-plumbed all three bathrooms, and refinished every hardwood floor, down to the nail heads. For the past two or three weeks, Katie had been working on three or four hours of sleep to make our home a palace. It was spiffed and scrubbed and ready to feature on one of those fluffy dream house shows on the double-digit cable channels.

We were proud of our house and rightly so. The old manse was decked out top to bottom with holly, magnolia, evergreen boughs and two Victorian Christmas trees. We had three fireplaces roaring, candles all over the place and tasteful holiday music that would have pleased the most cynical of the *New York Times*' critics. Tasteful, authentic, comfortable. After all, as newcomers we were honored to be hosting the Christmas Open House, a tradition in the Village since the neighborhood's incorporation almost thirty years before. Honored, but beat to a pulp. I was coming off the year from hell, having just finished my third, two-week malpractice case and I was running on fumes. My Christmas wish was to see the last guest safely out the door.

After Jerry and Lynn arrived, guests started streaming in from all sides. With parking such as it wasn't, they arrived from around street corners, by paths beside neighboring houses, and from the church parking lot, by way of the alley, that ran in the back of our home. Now I was really sweating. New faces, new names, a bunch of strangers in my house.

From my perspective, and probably their's, I was an outsider. Katie had grown up in the Village, living in the neighborhood until she went away to college, attending the old elementary and middle school and going to the city high school a few miles away. She and the neighborhood kids had been like siblings. Even before we got married, I knew that her dream was to return to the Village. I was all for it, but knew little about the neighborhood when we bought our house. I grew up in an undistinguished little bungalow in the northern part of the state. Any history I had concerning the Village was strictly what I learned by word-of-mouth.

Given my schedule at work, Katie was the one who got involved in community affairs and special projects like the Christmas Open House. No one ever asked *me* if we wanted to host the Open House—and that was okay. If they had asked I wouldn't have known what they were talking about. Then I would have blown it by giving the wrong answer—like, "maybe next year," or "why don't we wait until we've finished our restoration." Those would not only have been the wrong answers, they might have resulted in excommunication from the Village. Then Katie would have left me. Divorce courts. Alimony. Child support. Visitation. I shivered again at the thought of the bizarre turns my life would have taken if they had asked me rather than Katie. I was a mere private in my family's chain of command . . . a custodian of my house and my yard and the kids' ball teams . . . and I wanted to keep it that way.

So the strangers poured in, hugging and kissing me, grabbing my hand, and putting forth boxes of cookies and bottles of wine. For almost an hour, I kept my post near the front door, accepting the largesse of the season and trying desperately to memorize names. There were roughly a hundred people inside our house and I wasn't sure how many more could be crammed in without violating some kind of fire code. I looked across the street at Cobb's house and noticed there still wasn't any sign of the season, or of life, just a gray hulk.

Once the front door traffic slowed down, I was supposed to go inside, mingle, keep the logs stirred in the fire and watch carefully for any sign that Katie needed help—more food, punch, anything else—and especially more wine.

When I finally went inside, I found myself way behind. Our guests had already consumed at least one glass of wine or a cup of punch and their hands were spinning around, trying to keep up with the stories flying from their tongues. They were telling tales and trading gossip like they hadn't seen each other in years. As a newcomer to the party and the neighborhood, I tried to listen and circulate, answering questions or adding something when I could.

"Now, Joel, how many apartments were there in this place?" Tom Underhill was a local builder and one of the trustees of the Village Neighborhood Association. His eye was sharp and he was taking in every piece of crown molding, every ten-foot door, every shutter on every window.

"Four."

"You did a nice job of uncovering that old staircase. Last time I was in here, half of it was behind a wall."

"We just started tearing out drywall in the front hall where it didn't seem to belong." I smiled. "Pretty soon the bannister reappeared. With a little help from a carpenter, we replaced some missing spindles and put it back into business."

You would think I had created one of the wonders of the world. Oohing and aahing emitted from every beautiful wife who surrounded me. Accolades mounted and I began to feel like a Nobel Prize winner. Exclamations and congratulations flowed like the hot rum punch Katie was now serving.

"Too bad you have to be across the street from that." Underhill's wife, Fran, pointed to the Cobb house. The Nobel Prize dissolved into a city building citation.

"Mr. Cobb's got some work to do all right." I was trying to stay upbeat and neutral, still thinking the old man might have at least one friend amongst my guests. But that wasn't likely. Mere mention of the old man's name was like striking a dead piano key in the middle of a sonata. Gulps. Stares. Groans. Then silence. Eyes trained sympathetically in my direction.

"I wish we could just buy him out," Underhill noted, with an emphatic nod of his head. I knew he was thinking the words "lynch him."

"He's not very popular, is he?"

"That's an understatement!" Nancy Rivers slipped over from a circle of guests near the fireplace. Nancy was about Katie's age. They had grown up in the neighborhood together. She nibbled her Christmas cookie with increased animation and I sensed that Cobb's house was a hot button for her as well. Nancy and Randy Rivers had moved to the Village after college ten years before. They knew everything about everyone.

"So what's his story, anyway?" If I couldn't avoid the subject, I might as well find out more about it. With my question, four or five more guests joined our little circle.

Nancy took up the question first. "Well obviously, there's the house. I mean, I'm sorry you have to be across the street, Joel, but it's a real blemish . . . probably even a health hazard."

"Don't forget the rust heap in the back yard." Randy was ready to add to Cobb's indictment.

"The '55 Buick?" I asked for clarification.

"Exactly. It goes with the house. We've got bets on which one will turn to dust first . . . house, Buick or Cobb."

Though I didn't know much about the inner workings of the Village, its association, or the history of either one, I did walk my dog, Zeppo, up and down the alleys and all around the streets at odd hours in the early mornings or late nights. I had seen the Buick many times. It stood up on blocks, a tattered canvas drawn over part of it like a shroud.

"You know, those old cars are worth money sometimes," I said. "I wonder why he doesn't fix it up to sell or just sell it as is."

My question produced chuckles. "He just doesn't care. Sad to say, but he doesn't care how it looks." Tom Underhill was adamant.

"And he's always wandering around the streets at weird hours, walking that old, black dog of his like some bum." Nancy wanted to affirm that it wasn't only Cobb's bizarre abuse of property that made the old man a troublesome eccentric.

I looked down at my feet, guilty but not yet discovered. Under cover of darkness, I could have been their lurking prowler. In fact, it was while my dog, Zeppo, was tugging me around the neighborhood one early morning before dawn that I caught my first glimpse of Cobb. He was coming out of the side door of the Presbyterian church just up the street. At the time I didn't think anything of it. As far as I knew, he could have been the custodian. For that matter, he could have been a thief. Still later I wondered if he was begging for a handout.

He had left the church, looked around, seen me and seemed startled. Then he had composed himself, nodded once and moved on in the opposite direction.

Then there were the yard sale days. On Saturday mornings in the spring and summer I would crawl out of bed, make a quick cup of coffee, sneak out of the house before anyone else was up and take Zeppo with me. Sometimes we walked. Sometimes we drove, if the sale was outside the neighborhood. I had seen Cobb more than a few times. He was always picking up stuff that he couldn't possibly use—old ball gloves and bats, junky toys and bicycles.

"And sometimes we've caught him staring in our front windows from out there on the street," Tom continued. Now I was really feeling guilty. Sometimes I stared as well.

"One time I looked him right in the eye." Nancy Rivers snapped another cookie in two. "It was creepy."

"I went out one night to confront him," Tom said, "but he got away."

I wanted to point out that if Tom was so sure it was Cobb,

then the old man didn't exactly "get away," since everyone knew where he lived. But I didn't. "Did you report him to the police?" I asked instead.

"No." Fran glanced at Tom as if he had wimped out. "But we thought about it. He didn't come around again for at least two weeks. And then he walked on by."

"I'm one of the few neighbors who've ever talked to him." Randy Rivers didn't want to be overshadowed by Tom. "I bought an old bike from him."

"A bike? What would Mr. Cobb be doing with a bike?" The recollection of last summer's yard sales flashed through my mind.

"I don't know. I didn't ask him. But here's the really eerie part. I used to have this bike—got it for Christmas when I was a kid. I used to ride it all over the neighborhood, playing like I was a fighter pilot or whatever. Eventually I outgrew it and my dad sold it. Probably the one time in my life that I was really pissed at my dad.

"But anyway, I was out with my son one day and I looked over at Cobb's house and he's got a 'For Sale' sign on this old bike. I had to stop and look really hard, but I suddenly realized that this was *my* old bike. Somehow, hook or crook, maybe because Cobb hangs out at yard sales, he had come across my old bike.

"I didn't want to let on that I was interested. He was out walking around his house. I asked him how much he wanted for the bike. I probably would have paid some antique dealer a small fortune to get my old bike back, but I didn't want to let Cobb know that I was really interested. He looked me up and down. I could tell he thought he was about to drive a really hard bargain, and so I almost turned and started walking on when I heard him say "Fifteen dollars."

"I offered him ten bucks on the spot and he took it! I couldn't tell who was more excited, my son or me." Randy's pride over his skillful bargaining had him grinning and swaying—or that could have been Katie's rum—back and forth on his heels.

"Well, that's one good thing old Mr. Cobb's done," I noted, simply to hold up my end of the conversation. Randy and Nancy, Tom and Fran looked at me as if I had just walked into the room in my underwear.

"You can't say that," Randy said. "As far as Cobb was concerned, it was a piece of junk. He was making ten easy bucks."

"You're probably right," I said.

"Joel . . . darling . . . " Katie, oozing sweetness, was preemptively striking any resistance I might voice to whatever request was coming. " . . . More wine . . . ," she held an empty bottle up, " . . . there's some on the back porch and Zeppo is making an awful lot of noise in the back yard. Would you see if you can quiet him down?"

I hated to leave everyone, but I had almost forgotten that I was the host, not a guest, at the Open House. Katie and the few people we had hired to help were keeping the show going and I was getting all caught up in gossip. I excused myself and headed for the great outdoors.

* * *

Outside the sun had set. A few, gray clouds that had been dusting us with snow had moved on to the east. The sky was full of stars and the moon was bright enough to have been hung by someone who knew it was Christmas time. From the side porch, I could see inside the house, and it looked like a diamond absorbing and throwing off light. Nancy's trees sparkled, the soft candlelight from the mantels glowed and our antique chandeliers, dimmed for the occasion, made the scene take on a golden patina. Our guests seemed in constant motion, like so many hummingbirds, and the glittering outfits and jewelry of the women took the light of the room and scattered it into a thousand directions.

From the outside, I could also see Cobb's house across the street. Strange. For a moment, in a different light, it almost resumed its former grandeur. It's drab, gray color and the water stains on the bricks disappeared, pock-marked slate and dangling gutters became invisible. Instead, tall chimneys stood out against the moon and the graceful curves of the roof looked as if they were painted by an artist's brush. "Too bad for the light of day," I thought to myself, then grabbed more wine and moved to the kitchen.

The kitchen was like a party within the party. Gathered there was an entirely different conclave, mostly older neighbors from a different part of the Village. These folks had moved from the rambling mansions and three-story frames when their children had grown up and out. They had resettled in condominiums, many situated in the

Parkside, a twenty-story complex that was still considered new but had been completed fifteen years before, in keeping with the architecture of the Village.

Their perspective on the neighborhood was a little different than Katie's and my contemporaries. Towering above the rest of the neighborhood, their condos allowed them to look out over our rooftops. They were detached from the traffic and parking problems, from the pockets of derelict structures and littered bus stops below, from the homeless men and women who wandered through our neighborhood. In many ways, they were like neighbors in some parallel universe. They shopped the same hardware and drugstores, ate at the same funky restaurants and coffee shops, frequented the same bookstores and groceries, but they were removed from many of the thornier problems of the Village.

Still, the Parkside and other condo residents were members of the Village Association, and, like the rest of us, received invitations to the Open House. I had also sent out a few invitations to non-members of the Association who lived in the Village, but weren't Parksiders. I slid in between my senior guests as they caucused by the refrigerator, leaning comfortably against the center island or up against the sink. Like the twenty- and thirty-year-olds in the front of the house, they were talking and drinking, telling stories about the neighborhood and trading news about their children and grandchildren.

"Joel," a gray-haired, distinguished looking man in a turtle neck caught my arm as I inched by. "Thanks for hosting this event. Great job. Super house." I thanked him and he continued, "I'm Don Osborne. A million years ago I was the first president of the Association."

I had started to smile and move on, but now I was awestruck. Strange that it would hit me that way, but it was like meeting one of the nation's founding fathers—Washington, Madison or Jefferson right there in my kitchen.

"Wow," I heard myself saying, "I didn't know anybody from that far back was still around."

Osborne practically lost his drink on my floor. He choked on the sip he was taking and his hand started jiggling up and down as he laughed.

"You know how to hurt a guy."

"Sorry. But thirty years seems like a long time ago."

Osborne smiled. "It was a long time ago. Most of us were in our thirties back then. But I know what you mean. Just the same, there were a few titans older than us. They're the real ancients." He sipped again, looking over the rim of his glass with the sort of knowing expression that he wasn't really all that old.

"Those must have been exciting times."

"Well, we fought the church and the state and every developer who set foot inside of the Village boundaries."

"Only we weren't even called the Village." Osborne's wife slipped over to his side. "We were just part of the Highlands."

"Everybody wanted to make a quick buck on our neighborhood back then," Osborne added. "Houses got torn down in the night, or on weekends. Ugly apartment complexes popped up right and left."

"And there was a lot more crime than today," Mrs. Osborne nodded. "I'll bet you didn't know that a bunch of bikers lived in your upstairs apartment and the young couple downstairs had a nice little marijuana greenhouse right where we're standing. They were sort of a self-contained cottage industry—manufacturing, distribution, sale and consumption—all under one roof."

I laughed. These seniors were really funny. "So this was a wild and woolly block, eh?"

"You bet. The only respectable place left on the block belonged to Eddie Cobb and his family."

"Old man Cobb?"

"Well," Osborne laughed. "I didn't think of him as that old back then, but he was older than all of us. I guess he's dead now. Say, I couldn't help but notice his place when we came in. Must be apartments. Who owns it?"

Finally, I had the corner on knowledge. I hesitated for maximum effect, "Eddie Cobb—and it's not apartments."

"What!" Mr. and Mrs. Osborne's exclamation called the attention of others around us. Cobb seemed to have that effect on people.

"The once respectable Eddie Cobb is probably a stone's throw from us right now," I said.

"That's incredible." The voice belonged to Henry Motley, retired minister of our Presbyterian church on the corner. "I've been eavesdropping. I had no idea Eddie was still around."

"Well, if you all hadn't kicked him out of the church, Henry," Osborne winked at me, "you'd know."

"No one kicked Eddie Cobb out!" the minister protested—still with enough grins and insider winks that I knew he wasn't upset. Still, it was an odd statement. At least in the year that I'd attended, our church made it its mission to reach out to inner-city neighborhoods, foreign refugees, and homeless men and women who found their way to the new minister's office for a handout. As far as I knew, that handout was seldom rejected—though it usually took the form of a gift certificate to the local Arby's, rather than money.

"Well, Henry," Osborne addressed the minister emeritus as an old friend, "that may be true today—when you take in anyone! But not thirty years ago." Osborne turned back to me to explain. "That's when Eddie Cobb was head of the session . . . *and* on the first board of trustees of the Village. He single-handedly blocked the church from knocking down two of those four houses right behind the church. Parking, Joel. Problem then, problem now."

"Those houses are beautiful," I said, "but what do you mean four houses?" Here was a story close to home. No one would dare destroy a house in the Village today.

"Truth be told . . . they were pretty crappy at the time," Osborne noted. "The church bought them just to tear them down. The neighborhood was up in arms."

"And so was the congregation," Henry Motley added. "In their minds, those old frame houses were a public health menace. They figured they were doing the neighborhood a big favor. And they were mad as hornets when the neighbors put up protest signs and had the newspaper snooping around, writing stories."

"So where did Eddie Cobb figure in?"

"Well, Eddie wanted to save them all," Motley recalled, "but there wasn't any preservation ordinance back then . . . so Eddie forced a compromise—save two, destroy two. And looking back on it, of course he was right. We should have saved them all."

"So he saved two houses," Osborne picked up the narrative, "but the real die-hard preservationists called him a wimp and a traitor."

"And the congregation nearly tarred and feathered him," Motley added. "I tried to make peace, but without much luck. After that, Eddie stopped coming to church and nothing I could say convinced him otherwise. After a year or so, I gave up."

"Well," Osborne held his glass upwards in an imaginary toast, "he was a man before his time." He sipped. "The Association wouldn't have saved squat. Eddie did what he could. And after that, whenever some old house came up for sale or was about to get turned into apartments, Eddie and his wife were right on top of it. His son was into that stuff too."

"Son?"

"Yeah, sort of a pre-hippie, beatnik sort. Drove around with Eddie in some old fifties Oldsmobile or something—policing the neighborhood. That boy was the last guy you'd think would go to Vietnam. But when they drafted him, he went. Never came back. Real shame. They were quite a pair."

"And his wife?" I asked.

"She and Eddie separated after that. I don't think she forgave Eddie for not doing something to keep the boy from going. Back in the early days of Vietnam, if you had some pull with the draft board folks, you could usually get around service—or work it out here in the States. Anyway, she moved back to live with an aging mother in Michigan or Ohio or somewhere—I've forgotten."

"Joel," my wife was at the door. I'd done it again. The three bottles of wine were still in my hands, unopened. "More wine?" Katie's eyes immediately forgave me for getting caught up with our guests. But I knew it was time to get back to work.

I wanted to stay. The history of our neighborhood's rejuvenation was as interesting as talk at the Open House was going to get. Katie had gently warned me to "keep it light . . . no politics, local, national, anything . . . ." So history seemed safe—and interesting. Apparently the story of the Village wasn't always a happy one. Beautiful homes that had once given large families room in which to interact with other large families were torn down or allowed to deteriorate. Many that were saved were condemned to becoming rooming houses or efficiencies. Property values dropped. A whole generation exited to the suburbs. Interesting saga, but I knew I had to keep the wine flowing.

In the dining room, the evergreens filled the room with a scent unique to the season. The burning logs, which I realized needed another poking, added just enough musty smoke to make it all cozy, even in a house jammed with a hundred people. The Christmas music I had selected was all but smothered by the buzz of neighbors eager to share their stories, their gossip, and their recent life experiences. But whenever there was a fleeting lull, smatterings of tunes surfaced, giving the party an ambience that was reflective of parties twenty or even fifty years before.

"My last party in this house must have been in '55 or maybe '56." The attractive, snowy, white-haired woman who snuck up on me was a stranger. But then most of my guests were strangers to me.

"I'm sorry, but I don't think we've met. Do you live in the Village?"

"I did. Before the War and up through the early '60s. My name's Virginia Walker. I'm visiting my grandkids this week and they brought me along."

"And they are?"

"Nancy and Randy Rivers. Nancy's my granddaughter. I saw you talking to them a few minutes ago. They brought me along for nostalgia—mine that is."

"That's neat. And you lived . . . ?"

"Next door. The Baumeisters lived here, in your house, back then and they were always giving parties. The three families used to alternate years giving the big Christmas affair."

"Three families?" I was trying to follow her, but her voice was soft and the din of voices drowned her out. "You and the Baumeisters and . . . ?"

"And the Cobbs. I'm sorry. Sometimes I forget. It's just that it used to be second nature to think of the three families as one, extended family."

"The Cobbs had parties too?"

"Did they have parties! Good Lord, the Cobbs gave the best parties of all. Eddie was the original life of the party. He would play Christmas songs on the piano and he did impressions—Bing Crosby and Perry Como and Vaughan Monroe—all the singers of those days. And we would sing along and toast the season with the best spiked cider you ever tasted."

"Do you keep up with him now?" I wondered if he could really be one and the same with the troll everyone loved so much to hate.

"Oh sweetie . . . they're all gone now. We lost touch years ago, before they died off."

"You're the second person I've talked to who thinks he's dead."

She had been holding her cheeks up in a perpetual, but charming, smile until that moment. Her entire face seemed to collapse, her bright rouged cheeks drifting downward. "You're saying Eddie Cobb is still alive?"

"Yes."

"He was older than all of us."

"That fits. He still lives across the street."

She seemed startled, almost shaken. "I can't believe Nancy and Randy didn't tell me."

"Maybe they didn't know. Did you ever tell them about Eddie—or the parties or whatever?"

"No. I suppose not. My daughter—Nancy's mother—knew. After all, she grew up next door. She came this close." She pinched two arthritic fingers together to illustrate her point, "to marrying Ed, Jr." She fluttered her hands. "But Eddie, still alive. Incredible! He must be the treasure of the neighborhood."

I was about to respond, to tell her just what I had been able to gather in the last hour or so when our front door bell rang. Reaching the front door to answer would have been like swimming through molasses. The best I could do was excuse myself and start squirming in that general direction. Someone else reached over and turned the knob. The door swung open.

There stood Eddie Cobb. Not the Eddie Cobb I had invited as an afterthought days before when I was walking Zeppo. Not the Cobb who peeked out of his front window as I slid the invitation under his screen door, half hoping he wouldn't come. That Cobb was scruffy and unshaven, sporting torn shirts that were a map of wrinkles and an old leather jacket pock-marked with holes and the patches where holes had been.

This Eddie Cobb was overdressed for the Open House, like the men a little younger than him back in the kitchen. He wore a navy blue blazer and an old pair of triple pleated gray flannels. His blazer was parted, revealing a red vest and a tie erupting in Christmas colors of red, green, and white. His starched, white shirt was frayed but pressed, though I wouldn't guess in what decade it had last seen an iron.

His eyes roamed the room and he found me. "Good evening, Mr. Fleming." He spoke so softly I could hardly tell he was speaking, but somehow my guests recognized in seconds that the stranger at the door was the Cobb who had been such an easy topic of conversation. The rat-tat-tat of cocktail chatter simmered quickly into silence.

"Merry Christmas, Mr. Cobb." I squeezed through the crowd and shook his hand. Throughout the parlor and dining room, significant conversation ceased. After all, much of it had been about Cobb or his house or his junk car or his mangy dog. With him present at the Open House, it was hard to keep up the pace of story-telling.

He looked around, wary. Why shouldn't he be, knowing how people talked about him. He looked old, but not stupid. No one had ever accused him of that. Instead of walking from the doorway into the main hall, he seemed to take a step back.

"I think this was probably a mistake," he said softly, "I should be going."

My guests were silent and staring. The seniors clustered in the kitchen squeezed towards the front of the house, wondering what made everyone and everything so still. I looked at Katie. Not a hint. She didn't know that I had invited him and I wasn't about to tell her. This was my problem. We had a plan for everything else. The music, the fires, the candles, the greenery, the food and drinks. But we didn't have a plan for receiving the derelict old man from the wreck across the street. Plan or not, I was going to have to deal with it.

"Everybody . . . I think you all know Mr. Edward Cobb." Not a word from any of my guests, only an isolated gasp or two. I was going to have to keep talking, just so people could start breathing again. I took Cobb gently by the arm and eased him a step or two away from the door.

"He's lived in the Village about as long as anyone here." I looked over at Nancy's grandmother and smiled. "Some of you can remember when he and his family gave Christmas parties with a lot more music and fun than mine tonight. He was friends with the family that built this house. They were leaders of this neighborhood before many of us were born. They were leaders of the city itself, and I know Mr. Cobb was a leader in the Presbyterian church."

The Reverend Henry Motley inched forward from the kitchen crowd. "And he still would be, if we hadn't been so bone-headed!" Motley boomed in the same voice that had once made his sermons legendary.

I could hear the faint and welcome tinkle of my guests' wine glasses as they began to resume sipping. Their initial shock had passed. They were relaxing into the Open House again, but I wasn't about to lose their attention. They were listening. I had to be careful what I said. There were things I knew and things I could only surmise. But I wasn't about to stop.

"Now, you wouldn't believe it . . . but thirty years ago, the church thought a new parking lot was about the most important thing in the world. Knocking down a few old houses wasn't a big deal. The neighborhood wasn't even called the Village back then. Well, Mr. Cobb saved at least two of the houses and because of it, his own congregation made it pretty uncomfortable for him to stick around. So he made it more comfortable for everyone—except maybe himself—by just not coming to church. And eventually, people forgot about the parking lot and they forgot about Mr. Cobb.

"Now, I'm guessing that not coming to church didn't stop Mr. Cobb from helping out. I don't know that he'd want me to tell this, but like I said, I'm guessing anyway. Anyway, for quite some time he's been slipping into the church before the staff arrives and he's been leaving money when he could, maybe some items of furniture or clothing that he's been able to pick up at neighborhood yard sales. Things for special causes . . . refugees, homeless people and so on."

Wine glasses were moving more briskly. I could hear an undercurrent of whispers, though I had no idea what was being said.

"Please," Cobb said under his breath, "that's enough. You're embarrassing me."

"We're the ones who need to be embarrassed," I whispered in response.

"Of course," I continued, "that wasn't Mr. Cobb's last gasp for preservation. Back when some moron cut this house into four apartments, Mr. Cobb stuck it out in his house. He could have sold to the absentee landlords or the developers and be living in the Parkside Towers. And I'd have some concrete block piece of crap across the street, or maybe next door too, and none of the new apartments would look very Victorian. But he stayed put and so did the old zoning." I didn't dare look at Cobb for fear he'd stop me.

"There are some irritating things about Mr. Cobb." I laughed, looking around at my contemporaries. "We wouldn't dare talk about it much, but I'll give you a for instance. That old '55 Buick parked in his back yard. It's an eyesore. He'll probably never restore it. But you see, that was Mr. Cobb's son's car. Father and son drove it around together before Mr. Cobb's son was killed in Vietnam."

I glanced over at Cobb, wanting very much to apologize for talking about things that probably weren't my business. But then on the other hand, if I didn't do it then, chances are it would never be done, and I had decided that that would be the greater tragedy.

"I guess it's sort of like Randy Rivers' bike. Now once again, I don't know this for sure, but I bet Mr. Cobb bought that bike because he remembered Randy riding it around the neighborhood thirty years ago. I was there the Saturday morning he bought it. I know it cost a lot more than Randy paid Mr. Cobb—the people selling it claimed it was an antique. And it was. Mr. Cobb bought it for Randy's son and he sold it for next to nothing because he didn't want to let on that he knew what it was worth to Randy." I looked at Randy and winked. "'Cause we all know how sentimental Randy really is beneath that crusty shell of his."

Randy straightened up. "Well, yeah. Like Joel said, I really appreciate what Mr. Cobb did."

"Now I also know it's irritating to see Mr. Cobb walking his dog around, stopping and looking at houses. But you know, I sort of met Mr. Cobb when I was out walking Zeppo one night . . . and when Zeppo stops . . . I stop. And especially when you're feeling a little lonely or blue or whatever, you stop a little longer and stare into the light of other people's homes. You're not really looking at the people, you're imagining what life is like in a home that looks so inviting. And you're remembering how warm and cozy it can be to have family all together.

"Well, anyway, when Mr. Cobb's wife moved away, he should have done himself a favor and moved too but, you see, he's been part of this neighborhood for so long, I guess it was just too damned hard to give up."

I couldn't think of anything else to say. What I had just said seemed to come together like the end of a mystery novel or the pieces of a jigsaw puzzle. "So, anyway, I'm sure you all know Eddie Cobb a lot better than I do." I hoped Cobb would stay, but I couldn't hold him any longer.

He looked around the room, his eyes focusing on first one, then another, of my guests. It took me a second to realize that he was looking for someone—anyone—with whom he could connect. Without some bridge between his past and the present, there was no sense in his remaining at the Open House. All of my closing argument to correct the corporate impression of my neighbor across the street would remain well-intended but ultimately ineffectual. Then, without my ever noticing that she had somehow crossed the same unnavigable gulf of people that I had struggled through moments before, Nancy Rivers' grandmother slipped past me, hugging Cobb like a lost lover.

"Virginia?" Cobb spoke her name and the bridge was complete.

She slipped her arm through his. "We all had such good times in this old house."

And that was all that it took. I found myself nudged to

the side, then drifting further and further away from Cobb as Osborne, Henry Motley, their wives and an irrepressible wave of seniors from the Parkside clustered around Cobb as if he were some aging, but venerable, film star. Minutes passed and darker hair began to dot what had been a sea of white.

I found myself edging up my much heralded staircase until I was above and completely apart from the rest of the party. At first some very un-seasonal thoughts occurred to me about my neighbors and myself. We were such hypocrites, one moment gossiping and, the next, embracing this relic from a totally different era. Then, with a realization far more consistent with the season, I saw what had really happened. A different light had been cast on the person of Eddie Cobb. Cobb was still the person who lived in the house that everyone talked about. He was a hermit of sorts. But like the image of Cobb's house I gained from the vantage of my back porch earlier in the evening, what they now saw was just as true, just as real and perhaps more in the spirit of an Open House.

I smiled. In the end, I was glad that my neighbors, like myself, were simply human. And I was glad that in the spirit of Christmas, helped along by Katie's punch and party prowess, we were all just a little more humane.

"More wine?" Katie had slipped up the back stairs and hallway and was standing behind me on the front staircase. This time, instead of an instruction, it was an invitation. I took the glass she offered, gave her a kiss, and held it up to toast our Open House.

TO HEAR THE ANGELS SING

The Blue Moon Bar and Grille was the only place open that Christmas Eve. It wasn't their first choice, or their second or even their third, but Ike Moon risked his liquor license serving weak beer to the college crowd, and Alex and Benny were just barely the college crowd. The two hunched over their lukewarm cheeseburgers, fries scattered over the checkered oil cloth, resting half-in and half-out of splattered pools of beer. Benny chewed his sandwich in silence. Alex sipped his beer, staring at the decorations—such as they were. The Blue Moon's decor was frozen in the fifties. A two-foot plastic tree was propped cock-eyed next to the T.V. over the bar. Some deteriorating gold tinsel had been draped haphazardly around the mirror. Brands of beer long extinct still lived in the bar's clocks, lamps and dart boards. Ike Moon, owner for all eternity, stood behind the bar, expressing his nicotine-tinged breath on the glasses as he dried them.

Alex and Benny had munched in silence since their food arrived. Benny wasn't asking why Alex had called him on the phone. They were avoiding the topic, talking in disjointed half sentences about bits and pieces of everything else. Alex recounted his road trip home from Boston. Benny told him about the high school's football season.

"They won the conference, but they lost the championship. They could've used you."

Alex grunted, as if to say "Who are you kidding?"

Their words were exchanged in brief spurts and long lulls. Alex asked about home and Benny assured him that nothing had changed. Alex inquired about Benny's parents and Benny told him they were fine. Alex described what school back east was like and Benny listened in awe. Then Alex trailed off and Benny remained silent. They had always known each other, and it had always been the same. Alex led. Benny followed. Alex spoke. Benny listened. Alex joked and Benny laughed. Usually it worked. Tonight it was different. Tonight things were all backwards.

"So why *did* you call me tonight?" Benny finally asked the question that had been hovering around their words. He caught Alex with a mouth half-full of cheeseburger. Benny was never that direct.

"I don't know." Alex swallowed. "I just thought I'd give you a call. You know. Just get together."

"On Christmas Eve?"

Alex fumbled for an answer. He wasn't accustomed to Benny asking him anything. That was probably why he had called Benny. Friendship with Benny wasn't dependent upon words or deep analysis or well-expressed or well-taken advice. They simply sensed comfort in each other's company. Usually they did no more than bide time together.

Even if they hadn't written or called each other on the phone since Alex went away to school, Benny was there. Benny was always there. Alex had considered calling some of the other guys first. After all, unlike Benny, they had broken up with girls before. Benny had barely gotten a date for the prom. Yet Alex had picked up the phone and called Benny when he felt like he was going to cry again.

"I just needed to talk."

"What about?"

"I, uh, don't want to talk about it."

Benny scratched the side of his head. He never pressed, but Alex's nonsequitur wasn't meant as a joke. Neither one of them was laughing.

"So what are you getting for Christmas?" Benny asked. Maybe Alex would eventually get around to what he was really thinking.

"I don't know. Gloves. A sweater, I think. Who cares?"

"You don't sound too excited."

"I'm excited. I'm excited." Alex held out his arms in mock joy.

"Sure you are."

"Okay. I'm not excited. What does it matter? So how was the Christmas parade this year?"

"It was good. Mark Garrett played Santa Claus again, Deke was one of his helpers. The fire department made a lot of noise. One of the balloon floats got tangled up in the telephone lines."

Alex laughed for the first time. "I wish I could have seen that."

"I wish you could too. Things are a little lonely without the old gang." Benny sipped his beer. "So how's your little brother doing?"

"He's doing whatever he wants. He practically owns the house now."

Benny laughed. "Well, you're away at school. That makes a difference."

"Why should it? I was supposed to go away, wasn't I?"

"I didn't."

"But you never wanted to go away. You never applied to anyplace but State."

"I like home."

"Well, I do too."

Benny's face sobered. His finger drew figure eights with the watery beer collecting on the tablecloth. "So that's what's bothering you!"

"No. No," Alex repeated. "Well, not exactly. That's part of it."

"So what's the rest of it?" Benny's innocence was disarming. Alex didn't answer. Instead, he sipped his tepid beer and stared, unseeing, at the television. Christmas had ended the night before. The thought came clearly to him for the first time.

Christmas was over already. She had boarded the jet and flown away, coming to his hometown just long enough for him to introduce her to his family. Then she had told him they should *just* be friends. His present for her was still under the tree at home. They would never date, never kiss, never say they loved each other again.

"Something's bugging you." Benny persisted.

Alex finally nodded. He was ready to talk. "Patricia and I broke up last night."

Benny nodded. He didn't know her, but he knew about her. "The girl from up east?"

"She goes to school near Boston, but she's from Arkansas." Alex felt a little guilty that he'd told his other friends about Patricia, but not Benny. Benny was rooted to his hometown and the past. Patricia was supposed to be the future.

"You all were pretty serious?"

Alex shrugged. "I thought so. I mean, we only knew each other six weeks. But it seemed like forever. I fell in love with her." Alex let out a deep breath. "And I thought she fell in love with me." He thought he might start crying again.

"How did it all happen?" Everyone else had gotten the story as it unfolded; exuberant letters, cheery Christmas cards, manic phone calls where Alex extolled his and Patricia's miraculous love. Benny was the first to hear it as history.

Alex answered slowly. "We met on a subway. You know how Boston is."

"Not really."

"Well, we just met and started talking. I was with some friends and she was with some other girls. She heard me talking and asked if I was from the South."

"You don't have a southern accent."

"Well, she thought I did. Anyway, she came back to our room with her friends and they ended up spending the night."

"She spent the night!" Benny screeched. A cadre of Blue Moon regulars jerked their heads around. Ike frowned and returned to the Blue Moon's fine crystal.

"It wasn't like that," Alex crouched towards Benny, embarrassed, motioning for his friend to calm down. "We didn't do anything. The whole six weeks we didn't do anything. I mean we kissed and made out, but we didn't have sex. We just fell in love."

"Sounds kind of old-fashioned."

"It was. Very," Alex's voice trailed off again, "romantic. We only saw each other on weekends. Football games, a trip down to Philadelphia with my freshman debate team. Then she invited me to a Christmas dance. I went. It was . . . wonderful."

"So what happened last night? You get into a fight or something?"

"No, nothing like that. It's just that when we weren't together, during the weekdays, she kept convincing herself that it wouldn't work. She had something going with an older guy back in Arkansas. They broke up, but he kept calling her. We kept talking about that."

"You mean, *you* kept talking about that?"

Alex wondered how his unsophisticated friend had become so suddenly perceptive. "Yeah, I guess so."

"Well, it sounds like she's a little confused. Maybe about who she really wants to date."

"Well, yeah, I guess so. But we loved each other. We even talked about getting engaged."

"Engaged!" Benny's screech. Again, the stares from the bar leaners. "Alex, you're only eighteen."

"I know. I know. It was more her idea than mine."

"Alex, I mean last year we were going to the Senior Prom and football games and stuff. Engaged?" Benny spoke the word as if it connoted mystic rites, "I just can't imagine any of us getting engaged."

"Well, that part's a little hard for me to believe, too. But we were in love."

"So what happened last night?"

"I don't know. She flew in yesterday morning. She was really tired. Exams wore her out. I introduced her to my mom and dad and Kirk."

"I'll bet they were all real thrilled about you getting engaged."

"Yeah, thrilled wasn't exactly the right word. Try shocked and then really ugly. Things have been a little strained ever since I told them about her." Alex had no desire to churn up the extent of his father's frostiness, his mother's horror or Kirk's seeming oblivion to the entire situation. "Patricia and I had a long talk before her flight out. She picked up on my parents' feelings. Wasn't hard. That made her down on everything. The more I kept saying things would work out, the more she kept arguing with me."

"So, you had a fight?"

"No. We never fought. She kept talking around everything and I kept trying to convince her that if we loved each other, it would work out."

The two examined and re-examined Alex's anguish, his self-pity and self-consciousness. Alex set forth his tale in bits and pieces and Benny gently persisted, probing like a mother removing splinters from a prickled palm. Alex's pain spilled out and Benny absorbed it, comforting more with his ear than by his words. Eight o'clock became nine and then ten. Christmas Eve expired as it had never expired for either Alex or Benny. When Alex felt all the sadness he could feel and spoke of his sorrow until he could speak no more, the two grew silent again. Through it all they sipped their pallid beer and Alex began to feel human again. They weren't drunk. They weren't even close. They were simply together, and they hadn't been together since Alex had gone away.

Alex looked up from his empty glass and smiled at Benny. "Thanks."

"What do you mean?" Benny knew, but he wanted to hear it from his old, lost friend.

"You know. Thanks for listening. I hate to be such crummy company."

"That's okay. Besides, I would have had to go to Mass with Mom and Pop."

Alex wondered whether his friend meant what he had said. "You didn't want to go?"

"I don't know. I don't know what I want to do."

Alex leaned slowly back in his chair, a jumble of half-formed questions bubbling up. He started to say something. Stopped, then started again.

"What *would* you do," he paused, collecting his thoughts, "if you could do anything on Christmas Eve?"

Benny's lips formed into a whimsical grin.

"I don't know. I mean, I never thought about it." Benny's short life had been spent pursuing actions initiated by others.

"Okay, Benny, I'm Santa Claus. I can make wishes come true. What wish will I bring you?" Alex relaxed a little, his mind off of Patricia for the first time in days. Benny puzzled over his friend's question. Benny had always taken Alex seriously. Alex saw the faint glimmer of a desire in Benny's eyes and he murmured, "Hmm?"

"Well, you remember when Alice Taylor asked me to the prom last spring?"

"Yeah."

"Well, I wish I'd said 'yes'."

"Alice is sort of a loser."

"I know. But I am too. And she ended up not going because I turned her down. And Alice helped me pass chemistry the fall of senior year. If I hadn't passed chemistry I wouldn't have graduated with you guys."

Alex nodded. "I see what you mean." He searched for words to make Benny's decision sound like the right one. "But you still shouldn't have to go with someone . . . "

"But I actually liked her."

"You liked her?" Alex scratched along the crown of his head. "Then why didn't you go with her?"

"Because I knew you guys thought she was a loser. And so I was too embarrassed to go with her."

"Oh, shit," Alex's voice went as flat as his beer. Alex the wannabe wish-maker had become Alex the wish-breaker. "I'm really sorry. I wish I'd known."

"That was my fault. I should have told you guys." Benny squirmed in his chair and it made a grating noise. "What about you? I'll bet you wish Patricia hadn't flown away like she did."

Alex started to nod his head "yes," then stopped. He suddenly realized that the answer wasn't that easy. He chewed at a piece of burger that emerged from his gum. "No, I wish it was different. That's for sure. But I don't know what I could wish to make it different." He looked down at the table for a second. His thoughts were a jumble of wishes and desires, but none of them seemed to matter. No one wish seemed that important. Then he remembered. Something that had been in the back of his mind for months. Something he had dismissed a dozen times as silly, but simply wouldn't go away. "If I could make a wish to change something—to do something right that I did wrong, I think I would have thanked someone who was really kind to me. Someone I should have thanked, but didn't. Maybe that sounds crazy, but Patricia falls under 'what's done is done'."

"That doesn't sound so crazy. But who was it you didn't thank? And for what?"

"Remember last summer when I worked as a mailman?"

"Sure, I remember."

"Well, every day it seemed like I had a different route. And one week it was really hot. I mean over a hundred degrees. And I was delivering mail to this little rundown neighborhood over in the west end. No one place got a lot of mail, so I had a zillion addresses. I was trying to figure out which apartments were which and I must have looked like I was dying of thirst—and I felt like it too. Well, anyway, all of a sudden there's this really old lady standing on a porch calling to me. I mean she was really old—and not too well-kept. She was in a bathrobe and her skin looked like a wadded-up dish rag and her fingernails were long and starting to curl under."

"Sounds pretty gross."

"It was, but she told me that I looked hot. I said I was, and then she handed me seventy-five cents. I mean, she didn't look like she had seventy-five cents to spare or any family who would give her any money if she needed it. But she gave me seventy-five cents for a Coke. I tried to give it back to her, but she wouldn't listen. She just kept smiling and telling me that I looked so hot. Then she told me that years and years before her son was a mailman and that he always appreciated kindness from people on his route. She said, "It's been seventy years since he was a boy like you." Well, I got so turned around and surprised that she went inside before I had a chance to really thank her again. Next day, they switched me to another route and I never was on her street again. Every day I meant to go back and thank her and maybe take her something. But I didn't. Then I left for school. See what I mean?"

"Well, yeah, I do, but it's not like she expected you to pay her back or whatever."

"But that's not the point. I'll bet nobody goes to see her. Ever. Let alone at Christmas. Nobody thanks her for anything. So there she is handing out money she doesn't have to spare, to thirsty mailmen in a rundown neighborhood, with nobody to visit her. I mean, if she had a big family or something it might be different. And maybe she does, but I don't think so."

"So go and see her."

"I can't. We're going to my Aunt Dorothy's in the morning and then over to my Aunt Helen's for dinner. Besides, I'd want to take her something and there's no place that would be open."

"Too bad."

"Yeah."

Their beer-mellowed tongues were silent. They had told their tales and exchanged their wishes. Alex examined the grease-splattered clock next to the television. Ten fifteen. An hour or two before, he would have been satisfied to welcome Christmas in the company of the Blue Moon's most faithful patrons. His mood had matched the melancholy on their faces. Now the intensity of his pain had lessened. Patricia seemed further away, both in space and time. Benny's willing ear had given him a release, and the space created by that release began filling with a short list of regrets and recriminations. For the first time since getting home, he wanted to do something, anything. Instead he sat in his chair, his eyes only half-focused on Benny, trance-like, mute of voice, inert.

"Don't you boys have somewhere to go tonight?" The voice of Ike Moon resounded like a growl from their side.

"Uh, we're just talking . . . " Alex found his mouth open, words locked up in his mind.

"I'll bet you've got family you could be with," Ike's eyes seemed to mellow as he assessed his young patrons.

"Well, yeah, but we just wanted to talk here." Alex stumbled across a few more words and Benny nodded in agreement.

Ike Moon flung his towel across his shoulder. He had suffered their foolishness long enough. He knew where they wanted to be and where he wanted them to be. Most of all, he knew where they should be.

"Okay, fine," he said, "You want to stick around, that's great. But I'll tell you right now, if these other guys here had anywhere else to be—yours truly included—we would be." Ike caught his breath. "By the way, let's see your I.D." Ike folded his arms and jutted his spear-like chin outwards.

Alex and Benny were catatonic, mouths half open. Ike Moon never carded anyone. That was the only reason the college crowd ever went to the Blue Moon Bar and Grille.

"I left my wallet at home," Benny lied.

"I, uh, well . . . I think I left mine in the car," Alex's mouth had gone dry. "What do you say we go somewhere else, Benny?"

"Okay," Benny rejoined. "Yeah, okay." The two stood

up and dropped a few coins on the table, then started to walk away.

"Be sure to come back when you got more time to stick around," Ike called after them.

Alex did an about-face. He couldn't tell if Ike Moon was laughing at them or just smiling.

"Merry Christmas, Mr. Moon," Alex said. They were through the front door before Ike Moon's face alighted in a crescent-like grin.

"Merry Christmas, son," Ike muttered to himself, "Now get on home."

Cold spits of sleet took the flush from their cheeks. The cars on Main were moving slowly with the change in the weather. Traffic was light. The church-goers were another twenty minutes from leaving their homes for late services.

"Well, what do you want to do?" Benny asked.

"What do you want to do?" Alex asked, though he knew exactly what he wanted to do.

"I asked you first," Benny retorted.

"Okay," Alex motioned towards his car. "Hop in and I'll show you."

Alex pulled away from the curb. The only decent F.M. rock station was still playing its usual. Not tonight, Alex thought. His fingers danced over the face of the car radio, switching it to an A.M. station he knew was playing Christmas songs. Christmas had been on hold long enough. Perry Como crooned that there was no place like home for the holidays. Alex and Benny listened in silent agreement. Benny knew his friend had a plan of some sort. It was good to have Alex back. Back in town and at least for awhile, back from the doldrums of losing Patricia.

Benny didn't pay any attention to where they were going. The sleet was turning to snow and the streets were beginning to look like a city-scape from one of those old forties Christmas movies Alex liked to watch. Benny was happy just to be along for the ride, watching the city take on its white frosting. There wasn't any place in town that was more than fifteen minutes away from any other place. Benny wondered if they were headed for another bar down on the river. When Alex pulled the car over, Benny was caught off guard. This wasn't the destination he had expected.

"What are we doing here?" he asked.

Alex smiled. "What do you think?"

Benny gulped. "Come on, Alex, I haven't seen Alice since the summer. I don't even know if she's in town. And even if she is, it's awful late. I don't want to get her parents all mad."

"Come on," Alex chided, "it's Christmas Eve. Mr. and Mrs. Taylor aren't going to be too tough on us tonight."

"Yeah, I know, but . . . " Benny was still fumbling for excuses not to get out of the car as Alex threw open his door and started running up the walk of the little brick bungalow.

"Come on," Alex cried, waving his arm, "I can't do this alone."

Benny drew a quick breath and threw open the passenger's door. The wind had softened, but the wet snow against his face made him wince. "Okay," he cried, blinking, "okay, I'm coming. But what are we going to do after we knock on the door?"

"We'll figure that out later," Alex yelled back.

Their feet scraped prints in the thin film of snow covering the Taylors' front walk. All the lights were on in the living room. Alice and her parents were lined up like three chubby little dolls on the couch, watching television.

"Now what?" Benny's voice broke. Embarrassment awaited him in the lighted arena of the Taylors' front porch.

"Well, first, we're going to sing!" Alex was almost manic. "We're going to serenade Alice."

"Huh?" Benny froze at the prospect.

"'It came upon a midnight clear, that glorious song of old,'" Alex began, "'the world in solemn stillness lay . . . '"

Benny grit his teeth and started singing in his own distinctive monotone, "' . . . to hear the angels sing. Peace on the earth, good will to men . . . '" they sang until the first verse was over. Then they started on *God Rest Ye Merry Gentlemen.*

Alice and her parents jumped up at the first explosion of Alex's voice. They moved to the window and stared into the darkness, visible to Alex and Benny, but unable to see the two boys at first. Their eyes darted from left to right, straining to focus on the two figures in the shadows. Alex grabbed Benny and drew him into the yellow light cascading from the porch. Their voices made up in volume and energy what they clearly lacked in quality. If their caroling could get them in the door, then Alex's spur-of-the-moment plan would be a success.

Alice was the first to come to the door. She opened it and stepped out on the porch. Alice was smiling. Her father was not.

"Now look here, boys," Mr. Taylor began.

"Daddy," Alice turned to her father, her face reminding Alex of a jelly roll. "These boys are friends of mine from school." Mr. Taylor jiggled his jowls in a brief acknowledgment. Alex inched towards him.

"Sorry for the racket, Mr. Taylor." His mind was spinning for a reason to be at the Taylors' front door at nearly eleven on Christmas Eve. "Merry Christmas, Mrs. Taylor. How are you doing, Alice?"

"I'm okay. I didn't know you were home from school."

"I'm back alright. Finals ended Wednesday." The perfect lie began to flow from his lips. "In fact, I'm the reason Benny didn't ask you to the Candlelight Mass like he wanted to. I had him out listening to my problems. Right, Benny?"

Benny listened and watched in amazement and simply nodded.

"And, since it was all my fault, I thought I owed you a carol or two before you came to church with us . . . I mean, if that's okay with your mom and dad."

Alice turned quickly, giving her father little choice, though he was already in the process of saying, "Yes."

"We won't be out long after midnight. I know everybody's gotta get up early tomorrow morning . . . " Alex babbled on for a second or two while Alice grabbed her coat. Benny was still too stunned to speak.

Nothing was explained on the way to the service. If anything, Alex avoided long explanations, choosing instead to raise the volume on the continuous stream of Christmas songs. When they arrived five minutes early for the service, the church parking lot was full. Alex pulled up to the front entrance of St. Dominic's.

"Hold a spot for me inside." He grabbed Benny's sleeve. "Over near your folks. I'll be back as soon as I can."

"There's a parking spot in the next block. I can see it from here," Benny pointed down the street.

"Don't worry. I'll find a place. See you in a little bit."

Benny and Alice jumped out, still uncomfortable in each other's presence, still a little surprised that they were at Midnight Mass together. Alice turned to thank Alex for letting them out at the front door, for asking her to the service, and most of all for serenading her with carols. She knew Benny wouldn't have done it on his own. But Alex had already pulled away.

Alex turned at the next block. He didn't park. Instead, he headed for home. With Benny and Alice gone, his loneliness returned. Where was Patricia now? Was she at some church service somewhere? Or with friends commiserating over love lost? Or had her old boy friend already surfaced? The same thoughts that would haunt him off-and-on through the holidays were neither resolved by his evening with Benny nor a dozen evenings with various friends before he went back to school. Only time would make the hurt fade until it was merely a memory of heartache.

Alex approached his own front porch more cautiously than he had the Taylors'. The lights in the living room were turned down low. The television was on, but he couldn't see anyone. Alex nudged the door open. It stuck. It always stuck, a warning to both parents that someone was entering. On the television, a cathedral choir was singing. His father was asleep on the couch.

The presents under the tree had been rearranged in the process of adding a few more. Alex dropped to his knees and started rummaging. A glass ball ornament tinkled and almost fell. He caught it, let out a sigh, and started searching behind some other packages. Finally the small oblong box he had been searching for emerged. He grabbed it, stood up and started for the door.

"You okay, Alex?" His father's voice was soft but alert. He had been feigning sleep.

"I'm okay, Dad. I got an errand to run before I go back to church."

"Church? Well, when you come back, wake me up if I'm still on the couch. They're showing one of those old Christmas movies on the late show. We can watch it or talk or whatever."

Alex turned to his father. If he had never left home this evening, never met Benny, never killed time at the bedraggled

Blue Moon Bar and Grille, he could never have said, "okay," but he did them all, and when his Dad returned his "okay" with a smile, Alex felt the anguish of this Christmas Eve continue to dissolve.

Ten minutes later, he found her neighborhood. Several street lights were out. No one seemed to have any Christmas decorations on her street. He had been there in the day and during the summer. It took him another five minutes walking around to find the right apartment. When he did, he wasn't sure if she was still there. He stared at the mailbox names and he recognized hers immediately. Mrs. McNeill was still among the living.

Alex looked around, trying not to be noticed, but at the same time trying not to look so suspicious that he might be mistaken for a burglar. Mrs. McNeill's lights were out—except for a diminutive, two-foot Christmas tree, standing on a table, its few strands of old-fashioned, fat bulbs casting a good bit of light. He tore off the tag on the package under his arm, grabbed his pen and printed neatly on a white part of the wrapping itself: "Thanks for the Coke money you gave me last summer. I was your mailman for a day. Merry Christmas!"

Alex started to sign his name, but didn't. She would know who it was. Maybe in a day or two he would come back and make a formal introduction. Maybe the whimsy of Christmas would pass and he would never come back. For now, it didn't matter. He would be happy if she had any use at all for a bottle of cologne. For an instant, standing in the dimly-lit hallway of the apartment house, a strange thought ran through his head: he'd had the right present, but he'd almost given it to the wrong person. He placed the package in her doorway and left the inner hallway. One last glance back at her glowing Christmas tree and he was gone.

Alex sped faster than he should have through the silent streets. The Christmas Eve service would be more than half over, but he would make something of it. He would slip into the pew next to Benny, unnoticed, just as if he had been there all along. Midnight had nearly come, bringing Christmas. Alex turned off the radio and rolled down his window. Big flakes of snow swirled in around him. The quiet created by the whitening of the streets and trees served as a backdrop for his jumbled thoughts. It had been his first Christmas Eve back from school, his first not spent with his family, his first wrangling with the sorrow of love lost. The characters of the night filled the stage of his mind. Patricia, Benny, Alice, the Taylors, his Dad, Mrs. McNeill—even Ike Moon. Nothing would ever be black-or-white again, simple and pure, offering easy answers. But he had learned the need for angels to sing and wise men to bear gifts and for lesser humans to imitate them both.

THE ROAD SHOW

1.

She was late. Christmas Eve and almost Christmas. The fact that it was almost Christmas mattered less than the lateness of the hour. I learned years before that Christmas began when we were joined together as a family. That moment might come a day or two before or after Christmas day. Liza had forever split Christmas between her mother's home and mine.

Liza was eighteen now, her "baby" brother, Joe, fourteen. The years of setting out cookies and hot chocolate for Santa, celery and carrots for the reindeer were gone. So were the Christmases of play lipstick and Barbie dolls, elementary school programs with a cast of hundreds, and heroic efforts by me to transport her from one home in Cincinnati to another in Louisville with minimal anguish. All of these Christmases had suddenly burned brightly and extinguished, like memories of my own childhood Christmases a million years before. A cascade of photos, a handful priceless, were the only evidence that my children had once been young and full of whimsy, ready to believe in the myths and the realities of Christmas. There were Christmas memories to come, but on this particular Christmas Eve, Liza was still on the road, somewhere between Indianapolis and Louisville, snow and temperatures falling.

I poured a glass of wine and walked to the front window. No Liza. No call. Beth, Joe and I had trimmed the tree two weeks before. It stood almost ten feet tall, twinkling lights and a potpourri of mostly wooden, signed ornaments sheathed in garlands of shimmering foil. Presents were wrapped with ribbons and stacked under the tree. Unfortunately, this postcard-perfect setting blocked my view of the street as I squeezed past pine limbs and over unopened presents to gaze outside. Though not a gift had been opened, not a moment of Christmas spent, I was already feeling the familiar pangs of loss that follow the passage of Christmas. No matter how long I live I will always feel it—and this year, Christmas's coming was suspended until sometime after a snowy drive home.

The dusting had begun. Just as the weatherman had warned. A cold front was coming out of the Dakotas and across the Midwest. Warmer Gulf Stream air was meeting it at St. Louis and moving east. Great. White Christmases were a rarity. South of the Ohio River, it might never accumulate at all. If Liza were driving in from Cincinnati, she might never see a flurry. She'd be south of the river all the way down Interstate 71. But there were college friends, or, I suspected, one special boyfriend in Indianapolis and, even though it was Christmas Eve, she had resolved to drive there first from Cincinnati before turning down Interstate 65 for Louisville.

The highway between Cincinnati and Louisville was familiar. Year after year, we had driven back and forth from Cincinnati, meeting her mother halfway. We knew every mile marker, every exit, the hills, the curves, cafes and motels, gas stations and convenience stores. Safely strapped beside me, she seemed to have grown up in the passenger's seat of the Volkswagen I wore out driving up and back. One day she was a little, blonde-haired girl with chubby red cheeks. The next she was a dark-haired teenager with one dyed blonde strand who, for all of my fatherly love, could not be delivered from the insecurity of her age. No road is without danger, but at least the road from Cincinnati to Louisville was like an old friend.

Interstate 65 from Indianapolis was different. I knew it, but Liza didn't. The towns, the exits, the gas stations—all more polished and spotless than those in Kentucky—were unfamiliar to her. Why couldn't she have chosen another time to visit her fellow Kalamazoo College freshmen? Why couldn't she have left Cincinnati earlier and gotten on the road from Indianapolis before dark?

"I'll leave Cincinnati by noon," she told me the day before, "Indianapolis is, like, two hours away. I want to see people for coffee and presents. I'll leave as soon as I can. I'll be in Louisville by ten. I'll be fine."

"Liza, I know you too well. I'll bet you'll be out partying tonight."

"Well, yeah, but . . . "

"That'll mean you'll sleep late Christmas Eve morning, won't get to Indianapolis before three and won't leave there until after nine."

"No . . . I told you," her voice had that slightly frosty edge, "I'll be with you guys by ten."

There was no arguing with Liza when her flag of independence was waving, especially if her 'friends' were really one special friend. The more subtle Liza tried to be, the more I knew there was some detail or details that she knew were absolutely none of my business.

I didn't expect her before eleven o'clock Christmas Eve, but we planned the evening as if she would be in by eight. The service at church was over by six and Beth made enough dinner for four. After dinner we told stories about Christmases past, half-listening to an old recording of *A Christmas Carol* with Lionel Barrymore as Scrooge. By eight-thirty, we had nested in our respective spots. Beth and Joe trusted my choice of movies as long as I didn't choose *Bells of St. Mary's* (my most maligned favorite). So I chose *The Bishop's Wife*. Beth drifted off to sleep on the couch just before the angel, Dudley, assured the Bishop that he would leave and never return. Joe made it to the Bishop's sermon at the end, but surrendered to the upstairs and a warm bed with the closing credits. Beth wakened enough to smile and murmur that she was sorry she couldn't stay awake for Liza. Then she followed Joe upstairs, exacting a promise that I would wake her once Liza was safely home.

The house was silent. No Liza. I read for a few minutes and finished a Christmas story that I had started and put down earlier in the day. I found myself reading paragraphs over and over, waiting for the phone to ring. If Liza was in trouble, she'd call. Or would she? She was stubborn and self-sufficient, as well as independent. I put my book down and fidgeted through magazines and catalogues, the newspaper and Christmas cards, waiting and helpless.

I paced and chafed as one Christmas memory transformed into another. My first year home from college I had almost died on a snow-bound interstate between Buffalo and Cleveland. Five of us were sharing a ride in an old Volvo, twenty years older, but otherwise just like the one Liza was driving over Indiana flatland. Our driver was an archetype of his era—long hair held back by a bandana, wrinkled blue work shirt, and worn-out, shiny blue jeans with holes in the knees. The Volvo sent snow mush spraying around us as he passed three semis in a row. Then, as he moved back over in front of the lead truck, the Volvo started spinning like a merry-go-round. Squeezed into the back seat, I closed my eyes and wondered for a millisecond what the semi's impact would be like when it came. When I opened my eyes we were careening off into the median, missing an abutment by only a few feet. The semi's roar was a sound I remember to this day. They showered us with salty slush, but the Volvo eased to a peaceful rest and the crisis passed. The worldly junior who owned the car and endured the near-miss from the front passenger's seat calmly confronted his friend and driver with the words, "Well, I guess I'd better drive for a while."

I caught myself smiling, then shuddered. It could be Liza this time. No longer possessed of a youth's misplaced sense of immortality, I was the parent waiting helplessly for an ominous call.

I had waited before. Outside of elementary schoolyards, knowing that if I went inside too early I would disrupt her teacher and classmates; at the stage door after high school holiday concerts, ready with rose in hand to congratulate my talented teenage diva; at the truck stop where her mother and I met on Friday nights to begin Liza's weekend with me. I had waited in good weather and bad, in the coolness just past dawn and in the humidity of a summer's sunset, in dismal rain and in crystal blue skies and sunshine. And I had waited and traveled in the snow. But I had never waited secure, at home, while Liza made the trip alone. Was she sufficiently skilled to drive on ice or careful enough to know her limits?

Was the Volvo in any shape to drive? Liza had promised to have it checked while she was home for the holidays. Oil, belts, timing, suspension, muffler and, most importantly, tires. The list had been included in my last letter to her, along with a check to cover all of it and then some. I also knew she would be busy visiting friends, working part-time, and doing her Christmas shopping. Hanging around repair shops wasn't Liza's idea of a good time. So I gave her the short list too, beginning with tires. Would she do any of it? I doubted it and now I wasn't just miffed, I was scared—parent-scared.

Eleven thirty Christmas Eve was becoming midnight and Christmas. I wandered into the kitchen, opened the refrigerator and stared inside. What did I want? All I really wanted, or needed, was for Liza to call and to be home where she belonged. I walked back to the parlor, poked my head around the tree to stare out the front window again, found my glass of wine and finished the last sip. I would've called her friend, but he didn't have a name or phone number. Calling Liza's mother would have only worried her. Besides, one worried parent was enough. Another ten minutes passed, then I'd had enough. Christmas Eve or not, I was through sitting in the house getting depressed and driving myself crazy—or crazier.

The sensible thing to do was to wait at home. I told myself again that she'd be along any minute. If she wasn't, then she'd call but, of course, she should have called two hours before. I was beyond rationalizations. For eighteen years of her life I had always done something. Not always the right something, but something. Why turn pacifist now?

I went upstairs and into our bedroom. I cleared my throat and shuffled around. Beth didn't move. She was in for the long winter's nap. I turned a light on in the corner. She stirred, turned and slipped a pillow over her face. I turned on the light next to the bed and started nudging her as I spoke.

"Honey, wake up," I jostled her a little harder. "Honey, I need you to wake up for a minute." No more whispers.

This time she sprang up like a jack-in-the-box. "What is it?"

Her eyes were wide open, her pupils dilated.

"Liza's not here yet. I'm going out."

Beth had more sense half-asleep than I had fully awake and, despite my glass of wine, quite sober. "You are what?"

"Going out."

"Where?"

"Up the road."

"Like I said, where?"

"Well, I figure . . . "

She took my arm, "I know you are worried—but you need to stick around here."

"I'm going. Here's the cell number just for convenience," I wrote it in big numbers on the message pad by the phone. "I'll go up I-65 for about an hour, then I'll call in. If Liza calls, find out where she is. If everything's okay, have her come on in, then call me and I'll turn around. If she's in trouble, tell her to stay put, call me and I'll go wherever you send me. No matter what, I'll turn around after about fifty miles."

"You're crazy. Stay here."

"I love you. Remember, call me if you hear anything."

"I'm going too," the voice from the door was Joe's. He was standing fully dressed in blue jeans, boots and warm sweater. No telling how long he had been awake, but I could tell there was no dissuading him.

I looked back at Beth. She sighed. "You two be safe. You're both crazy, but the old, crazy one needs company."

We left before she could remind us again how foolish we were and think anymore about having the whole family out on the road where we could get in trouble.

I threw on my bomber jacket and boots, grabbed my gloves and wool ball cap and Joe and I were out the back door, silently executing our exit like some para-military force from a bad movie. I unlocked the side door of the garage. Joe followed, popping the overhead door and slipping beside me in the aging black Mercedes I swore to love and protect through its first half million miles. It was a solid road car and now was the time to prove it. Half German high command, half Batman and Robin, we took off into the alley while the garage door was still rising. Joe punched the remote and I waited only long enough to make sure the garage door was closing.

Sliding twice on the alley's brick surface should have told me to slow down, but we were on a mission. The main roads were wet but not slippery, the snow sticking on trees and cars but not yet the pavement. For the few moments it took me to reach the ramp for the expressway, I marveled that the city was still awake early Christmas morning. We passed near one parish where the streets were filled with cars for the midnight Mass. Twenty-four hour gas stations and convenience stores still glared stark, bright lights. Automobiles sped up and down Broadway. We noticed these rumblings of humanity which seemed unaffected and untouched by the arrival of reindeer and oversized elves. We noticed, but largely ignored it, since our mission was more important.

II.

I should have left Indianapolis before nine. The streets were already snowy and I could feel the tires beginning to slide. I should have left Cincinnati for Indianapolis before two in the afternoon. I wanted to get to Indianapolis early, but I didn't. I knew that if Dad called Mom, she'd flip out. God, I am always late.

It's hard to admit when Mom or Dad are right. Not that I'd ever let them know. Why do we have to make all of these promises about when we'll be someplace? I felt so embarrassed. But anyway, Jeff.

Jeff made me laugh so much I cried. Jeff can do that to you, or at least he used to. Tryouts started it all. He was clowning around so much it almost made *Marat/Sade* seem like a comedy. We had the parts of inmates in an early nineteenth century insane asylum. We drooled and wandered around the stage. I greased my hair down and blacked out some of my teeth. "Just act like you do in seminar," Jeff said. "Oh, great, a comedian," I countered. "Sharp wit, lad." We kidded each other all of the time. But Jeff, what a talker.

He wasn't like most guys. Most guys don't have two words to say before they get physical. When Jeff spoke he had something to say. I thought so anyway. How did he see inside my soul so well? We talked all night sometimes. God, he was fun to talk to. At least he was fun to talk to at school.

Simple, dumb things were so interesting when Jeff and

I were together. We read parts of books aloud sometimes. Jeff even liked my favorite music. That was unusual too. Refreshing. Most guys don't know anything about Judy Collins or Joni Mitchell or Leonard Cohen and they don't like Fiona Apple or Shawn Colvin. Jeff does. After the play performances we must have seen a ton of old movies.

He liked old movies, foreign movies too. He's really funny at a movie with subtitles though. He makes up his own lines as the movie goes on. *Casablanca* is his favorite. Can you believe that a guy would like a romantic movie like that?

It's a good thing I got the oil and the antifreeze changed. I wished I had bought the new tires Dad told me to buy in Cincinnati. At least I didn't spend the money on other stuff. There was just so much to do during the holidays, so many friends to see, so many people who needed to know about Jeff.

Did I love Jeff? Am I still in love with him? Writing poems about love is so much easier than being in love. When Jeff first said he loved me I didn't know what to say. We kissed. Then I knew I loved him too. I guess I'd known for a long time, maybe even from our first time out. I wish I knew.

After the play, there weren't enough weeks. The weekend in Chicago. God, that was fun. Catching the train, hanging out with Jeff's older brother at Northwestern. Second City was really wild. I laughed more with Jeff than I did at the improv. Walking all over Old Town and Michigan Avenue was like something out of one the movies we saw. Being there as a couple was so different than being there with my family. You know, sometimes it feels like you're leading two completely different lives.

Jeff really liked the Museum of Art. Sunday afternoon we spent hours there, walking around, gazing at Van Gogh and Monet and Picasso. We even ate lunch outside. You wouldn't think that balancing an orange on your nose could be so much fun. Jeff made it fun. Just a dreamy, lazy day, sunny, but crisp—still warm for November and Lake Michigan.

Then there was the last weekend before Thanksgiving. God, it was awesome. You wouldn't think a swing dance could be so much fun. Jeff can dance too. What couldn't he do? We must have danced until two in the morning. That's when the snow started falling. The band played this swing version of "White Christmas." It already seems like such a long time ago now. Every couple in our group seemed to be in love. I'd never been that happy.

The road got worse the farther away from Indianapolis I drove.

New tires really would have helped. Whenever I slowed down or stopped, the Volvo wouldn't grip. Dad always says "hindsight is twenty-twenty". So, I should have listened to him!

The long Thanksgiving weekend was really hard. We talked on the phone every night, but things always seemed rushed. Jeff's parents always had someplace for him to go. That's what he told me. The one time I called and got his Mom she didn't seem too excited about talking to me. Maybe it was my imagination. I don't know. But something was different.

That Saturday I drove down to Louisville to see Dad. It seemed like all day Jeff and I kept missing each other. I'd call. He'd call back and we'd be out to dinner. Then late Saturday night I called again. I don't know why, but I felt really anxious, nervous about things. Joe's dad answered this time and he wasn't too happy about my calling after eleven. Joe was out with friends. He finally called Sunday morning and made up some story about being with old high school buddies. I think his buddies wore panties and skirts, but I didn't say anything—just that I'd see him back at K-zoo.

My roommate dropped out of school the week of exams. When I got back to school from Thanksgiving, she wasn't there. Half of her things were already gone. The other half didn't look as if they belonged to anyone. That really made me sad. I started crying. Too much going on. Too many crazy things happening.

Jeff came to the door. I was still crying. He held me in his arms and I got tears all over his new shirt. God, it felt good, just like it had been before Thanksgiving. I didn't feel like talking and Jeff understood. I just wanted to be held and that's what Jeff did. He didn't try to make me stop or try to make it go away. He didn't try to solve anything.

Christmas break comes so early at Kalamazoo, only one week after Thanksgiving. There wasn't any time for us to be together. We had just enough time to finish papers and take exams. Before I knew it, the week was gone. I wanted to go to Indianapolis with Jeff. I knew he could drive me back to Cincinnati in a day or two, or I could even catch a bus.

"Not a good idea, Liza," he said.

"Why not?"

"Mom and Dad have got everything planned for the first two weeks. I can't do that to you. You'd really feel weird. Trust me. How 'bout closer to Christmas?"

"Okay, but why don't you come over to Cincinnati?" I felt like some stupid married couple haggling over the details of whose family we would visit.

"Okay. How 'bout the week before Christmas?"

So that's what we planned. I must have seemed so desperate. I didn't mean to. I should have known that it was time to back off a little. Those next two weeks dragged. I saw friends and hung out and went for coffee. I saw a concert at Music Hall. My old high school chorus sang with Judy Collins. It felt like forever since I'd been with them, especially when I saw them up on stage while I was in the audience. Jeff and I talked, usually around dinner time. I talked more than Jeff. He just wasn't talking as much as when we met.

Finally it was time for Jeff to visit. Sharing him with my friends was so much fun. I took him to my favorite restaurants, places to hang out, the parks around my neighborhood. He stayed the night at my mom's house. That was fun, but a little strange. When he got back in his car, I started crying. The taste of those tears, salty in the wind, as Jeff got into his car.

"Well?" Jeff looked at me. I mean, what did I have to say to him? I had his present wrapped in tissue paper stuffed down in the pocket of my jeans. An antique, silver ring. I'd found it at an old jewelry store in Louisville on the Saturday after Thanksgiving.

"Let's get together in Indy soon."

"When?"

Jeff looked helpless. I should have just said something then.

I should have done something then. I feel so stupid now. Why didn't I just take control?

"Before Christmas? I don't know." Jeff was fumbling.

"Okay, Christmas Eve. I'll stop in Indianapolis on the way to Louisville."

"It's not exactly along the way," Jeff laughed. I should have known he was hinting that it really wasn't a good idea. Jeff kept talking when I didn't say anything. "Let's do it. We'll go to the afternoon service at my church."

I was fooling myself. I know that now, but at that moment, everything changed for the better. Jeff's invitation, if you want to call it that, was what I needed more than any Christmas present in the world. So I planned everything around Christmas Eve.

The drive to Indianapolis was lonely, lonelier than the worst Sundays when I'd have to leave Dad and return to Cincinnati. The sun didn't shine the whole way to Indianapolis. The air was damp, bone-chilling cold. Jeff's family had this late lunch planned and I was supposed to get there, all dressed up for lunch and the church service. I got a little lost in Indianapolis. I turned west instead of east on the beltway and it took me another twenty minutes to get back on track. I missed lunch. When I got there they were leaving to pick up Jeff's grandparents.

Jeff seemed really uncomfortable at the Christmas Eve service.

Down at the end of the pew, I felt like a complete stranger. I sure didn't feel like I was part of Jeff's family. Even with Jeff sitting next to me, it felt like he was there by mistake, more with his family than with me. Maybe that's normal. I don't know. Everyone was singing and smiling and filled with the Christmas spirit. And I sat there feeling like I'd gotten the wrong directions to the wrong church and the wrong family. Maybe they would have felt just as out-of-place in my church in the city as I felt in their church in the suburbs.

"What happened, Jeff?" I finally got him alone after the service.

"What do you mean?" Jeff knew exactly what I meant. It was just a matter of getting it out of him.

"If it's an old girlfriend, I could understand that."

"Liza, I don't know what you mean." My witty, sensitive, sophisticated, real man was slipping into the dumb male syndrome. This is so crazy. I don't know why I keep replaying this all in my head.

"Jeff, just tell me, are we going to be friends?"

"Liza, it's just," he paused, taking my hand. He started

again. "When I got home I realized who I really am. And it's not who I am at Kalamazoo." I felt like crying right there in his family room. But I held my breath. Don't cry. Don't cry. Not here.

Tears are running down my cheeks, now that I think about it.

But I was really good in Jeff's family room. I could feel my face getting red, but I didn't cry.

"You're saying we are going to be 'just friends' because I don't dress as preppy as your family would like or maybe I don't have the right connections in Cincinnati or Indianapolis? That's it, isn't it?"

Jeff denied it off-and-on for the next hour or so as we talked in front of the fire. We revisited what we'd "said and done and felt about each other" to quote the old Crosby, Stills and Nash song my dad likes so much. We talked around the possibility of seeing each other again when school starts. We broke our date for New Year's Eve. I never told Jeff how badly he was making me feel.

So much about that evening reminds me of stories my dad tells about some girl he was in love with his freshman year in college. He can picture certain moments with her as if they were in a movie. For me, it was like a movie being filmed, still very much in process. One where I couldn't turn off the camera. Even while it was happening, I felt like it was happening to someone else. The couch, the fire, the low lights and the family portraits that surrounded us in Jeff's basement. The Christmas tree in all white lights and red and gold glass ornaments. The constant flow of

Jeff's two little brothers parading through to irritate us. The rich, warm smell of spiced apple cider from a pot Jeff's mom had on the stove. The way the snow had begun to gather on the evergreen bushes outside of the glass sliding doors leading to the back yard. I felt like I had to get out of there. I wanted the twelve-foot ceilings of my Louisville home, the white tile wood stove in the family room and the gigantic tree filled with dozens of ornaments from all of the Christmases past. I wanted the corny old Christmas records my Dad played. I missed my brother who was so cool next to the brats Jeff called flesh and blood.

When I finally got up to leave, I was numb. Losing sense of time, I had no idea that it was past nine. I would have called home, but I just wanted to get into my car and drive. Jeff, at least, saw me to the car. I had a little trouble getting the door of the old Volvo open. Sleet had fallen before the snow and covered the door handle and lock with a thin film of ice. Jeff helped me get it open. I climbed in and had to slam the door three times before it clamped shut. I turned the engine over. Thank God, it started up. I waved through a window already fogging up and then Jeff walked away. I was on my own.

The streets were covered with snow and I knew the expressway might be worse. The snow was coming down hard and cars were beginning to shimmy just a little at stop lights. This was what Joey and I had always wanted—a real, white Christmas. I've got to admit that everything that had seemed drab and run-down on my drive into town now looked like Bedford Falls, the town in *It's A Wonderful*

Life. I guess that's why a white Christmas is supposed to be so special. Even run-down neighborhoods look like a set from a fairy tale.

Once I got onto Interstate 65 it wasn't so magical. There was construction just south of the city and that backed up traffic even more than the snow. I couldn't believe there were so many people still traveling on Christmas Eve. Why weren't they at home with their kids, feeding reindeer and warming up hot chocolate for Santa? I felt sorry for them. Then I felt sorry for myself. I was one of them. My family was in Cincinnati and Louisville and I was a hundred miles from either one. Jeff might as well be a million miles away because he had suddenly become part of my past.

After awhile the highway traffic thinned, but when it did, another thing happened. The cars and trucks had kept a path cleared in the slow lane while the fast lane had sheeted over with ice and beaten down snow. Now, as the snow fell even harder, the ice ruts in the right lane began to fill. I turned up the radio. Most of the stations were playing Christmas songs with no talk, but after about fifteen minutes, I finally found a station with a live voice. Poor woman. I'll bet she was the disc jockey intern having to serve Christmas Eve duty. She didn't tell me anything new—snow, ice and disasters on the road were becoming old news.

I had started out driving sixty-five, then fifty-five and before I knew it I was lucky to be going forty. I figured out that I was safest behind one of the big trucks still on the road. So I stayed right behind one, my car wobbling right, then left.

I knew I really should have left sooner. I'm so stupid. Jeff and I would have still broken up. Nothing would have turned out better or worse. I began to miss my family in Louisville. I remembered past Christmas Eves we had spent together, reading *Best Christmas Pageant Ever* or listening to Perry Como albums or watching an old Christmas movie. Would I even get there tonight? What if the Volvo went into a skid? Could I control it? Could I swing it back on track?

When it happened, I didn't expect it. I was paying attention, my eyes on the road, not fiddling with tapes or CD's or anything else. There was an exit ahead. I thought if I could get some coffee to stay awake and find a telephone I could call Dad and let him know I was okay. I would be better off than staying on the road. I moved over to line up with the jagged tracks leading up the exit when the car seemed to start floating. That's when I knew I was in trouble.

III.

Even the bridge into southern Indiana was more treacherous than the highway a hundred yards south. The weather got worse by the mile until a light dusting became a barrage of snowflakes, dancing around us like fireflies. Big and cottony, they collected on the windshield and coated the side windows. My vision became more obscured with every mile. It wasn't a road for my little girl to be on. It wasn't even a road for me to be on with Joe sitting next to me. He and I had driven to Liza before, though he was little more than a baby. We had driven in the snow, but that was during the day and there were cars and trucks around to help. On Christmas Eve, every single human being should be someplace they call home with someone they call family. We shouldn't have been out, but we were, and I think we were both glad to be nowhere else until we found her.

Liza had probably passed me going in the opposite direction.

At least I hoped so. I would get a call from my wife telling me to circle back home and Liza, laughing, would get on the phone to poke fun at her father and brother. She would slough off her late start and avoid telling me that some boy was the reason. In my head this was the scenario playing out.

In my gut, I knew that something was wrong. I sensed there was a problem, even though I didn't know what it might be or whether Liza was safe. Sleet had combined with snow and I was slowing down. I kept a constant watch over to the left, knowing that if Liza had trouble she might be stuck on the shoulder or in the median.

Joe fought to stay awake. Since he was a baby he had learned to fall asleep whenever we drove in a car for more than twenty miles, day or night. Not tonight. Our adventure did not conduce to slumber. Instead he turned up the radio and surfed channels, not for current rock this time, but for Christmas songs he hadn't heard a hundred times in the last three weeks. All the while he helped me keep watch to the left.

We had gone about forty miles when Joe cried out.

"Dad, look. Over there," he pointed to the far side of the median. "A car."

I slowed down, the back of the old Mercedes immediately wriggling right and left. My breath was fogging the driver's window and all I could see was a vehicle of some sort. I slid the window down and spits of snow and ice pelted me. Instead of the glass, my glasses now steamed up and I saw less than before. I used my fingers as wiper blades and squinted through drippy lenses. It was a car all right, but it wasn't Liza's. Two guys who looked like college students were standing in front of a well-traveled Toyota. Stranded. The decision to move on should have been easy. I wasn't exactly killing time out there on the highway. Liza was somewhere ahead. She was my daughter. They weren't my sons. But I looked at Joe and he nodded back at me. Christmas guilt set in. Good will toward men and peace on earth overwhelmed us. I pulled the car over on the shoulder. We both hopped out.

"Hey," I cried back towards the car, "you guys need some help?"

Even while they cried out, "Yeah, thanks," they were jogging towards us in slow motion, bogged down in the snow.

"What happened?" Joe screamed.

"Broken fan belt," one of them yelled.

I had to smile again. Another road memory. On one trip back to college after the holidays a fan belt on my old Maverick twisted, then loosened too much to recharge the battery. Two friends and I were stranded in the middle of Pennsylvania at just about this time of the morning.

They reached us, panting and red-faced. "Where are you fellows headed?" I asked.

"Louisville. Home."

"That's where we're going," Joe blurted out.

"I hate to tell you," the taller one said, "but you're going the wrong direction."

"I'm looking for my daughter. I'll be turning back or stopping for awhile up ahead if I can't find her."

"Find her!" the shorter, apparently younger one exclaimed.

"You mean you don't know where she is?"

"You won't find her in this muck," the taller one said.

"Yes, we will," Joe noted without hesitation.

"You can come with us, or we'll come back this way in a half hour or so," I said.

They looked at each other. Then the one who had first spoken, spoke for both of them. "Mister, we've been here forty-five minutes already. Maybe the state police or a road crew will get by or maybe they won't. Your car looks warm and it runs."

"Then lock your car up and hop in. You can pick it up tomorrow morning."

In a few minutes they were retracing their steps across the median and jumping into my car. After a second of blowing on their hands they introduced themselves. The tall one was Scott, the other Brett. They were brothers, students at Indiana University, coming back from a day of skiing up north with friends. We never got the details. Details didn't matter. I was still focused on finding Liza.

I was expecting a call any minute. Even as I told them what had compelled us to start out, directionless, with only a general goal of finding Liza somewhere, I knew the phone would ring. The four of us exchanged small talk about Louisville. We found out where they lived, how long they had lived in the area, where they had attended high school—which turned out to be Joey's school—and their intentions after graduation. In the process, both Joey and I lost track of time, a fact Brett nonchalantly brought to my attention.

"What time is it anyway?"

I looked at the clock on the dash. One-fifteen. I might as well have seen Santa Claus and eight reindeer careening towards us. "Oh no!"

"Aren't you a little late turning around?" Scott asked.

"She was supposed to call. My wife was going to call." I started to rant and rave in frustration when Brett interpreted.

"Is your cell phone turned on?" he asked innocently.

"Well, of course . . . " I started to answer, pushing any button—except power—on the extra powerful cell phone I insisted on carrying with me on the road. Nothing happened.

"Great, Dad," Joe exclaimed, "*We* forgot."

Gallant soldier that he was, Joe had included himself at fault. But I was the captain of the ship and I had forgotten. I wasn't embarrassed. I was too scared to be embarrassed. Liza might be home already. Or she could be on the road, stranded and in trouble while my wife was trying to get good-old-Dad on the cell phone.

I jammed the power button. The phone sprang to life with a loud beep. "Joe, dial home."

Joe was dialing even before I spoke. Beth must have answered mid-ring. "Hi, Mom, what's up?" Joe asked. He paused, laughing slightly, "She wants to talk to you." I could well imagine. I took the phone, eyes still roaming the road ahead and to the sides.

"Where have you been?" Not "hello" or "any luck?" or "glad you're not in trouble". I couldn't blame her.

"Sorry, the power was off. My fault. Any word from Liza?" She hesitated. A lump crept into my throat and I held my breath. "No," she said. I let out a sigh and kept driving.

"Not a word?"

"I just said 'no'."

"Sorry . . . thinking out loud."

My eyes focused on the road but my mind was on a dozen alternative endings to our little adventure, most of them bad. I would have seen an animal darting in front of the car or the headlights of another vehicle, but like chewing gum and walking, talking on the car phone and paying full attention is an oxymoron. Thank God for Joe, Scott and Brett.

"Hey, Dad . . . " Joe spoke first.

Then, "Mister, look back there . . . " from Scott.

"Who was that?" Beth asked.

"Long story," I mumbled, glancing in the driver's side mirror. I craned my neck around to look back.

"What was it?" I asked.

"Who are you talking to?" Beth sounded more confused.

"Later . . . I'll call you back," and without warning or goodbye I hit the "end" button. I pulled over to the left shoulder, put my own emergency lights on and jumped out of the car. Down the road, almost a quarter of a mile away now, I could see tail lights, a soft, barely distinguishable on again, off again, glow.

"I can't tell what it is . . . " I said to everyone and no one in particular.

"Look," Brett said. "I'll go back. You turn around up at the next exit."

"What if it's not his daughter?" Scott asked.

"What if it is?" Joey responded.

"Offer accepted," I said to Brett. "If it's not Liza, then it's somebody else who needs help." A sixth sense told me it wasn't Liza, but I couldn't take a chance and I couldn't leave someone else stranded in the storm. "If it's Liza, she'll have an old Volvo 240. Light brown hair—unless she's dyed it again. We'll get back as soon as we can."

Brett slid down the median into the culvert at its middle, then struggled up the other side. He started sloshing southbound and we jumped back into the car and pulled back onto the expressway going north. I tried to speed up but the car slid halfway across the right lane.

"Easy, Dad . . . " Joe's voice reminded me for an instant of the college junior who had calmly taken over the wheel of his car after our near-collision almost thirty years before.

"Got ya," I chuckled. "Better call Mom," I told him.

Joey pushed the "recall" button and handed me the receiver. "Was it Liza?" Beth asked before I could say anything.

"Don't know yet. We're heading back. I'll call you if it's her. This time we're definitely keeping the power on."

"Is someone there with you and Joe?"

"Oh yeah. I helped out two brothers. We're giving them a lift back to Louisville . . . eventually."

"Okay . . . " the cast of characters was as confusing to Beth as the plot of our highway adventure was becoming to me. "Be safe."

"I'll call if I hear anything." We hung up.

The next exit was only ten minutes away. I accelerated at the ramp, turned onto the overpass and looped back on I-65 going south. When we got to the car, it wasn't Liza's, but what I saw made me thankful that we had turned around.

The car was an antique Chevy from the 1950s. What we had thought were emergency flashers turned out to be the Chevy's owner, flicking the lights on and off in an attempt to get someone's attention. Brett wasn't by the car when we pulled up, but as we jumped out, slipping and sliding towards the old Bel Air's driver's door, he rolled down a back window.

"Glad you got here, it's getting pretty cold." We leaned over and stared inside. Brett was sitting between an old man and woman, Brett's coat around the old woman, his sweater around the old man. The couple were ancient, huddled around Brett like little elves or gnomes, so aged they had clearly shrunken from their size of thirty or forty or even seventy years before.

"Meet Mr. and Mrs. O'Donnell." Brett continued. The couple nodded, trying to smile, even as their teeth chattered in the cold. Brett continued. "They were visiting their daughter in Chicago and heading to see their son in Louisville. I think they got lost."

"We made a-a-a wrong turn-n-n-n or two," Mr. O'Donnell stuttered.

"Harry's driven all over the country," the little old woman said, "he's a veteran you know," she cleared her throat and I expected her to tell me World War II or Korea, although he looked too old to have fought in Korea. Then she continued, " . . . World War I . . . Harry will be ninety-eight next week and he can still drive anywhere."

"Including into this ditch," Harry wise-cracked.

"You two are pretty nervy to be out in weather like this." I wanted to say "stupid." More than anything else I was dumbfounded; beginning to sense that if Santa and his reindeer suddenly appeared it would simply be another night on I-65. My eyes ached and I had the dull buzz of someone who can't sleep but isn't alert.

"We didn't mean to be so adventuresome. Harry drives slowly."

"I drive slowly on purpose." Harry defended himself through teeth clenched by the cold. In the dull light I could see that his lips were a pale blue.

"As far as I can tell, they ran out of gas," Brett explained.

"I thought we had enough to get us to the next stop," Harry confessed.

"Let's get 'em into my car—quick," I said. I couldn't tell how long they'd been out, but it had been too long. I convinced Harry and his wife, Dot, to lock up the car and leave it. That wasn't easy. He had bought the classic Chevy the year that he retired. Then I bundled them into the back seat of the Mercedes with Scott and Brett squeezed beside them. I figured the more body heat the better. Joe kept watch in the front seat, alternately eyeing the road and then the phone . . . as if that might make it ring.

"So what now?" I asked Joe.

"You sure can't cross the median. We'd get stuck before we got started."

"Agreed. So that leaves us heading south until we come to the next exit. And that's not for another fifteen miles or so."

"You still think Liza's north of here?" Joe asked.

"That's what I think . . . but I don't know . . . I guess we'll decide up ahead."

I turned the heater up and the snow fell harder. Whenever I could I turned around to see if the O'Donnells were all right. As far as I could tell, they had stopped shaking and I thought I glimpsed color returning to their faces and lips. Harry caught my glance once and winked. They were definitely pinking up, but there was no doubt that if Brett hadn't run back and found them, they would have made the holiday headlines as casualties of Christmas. I wasn't positive they were out of the morning and evening news yet.

Dot became chattier as she thawed out. Harry had retired thirty years before. Most of their married life had been spent in Chicago. Now they lived in South Carolina, but drove all over the country. She was a mere child of ninety, probably keeping him young. I marveled that their children or grandchildren allowed them to drive the expressways. I marveled even more that Dot and Harry were doing it at all.

Even as I realized that my ski bum passengers, along with Joe and I, may have saved the O'Donnells' lives, I was afraid that I'd lost precious time in finding Liza. Exhausted and foggy-brained, I was still convinced that Liza was out there. The brothers were more than a little chilly when I picked them up. The O'Donnells were well beyond chilly. What about Liza? She was young and had plenty of clothes packed, but what if she had a wreck and wasn't conscious? I kept imagining the ultimate parent's nightmare.

I alternated between "it will be all right" optimism and flashes of the worst. The thought of Christmases past became an ominous reflection on something that might never be again. Before, back home, I had spent more than a few moments feeling sorry for myself that the kids were grown. Now I faced the possibility of losing Liza forever. It happened all too often in America and usually involved a car and a highway. I looked at Joe. "Grow up," I thought. "That's the whole point. Grow up and enjoy life and start your own family and forge your own memories. You and Liza both."

As I neared the next exit, I picked up a shape on the right shoulder of the road. This time her car was unmistakable. A Volvo 240 DL, once maroon, now blotched white with snow and ice, angled off to the right as if it had careened from the highway. I almost hit it veering off. My front wheels locked. My back wheels shimmied. The car stopped. I jumped out and ran back to Liza's car. Empty. Locked. That was a good sign. Emergency lights blinking. Maybe she had walked to the exit just down the road. Maybe she had gotten a ride.

I dove into my car, almost knocking Joe in the head.

"It's Liza's car, all right, all locked up. She must have gone this way." Before anyone could agree or comment I was ricocheting snow and ice like bullets from my back wheels as I gunned the engine and took off. I almost missed the exit, going too fast, turning too quickly, nearly spinning into the small ravine that separated exit from highway. I straightened the Mercedes and accelerated up the ramp. There were gas stations to the right and left, but only the left was open. Another quarter mile away and across the overpass, but at least it was open. I started to turn left, then stopped. I don't know why. In my moment's hesitation old Harry O'Donnell had allowed his eye to wander.

"Over there," he said, his throat hoarse from the cold.

"Yeah, Dad, that phone booth there," Joe pointed to the right, as far away from us as one could get and still be on the lot of the service station that was closed. I twisted the wheel to the right and gunned the engine, then almost as quickly braked as I turned into the station. The car slid to a stop. I flung open my door and the car phone rang. Joe answered, and as I scrambled from the car I could hear him say, "Yeah Mom, we're here . . . ."

IV.

I must have moved over too quickly. The ruts caught my tires, the Volvo skidded to the right and I was out of control. I braked—again too quickly—and the car lodged in a snow bank.

For a second I sat shaking. Minutes passed and I kept the car running. I couldn't stay there. I couldn't be sure when someone might stop. I zipped up my coat, flicked on the flasher lights and got out of my car. I locked it and started walking towards the next exit.

That's when it hit me. I was really in trouble. It was cold and the icy snow stung my cheeks. I was looking right into it and I could only see a few feet ahead. I was scared. I wanted to be home. Louisville or Cincinnati, it didn't matter. Home was home. And I wasn't home or even somewhere that was familiar. I wanted to cry, but I didn't. I made it to the top of the ramp and found that the nearest gas station was closed. Duh. It was almost two o'clock on Christmas morning. Not exactly peak traffic time. There was a place across the highway. Could I make it? My legs felt like rubber. I wasn't sure.

There was a phone booth on the lot of the closed gas station.

I jumped into it. It felt good just to be out of the wind and ice. That's when I realized I might not have enough money for a long distance call. I reached into my jean pockets. Nothing. I fished around in my purse. Nothing. I kept reaching deeper and deeper, past my make-up and tissues and a paper with directions to Jeff's house. Nothing. Then I remembered that even without change I could get an operator and make a collect call. I did and the operator answered.

"Yes, collect call for anyone from Liza."

The phone rang. Even that made me feel better. Beth answered. "Long distance call for anyone from Liza."

Maybe I was imagining it—I was pretty scared by then—but Beth seemed to hesitate, confused or whatever and I almost cried out. Then Beth's voice.

"Of course."

I started crying. I couldn't help it. "I'm stuck on the road.

The car slid . . . "

"Are you all right? Are you alone?"

"I'm fine. Alone."

"Where are you?"

I told her as best I could. I remembered the name of a town and the number of the exit.

"Your dad's out looking for you. He's on his cell phone. Is there a number where you are?"

I looked. There was. I gave it to her.

"Just stay calm. I'm going to call him. Then I'll call you back. I'll have him there in no time. You okay?"

I was choking on tears and gulping in cold air, but I told her I was. She told me everything would be fine. Her voice was so calm and reassuring. Looking back on it, I'll bet she was as scared as I was, but she didn't show it.

My face was sloppy with tears and snow. I wished for a miracle. I wished for my dad to be there, to pop right out of his big old black car and grab me up like he used to when I was a little girl. I wanted it to really be Christmas. I wanted to be warm and cuddled. I wanted to be safe and home and out of that filthy phone booth.

Just then I heard the roar of an engine and the swooshing sound of tires in snow. I looked behind me and saw a car full of people. The driver jumped out and started sloshing towards me in the snow mush. Dad. In another second one of the passengers joined him. Joe.

I threw open the door of the phone booth and started running towards them. In one big swoop of his arms he grabbed me up and we both almost fell over. Then Joe came after him, strong and sturdy. Dad was laughing, calling my name, squeezing me tight and, like me, crying.

I've never figured out how we managed to end up at the same exit, on the same expressway, at the exact same time. I found out later how he and Joe started up I-65 and I know that sooner or later Beth would have led him to me.

But the part that's so strange is that if either of us had done anything differently, we might have missed each other. I guess it was sort of a miracle.

When we finished hugging and saying how glad we were to find each other, Dad and Joe and I squeezed into the car with the O'Donnells and the brothers, Scott and Brett. We called and let Beth know we'd be home as soon as we got everyone safe and settled.

With everyone packed in the car, Dad, Joe and I in the front, and Harry, Dot, Scott and Brett in the back we crossed over to the open gas station and bought two gallons in a can—enough to get the O'Donnells' car started. Brett agreed to stick with them in their car once we got it going. Scott said he'd ride with me. The poor guy at the gas station must have thought we were drunk. We all went inside and I started singing Christmas carols and Joe and the brothers joined in. Then we told him our crazy story and he started laughing and talking about the weather and telling us how lucky we were to have wound up safe and all together. It turned out that in exchange for agreeing to work the entire Christmas Eve shift, he would get the next three days off—enough for him to visit all of his family in Ohio and Indiana. We were still sad to leave him alone as we pulled away and headed north on the expressway. Our plan was to get the O'Donnells back to their car, get it started first, then mine, and finally head for home.

Dad was in the middle of singing "Hark the Herald Angels Sing" when he remembered that no one had called Mr. and Mrs. O'Donnells' son in Louisville. As it turned out, he actually lived in southern Indiana. Harry and Dot were so tickled at the idea of using a car phone they started giggling. There was no way they were going to dial up the number and all of that, so I did it for them. Dot was so cute. When the phone started ringing I handed it to Dot and she giggled when her son answered. Then she started crying and handed the phone to Harry. Come to think of it, their son could have been seventy, but they talked to him like he was their little boy. They worked out a plan. We would meet at a Holiday Inn right off of the Expressway in Southern Indiana.

It wasn't all that long before Dad circled up the interstate and back to the O'Donnells' car, but in that short amount of time something happened—something really neat. Joey turned up the radio once we were through using the phone. Good old WHAS was playing all night Christmas carols and as one would start up, we would all start singing. Scott and Brett had a deep monotone, practically tone deaf and the O'Donnells' voices were sort of high and scratchy. Dad and Joe and I weren't all that great ourselves, but we held a tune. As I sat there, listening to all of us singing, poking Joey and coaching Scott on the words, I realized that Christmas had finally come. We were warm, safe and together. We might never see our "extended family" again, but at least for those few moments together we were all friends, all sharing Christmas.

Even after we reached the O'Donnells' car it seemed as if we were having some trim-the-tree party or something. No one seemed frightened or cold or even worried about how late it was. When the engine finally turned over, Brett jumped in behind the wheel and we packed Dot and Harry next to him in the front seat. The idea was to follow him down the road to my car.

The same thing happened when we finally returned to the Volvo. Like some caroling group pouring out of the car to troop through another neighborhood, Dad, Joe and the brothers all pushed and shoved until I could free my Volvo from the snow bank. Scott jumped in the car with me and suddenly we were a caravan of three cars.

We turned my radio to WHAS and I imagined that while Scott and I were singing Christmas carols and songs in the Volvo, Brett, Harry and Dot were doing the same in their old Chevy and Dad and Joe were at it in the Mercedes, bringing up the rear. In fact, I'm sure they were because, at one point, while the radio was playing the version of "Jingle Bells" with the goofy, barking dog, Brett, then Dad, and finally I started following the notes with our car horns. In the back of the line, Dad was trying to keep time as well by flashing his bright lights off and on. We were crazy strangers acting like old friends. As we continued our parade back to Kentucky, the roads got better and better. The snow let up and the further south we went, the more snow plows had cleared a path.

We passed up Scott's and Brett's car. They would be coming back for it the next day. There was no way we could fix a fan belt at two in the morning. Once we got to the Holiday

Inn, the plan was for Scott and Brett to drive on in my car and get it back to us sometime Christmas Day.

I think we were all beginning to feel a little sad that the adventure was over by the time our little party pulled off at the exit for the Holiday Inn. The O'Donnells' son was waiting for them and, as we stood outside of our cars together, it was like saying goodbye to my grandparents. We all hugged and promised we would check in with each other. Dad, at least, got their son's phone number. He's pretty good at following up with things like that. I'm not sure their son could figure out why we all seemed so tight and friendly, but he smiled and thanked us over and over again. Christmas was very much with us.

The most remarkable thing for me was that I hadn't thought of Jeff once since Dad had pulled into the gas station, and while I knew I wouldn't get over our break up for a long time, maybe never completely, I did give Scott my phone number. After all, we were going to see them the next day. After what we'd been through, it didn't seem unusual at all to trust them. I let Scott know I'd be around for the rest of the week.

Then I got into the front seat of Dad's car. Joe slipped into the back. He spread out and looked like he might fall asleep back there. He can do that in any car, anytime. We pulled out of the Holiday Inn and back onto the expressway for the last few miles until home. I turned the radio up. Behind us, we could see the lights from my Volvo as Scott and Brett followed us south across the river into Kentucky. Once across the bridge, they turned one way and we turned the other and I found myself looking forward to their dropping the car off and maybe coming in for some hot chocolate on Christmas Day.

We were so close to home, there really wasn't any time to talk.

So we didn't. There would be time for us to recount the tale of our road show adventure over Christmas breakfast. One Christmas carol ended and as the "Unto Us a Child is Born" from *Messiah* began, we all three let out a big sigh. Dad reached over and gave my hand a squeeze and I squeezed back, so much like all of the times, through all of the years, that he had picked me up and brought me back to my Louisville home. I felt like a little girl again, running back into his arms, the same as I had from schoolyards and my mother's car and at truck stop meeting grounds. I reached back and played with Joey's hair. He smiled. I couldn't help but find another tear or two. It was Christmas morning, and I'd already received the best gift of all.

Stein
30%
SALE!
SteinMart

CHRISTMAS ON THE DISCOUNT

She noticed him coming through the front door. Her eyes wandered over the shoulder of the woman she hoped was her last customer, drawn by the motion of another body entering an otherwise vacant store. Even from her station in designer clothes, a hundred feet or more from the front of Stein Mart, she knew the type. The late, male shoppers were always the biggest pain in the ass. Late in the season. Late in the evening. And they could never make up their minds. Even on the night before Christmas Eve they waffled on their purchase, as if they had forever. Overcoat open and flapping, scarf hanging awry to one side, as if it might fall off at any minute, scrunched down fedora pinched low over his brow. Typical old guy.

"I think this will be perfect for our New Year's Eve party at the Pendennis. What do you think?" Her female customer preened before the mirror, expecting her complete attention.

"I'm sorry . . . New Year's Eve?" Her mind had wandered, her focus temporarily lost.

She had failed the test of unflagging interest in her customer's social calendar. Through pursed lips and with raised eyebrow her customer let her know. "New Year's Eve. My husband and I are going to the ball at the Pendennis."

Well, that was rich, she thought. Heading down to the Pendennis in a designer gown via Stein Mart. At least she wasn't too proud to share that detail with a clerk. What she told her girlfriends at the Pendennis on New Year's Eve would be another story.

"And this gown will be absolutely perfect." She retrained her eyes into those of her customer.

"Just what I was saying."

"Well, the fit is perfect. And black is stunning on you. Do you need any accessories? There are some darling purses on sale near the front table."

"I think I already have a purse that will be perfect. I do need a few pairs of pantyhose."

"Right over by sweaters."

"Thank you." The woman, appeased and pleased, looked at herself in the mirror again. "I know you all are trying to close. I think I'll just slip out of this and let you hold it for me. My daughter's coming by tomorrow and I'll have her pick it up."

"That would be fine. We can hold it for twenty-four hours," she tried not to show her chagrin. The likelihood of a sale and thus a commission had just plummeted. The woman started back for the dressing rooms. "Just take your time. We've still got twenty minutes before closing." She didn't mean it. She would have been happy if her customer had simply run out of Stein Mart wearing the gown. The day had been long, the night longer. But she was old school and courtesy and professional charm were the tools of her trade.

As her customer disappeared, she captured her own reflection in the full length mirror just outside the dressing rooms. The end of a long and arduous day was personified in the figure she beheld. Her snowy white hair, no longer appropriately termed premature gray, still hung in a perfect page boy. Her red, wool suit, neatly accented with gold bracelets and richly patterned silk scarf, seemed almost as fresh and crisp as she felt stale and wilted. The days were past when she could keep up with the cut of her clothing. Her muscles ached from moving dresses back and forth between the changing rooms and merchandise racks. A recurrent case of plantar fasciitis plagued her more as the holiday season wore on, like an early Christmas present, along the lines of switches and coal.

Holiday hours were a pain, even if they paid the bills for the next two months. She approached the mirror like an old lover, drawn to its memory but wary of its content. From a jacket pocket she removed her lipstick and freshened her lips. She puckered and moved back a step. Not bad for fifty—plus a few years. It would be nice to get rid of the puffiness on her eyelids, and there was a sag to her jaw line that hadn't been as obvious before Thanksgiving, but that was outside of the budget. Unless she wanted to go without food for six months. Lucky that a boob job had been part of her fortieth birthday present. Hubby number two had been good for something, besides leaving her with a girl in college and a teenage son. Yet he had never missed a tuition or child support payment and there had been some good years. Oh well.

Out of the corner of her left eye she noticed an aging businessman wandering through jewelry. He was certainly taking his time, zig-zagging aimlessly like a politician trying to decide how to come down on an issue. At eight-forty he was moving through the store as if it was mid-afternoon, oblivious to the salt-of-the-earth working girl—that would be her—who was counting down the clock to nine and the wrap up.

He moved timidly beyond jewelry. Blessed are the meek, she remembered, for they shall take every last minute and more before closing time. She checked her watch against the round, quartz wall clock that hung over the front doors. Perfect synchronization. Her last smoke break at six seemed like a week ago. The shy guy would make it seem like another week before she could step outside and light up on the way to her car.

Of course, he might not head back to her department at all. What sweet deliverance that would be! Maybe he was doing some last-minute shopping for a son or daughter, a grandchild or even himself. Pray that it be so, she thought. Throughout her wishful musings, her observation of him became more precise. He wasn't ancient. Not as ancient as his tweedy overcoat and funky hat anyway. In fact, he was rather good looking for an old guy. She smiled. Who was she fooling? Old guy. He was in his late fifties, early sixties, not much older than she. And on second and third glance, his dress wasn't so outdated or shabby. Nice crimson-and-crème striped tie, starched white shirt, good crease to his trousers, attractive herringbone gray sport coat. Maybe he really was shopping for himself. The well-dressed older men often picked out their own clothes.

Maybe she had a lawyer, banker or an accountant on her hands. Professional type, someone upon whom others depended. A man of substance, but with an eye for value. Why else would he be shopping at Stein Mart?

"Okay, then." Her customer emerged from the dressing room. "My name is Fair . . . Vicki Fair. Do you need a phone number?"

She turned, startled. Twice, now, he had drawn her eye from the main chance. "No . . . well, yes, why don't you. I know you said your daughter would be by, but there's a chance . . . check the morning paper . . . that the whole store might be twenty percent off tomorrow. Some of the designer shoes may go for fifty. Slow season. If so, I'll give you a call. You might want to come in yourself."

Ms. Fair glowed, her confidence restored. "You are so nice . . . well, here's my number." She jotted it down on a piece of scrap paper from her purse. "Give me a call if you think of it."

"I will. Believe me, I will."

"Well, thank you . . . and Merry Christmas!"

"And Merry Christmas to you, Ms. Fair . . . you'll be stunning New Year's Eve." Her voice signaled a rally, a second wind as she neared the home stretch towards nine.

Ms. Fair laughed, waved and hurried on out of the store.

She watched her depart, pleased that a last-minute dose of old-fashioned salesmanship may have saved a commission. Then the pain of high heels worn for nearly eleven hours overcame the ebullience of the holidays and her smile sagged into a pained wince. Oh well, she reasoned, stalwarts of the retail trade like herself endured the torture of high heels like a lover's caress. She looked down, checking the back of her hose. For a moment it felt like she had a run. No, everything was holding up fine. Eight forty-five and counting.

She looked around for the man that was now Stein Mart's last customer of the night. In the exchange with Vickie Fair she had lost him and now he was nowhere in sight. Maybe he had simply left the premises. Worse fates could befall her, she thought, smiling. As her eyes scanned aisles and racks to make sure he was gone, she couldn't help but reflect on all of the holidays she had spent closing down some retail store or another. In the old days, before marriage number one, she had started as a sales girl in a real department store where, from Thanksgiving through Christmas and even after, it had the big-city feel of the holidays about it. Even after most of the downtown department stores had perished, the old Stewart's Department Store had put up its decorations and trimmed a tree on the main floor, garlands draping the massive columns that seemed to support the ceiling and holly wreathes festooning every elevator door. Back then, the whole place smelled like evergreen, like Christmas really. Not that her current employer didn't appreciate the need to spark up the drabness of mid-winter. The front of the store overflowed with colorful baskets, foil-wrapped candies and dried fruits, ribbons and all the trappings of the season, but once past the first two counters, it was business as usual. On the other hand, it was a job and it paid the rent.

But there he was, not having exited after all, feeling his way towards her department, and worse, her. Moving erratically from a rack of blouses to a table overflowing with sweaters, then on to women's suits and finally designer dresses. At each stop along the way, he seemed to give concentrated attention to whatever items were there. None was more nor less important, everything held his interest with equal fascination. After a moment, he would scurry on with a great appearance of resolve to the next items. Yet all the time he drew closer and closer, seemingly bent upon becoming her customer. Eight-fifty.

She tried to ignore him. If she did, maybe he would go away. Or simply disappear. If he would just turn away and head off in another direction for a moment she could slip away with a clear conscience. The store did close at nine. She was free to punch out as soon as the announcement was made, providing she wasn't waiting on someone. Everything was tidied up. Ms. Fair hadn't left piles of discarded gowns strewn about. The fine people who owned and operated Stein Mart had no desire to build up her overtime hours. Yet her sense of duty—strange though it seemed to owe a duty to a customer—compelled her to wait.

Years before, during that first stint in retail sales, customer loyalty and attention to the customer's needs went hand-in-hand with increasing one's income. The older ladies she worked with had taught her that. Besides,

Christmas was a time for everyone to get well. If you were good to the customer, the customer would be good to you. Old habits, once formed, were hard to break—even now that concepts of a loyal customer base seemed as quaint as pneumatic billing tubes or a little black book of preferred clients whose size and personal tastes were to be carefully recorded. If he needed help, that much-needed cigarette would have to wait.

She straightened up, pressing the sides of her skirt down around her hips. He was almost in her department. Five minutes before closing. She wouldn't make it, but she wouldn't hesitate to cajole him out the door if he was just hanging around. Customer loyalty was one thing, but she wasn't slavish to the rubric that the customer was always right. Maybe at quarter-till-three in the afternoon or at seven-thirty at night they were almost always right, but at eight-fifty, they had better have something very specific in mind. But as he got within twenty feet, she noticed a look about him that again prompted her to relent.

It was the lost look of the last-minute, husband shopper. Obvious and undeniable, it might as well have been written on his features with a magic marker. Nodding to himself, giving the appearance of certitude yet totally uncertain, he examined items, touched them carefully, then laid them aside as if the exercise had been a terrible mistake. Though blind and directionless, he was no amateur shopper. Her trained eye told her that as well. He noted size and price, manufacturer and material. No novice, this husband. Yet he seemed unfocused as well as lost, going to a cluster of four or five tables filled with sweaters, picking over several sweaters with seeming intensity, then ignoring the remaining tables as he raced on to gowns. The pattern was intriguing and, as last customers went, he wasn't an easy stereotype to peg.

Perhaps all of his skipping around was simply how he shopped. Maybe he was trying to put together an entire evening in his mind, an ensemble that would truly impress. Playing his thoughts and ideas out on the tables and racks that dotted the store. Maybe he was embarrassed, maybe it wasn't a wife he was shopping for after all, but a mistress. She had seen all kinds and served all types and nothing would surprise her anymore.

"The store will be closing in just ten minutes." The distinct Indian accent filled the store through its public address system. She glanced at her watch. Still in synch with Mr. Shankar's announcement. "Please take your final purchases to the check out. It is our pleasure to help our valued customers with any final shopping needs or, if we can be of any help, please let us know." Mr. Shankar's friendly, Indian way of saying "get the hell out so we can go home."

Okay, she thought. The *coup de grâce* of closing time. Her psychological guesswork needed to yield to old-fashioned, high-pressure "purchase or get off the pot." Needy or not, confused or simply indecisive, buying for his wife or his mistress, he needed to make a decision. She would love to grant him the luxury of perusing random items of clothes, dawdling over details, while she fretted over him rather than her efforts to punch out on time. Nice, she thought, but not tonight. She needed to jump right in. What would be his preference? Lingerie? A gown that would flatter without being gaudy? A nice, warm, terry cloth robe that would make that special someone happy? He looked like the type that might creep up on something sexy, never wanting to admit it, always using euphemisms like "cute" or "fun" or "mature" or even "intimate." Okay, whether he was shy or forward, subtle or direct, she would help him.

The minutes were ticking away as she finally approached him. Not long now. Another tiresome, tedious day with the timbre of Christmas about it. The last full day before the onslaught of the day after. There were worse ways to eke out existence among the near-bottom feeders. She had an apartment and a car, both current on their payments. There was a rack of red wine, enough groceries to last through the weekend and no medical bills. What more could you ask for? Except that her John Doe make a quick selection and get out of the store.

"Can I help you?" she asked.

He looked up, apparently startled, as if he hadn't seen her all along. She didn't know whether to be offended, given her idle fascination with him, or be glad for her anonymity and hustle him on his way. But he spoke, forcing the issue of overtime. "Well, uh, yes . . . as a matter of fact, I could use some help."

"And what were you looking for?"

"Well, I know it's late. But I was driving by and wanted to find a little something for my wife."

So there it was. Just a loving—or guilty—husband, unsure if he had filled the Christmas stocking to overflow.

Enough, that is, to show that he really cared, that he really loved her. And did he care, did he love her? That was always the question, she thought. Did his marriage have a little gray hair? Was it an ever-widening canyon? Or was this a new venture? Maybe a trophy wife for Mr. Conservative Banker. If that was the case, then he was dropping by the wrong store and driving into overtime fits the wrong shop girl. A package, no matter how gaily wrapped, from Stein Mart wouldn't win the heart or performance of a trophy wife. The gown or dress or cashmere sweater might, but on Christmas Eve or morning the box was half the battle.

"At Stein Mart?" she hated to sound incredulous, but it was getting late and she was getting tired and beginning to think out loud.

"Oh, she loves Stein Mart. Shops here all the time. Why shouldn't we appreciate value?"

No trophy, this woman, though maybe a down-to-earth, second wife. That's what *she* had been. "So what did you have in mind?"

"Well," he paused, looking around as if it was his first time on the *terra incognita* of women's designer clothing. "I'm not sure. Everything's so pretty and festive. How about something that has the look of Christmas?"

This one would be a challenge. Almost nine now and no idea whatsoever. "Well, you could always get her a pretty cashmere or alpaca Christmas sweater . . . maybe a red, satin blouse . . . though maybe . . . "

"No, I agree," he finished her sentence, "too predictable."

"Would you like dressy? A little glitz?"

"Yes, maybe so. That would be good."

"What size is she?"

He smiled, seemingly pleased with the memory of something. Then he looked back at her blankly. "I'm sorry . . . "

"Her size. Your wife's size?"

"Oh, I'm sorry. It must be getting late. My mind . . . "

"Yes, it is getting late," her words were punctuated with slight bursts of breath.

"I'm sorry, again. She's an eight."

"Any special color?" she folded her hands patiently within each other.

"Red . . . or black."

"Are those your favorites, or hers?" She laughed, wanting him to know that he was still the customer and always right.

"Let me rethink that," he chortled. "Her favorite color is blue . . . sort of a royal blue."

"She's a winter?"

"Beg your pardon?"

"Her colors . . . I forgot men didn't do colors. But that's a start. Were you thinking of a cocktail dress or something a little more formal?"

"Well, that would be nice."

"Which one?" She tried to maintain polite deference.

"I've spaced out again on you. Sorry. A cocktail dress, I think, or something for a nice dinner out."

She glanced at her watch. Nine o'clock. Her watch said nine. Make the announcement, she thought. Let him know we're closed. Help me out here. The public address system was silent. She glared towards the front of the store. Mr. Shankar was fussing around at the pick-up and returns counter, his head locked in a downward position. For an instant, he looked up, made eye contact and immediately dropped his chin. He was hiding, avoiding her look and her nasty thoughts.

"Okay, let's see what we have over here," she started walking as she spoke. It was an acquired skill, inbred in every seasoned retail clerk. Take the customer by an invisible hand and lead them to where you thought they would make a purchase. She reached a long rack of beautiful silks, wools and satins. Her hands glided easily along the top of the hangers to the size eights.

"I like this," she pulled out a royal blue cocktail dress with simple thin straps and a scoop neck.

"Well, that's good. I'm not sure about the neckline though."

"Too much or too little?" Her fingers were already busy flicking through other selections, the sound of clicking plastic and metal creating a retailer's symphony.

"Maybe a little too much. She's very modest. I was thinking of maybe something a little more like this," he made a straight motion across his chest, well above what would have been his wife's bosom.

"Hmm," she wasn't accustomed to men acceding to their wife's desire to show less cleavage. Perhaps this was the rarest of all creatures—the selfless husband. "Well, how about this?" She pulled out a sleeveless dress, blue with a neatly tailored jacket top of matching silk.

"I think," he hesitated, "that would be better."

"What?" Her lips narrowed. "What is it now?" Her patience was wearing even as her curiosity was concomitantly rising. Something about her last-minute holiday husband was slightly askew.

"It's just that she may already have a dress like that."

"Well, hon, I can't help you if you don't know what she does and doesn't have." Impatience was winning over curiosity. The beat of a moment passed. Mr. Shankar seemed finally to have discovered the intercom.

"Please, let me see just a few more."

"You know, I hate to say this, and I'd like to accommodate you. I'd be glad to see you tomorrow when we open, but we're officially closed right now." There, she had said it. The ultimate splash of cold water on the hot, Christmas shopper.

"Could I see just one more dress?" A plaintive, almost simpering request.

"You can see all you'd like. I mean it. They're right here. Not that many really. I mean, we had quite a few to choose from at the beginning of the holidays. But we really are about to close."

"Okay. Okay," plaintive ratcheting towards frantic. The change was sudden and dramatic, mimicking a seizure or heart attack.

"Calm down," his mood swing had unnerved her. He was a different man, verging on tears, breathing rapidly. She gently placed her hand on his and patted it. For a moment the thought occurred to her that she was witnessing an actual myocardial infarction. Her training in CPR had been years before and an image of delivering mouth-to-mouth raced through her brain. Then what? What were the techniques for chest massage? "Sir, are you all right?"

He took a deep breath and nodded.

"All right. You can look for as long as you'd like. Our manager is going to announce closing in a second, but you just look to your heart's content. Don't worry."

"It's just that I have to find *something*."

"Don't worry. Just take your time."

"I'll only be a moment. I promise. I'll just look at these." He bit his lip and went over to the rack again.

Whether or not the crisis had passed, she was still concerned. Maybe he was a head case. He had that clipped, choppy sentence cadence of the manic depressant; the slight twitch, previously too subtle to pick up. Emotional swings. She caught herself in mid-thought. He's my customer, not my patient. And I'm not a psychologist anymore than I'm a cardiologist. Focus. Just wait on him and allow the evening to wind to a close. God, he's beginning to wear on me.

"Sir," her tone was low and calm, "I'm serious. We're going to be here awhile tonight straightening up," she lied, "and I'll stay as long as you need me to stay."

He turned from his rummage through dresses, "I appreciate that. I truly do."

She waited silently for a moment or two that seemed like ten. "So what's the verdict?"

He selected a dress—the first one she had recommended—and handed it to her. She thought of making a joke about his coming full circle, then thought better of it. The dress was beautiful and his wife would love it. A six-hundred-and-fifty-dollar dress for a little under three. A bargain, even for Stein Mart, though it would still provide a modest commission.

"We don't usually gift wrap, but if you'd like, we have some boxes up front and I have some paper and ribbon at the service desk."

"Would you mind?"

"I wouldn't have offered."

"Thanks. That would be very nice."

"Not at all. I'll meet you up front. I've got one or two things to do back here, turn out the lights and so on. Mr. Shankar's the only other store employee here right now, but he'll check you out and I'll start cutting paper and ribbon when I get up there."

"Yes, of course. I'll take it up right away."

As she had watched him approach, she watched him walk away. Though she couldn't see his face, he looked different now. His shoulders were thrust back, his chin tilted up slightly and his step seemed lighter. He didn't wander, hesitate or stop.

Why had one cocktail dress made such a difference? And at that a dress she had picked out and he had rejected moments before? Maybe she had made a difference, channeling his vague intentions into something definite. After all, what was all this goofy retailing madness about during the holidays? An effort, with a gift, rather than words, to express affection? She wondered.

She had never been able to get her thoughts around the

question without the truth squirting away like a little spider. Gifts for the Christ child? If that was it, Christmas marketing and retailing were way off the mark! Remembrance of Christ was in charitable giving, not size eight blue silk cocktail dresses! Besides, most of her customers didn't connect Christ with Christmas shopping. She didn't. That would be a stretch for even her most devout Catholic customers from over at St. Pius. So what or who was being bought off? Was it expatiation of past, present or future sins with a dress from Stein Mart? Or was it simple conformity to Christmas past? Everyone always did it. You always did it. So you marched right out and did it again—late as always. Rote programming.

Rarely, there was someone who seemed to think that a size eight dress was a gesture of love. Maybe it related back to their own childhood, maybe to a connection with their youth, maybe to a gift they had received that meant something. Ms. Size Eight's man was that type. The dress wasn't a peace offering or a bribe or a token of guilt or a necessary evil to conform to the season. But what was it?

It was too late in the season and too late in the evening for the gift to be long considered. And then there was the Stein Mart factor. Great store, great employer, great stock. Not the top shopper's pick for finding the one and only, most meaningful gift of the season. So what was up?

"The store is now closed, customers. Please take all purchases to the front counter. The doors will now be locked. Thank you for shopping Stein Mart."

She checked her watch. Ten after nine. Why was Mr.

Shankar making the announcement now? Habit again. Plain and simple. Besides, he wanted her last customer to know that there would be no dilly-dallying around the front of the store looking over boxed chocolates and tea tins. A long, needy sigh escaped her lips like a last breath. Half a day tomorrow, then Christmas, and the onslaught of returns and sales on the twenty-sixth. And the cycle would start anew. A cigarette would be really good right now. Maybe she could bypass her boy up front, punch the clock and slip out the side door to her car.

He was standing at the end of check out, talking to Mr. Shankar. He was probably explaining how the nice lady in designer dresses had offered to box and wrap his wife's Christmas present. She really didn't have any option.

"Mr. Shankar," she called out, "it's okay. I promised a quick wrap. Lights out in five minutes." She hurried towards the front of the store. Purse, coat and time card were back in the tiny employees' lounge. They would have to wait.

Lord, it would be nice to have somewhere to go at Christmas. Living alone had its advantages, but not at Christmas. During the holidays, all the world was one big party, at least for the married, engaged or seriously dating. It had been ten years since she met the first criterion. And for the first few years after number two, not to mention before her marriages, she had met the second and third criteria. Good looks, a sense of fun and an easy-going manner were a great combination. She wondered to where and just when they had all disappeared. Overnight. In the last five or six years, the tide had turned against her. Ordinarily she could call one of her girl or guy friends, but timing for that was lousy at Christmas.

"I'm coming, Mr. Shankar. Close out the register if you don't mind and I'll have that dress wrapped up in a flash."

"Whatever you say, Shelley," Mr. Shankar winked at the customer. "You see who runs things around here. Manager is just a title they let me use." Both men laughed. Mr. Shankar busied himself with the register and she scooped up the dress. Fingers dancing over cardboard, she unfolded a gift box, bottom and lid and lined it with a triple layer of tissue.

"Gold or silver?" she asked.

"Hmm?"

Spacing out again, she thought. "The paper. Gold or silver?"

"Gold, please," he refocused.

"Ribbon? White or green?"

"White, please."

"Your favorite colors at Christmas?" she asked, pausing to see if he would correct her use of the pronoun "your."

"Yes. They are. I've always been partial to bright gold paper at Christmas."

The tips of her fingers played the folded edges of foil paper like a piano. Her mind flitted over what he had just said and his comments back at designer dresses.

"You know the return policy?" Her eyes riveted on the task of crossing the ribbon just right.

"I'll save my receipt. But I'm sure it's fine. If not, I'll return it within the week."

"You've got a month. Skip the rush. Don't worry. You've got plenty of time."

"Thank you. You're very kind."

"Kids?"

"Hmm? Oh, yes. Three. Two girls and a boy. All grown."

"Coming home for Christmas?" She knew she was being nosy and presumptuous, but the workday was over and Mr. Shankar wasn't about to fire her. Her fingers made the last twists on the white bow.

"I don't think so. Maybe New Year's. The girls live out-of-town. Married and kids. You know how that is. My boy's over in Iraq with the reserves."

"That's tough. I'm sure you're proud of him."

"I wish he wasn't there. But yes, I am proud. I certainly am." No "we." She wondered whether his wife was proud as well.

"Well," she finished her task, "that's it. Glad you found something you like."

"Me too. Thanks so much."

"Have a Merry Christmas." She slipped her masterpiece into a plastic bag.

"You too." He took the package and walked towards the door, fumbling with his gloves. He hesitated for a second and turned back. "It's raining like crazy out there. I'll bet it turns to sleet or snow before too long."

"Thanks for the weather report," she laughed. "Goodnight!"

"Yes, goodnight," he turned the collar of his overcoat up, pressed his fedora down on his head and charged out the door.

She walked around from the little booth where her day's work had been completed to watch him one last time. Large, cold drops of near-sleet were plopping into craters that had already formed in the well-worn asphalt of the parking lot. He jogged right through them, jets of water spraying in all directions. That fellow's going to have soggy shoes, she thought. He fumbled with his keys getting into his car, one of the dozen or so remaining in the parking lot. A cluster of lights on a pole high above the expanse of empty parking places now seemed to single out his car, like stage spots focused to capture him and him alone. Something—not time to kill, since she was past closing time—made her continue to watch him. No head lights came on. He was probably still fumbling with his keys. She watched a moment longer. Nothing.

"Hand me one of those umbrellas will you, Manish?"

Mr. Shankar turned, already hoping that the last customer wasn't having difficulty getting his car started. "Here, Shelley," he handed over a large, golf umbrella. "Problem with your customer?"

"I don't know. I hope not. I'll be back in a second."

As she shouldered open the front door the thought occurred to her that Mr. Shankar could have been gallant, heading into the weather instead of her. But Mr. Conservative Banker was, after all, her customer. And Mr. Shankar's charge was the store itself. A gust of wind slapped her in the face. Cold, twenty degrees colder than when she had been out during her break at six. The rain plopped in slow, engorged droplets on the broad, vinyl umbrella. It was hard to run in heels and a skirt. But she wasn't about to walk. Unlike her customer, she tip-toed around the little lakes of rainwater and snaked her way to the car. Through the windshield she could see him leaning forward, his head on his left forearm. She tapped on the driver's window and his head jerked back. He turned and saw it was her. The window powered down slowly.

She huddled beneath the partial shelter of the umbrella, growing more uncomfortable by the second, staring into the half-light and shadows of his car. His face was flushed, his cheeks glistening. His fingers clutched the steering wheel, reducing the effect of his labored breathing to a faint tremor. No longer her customer, a sale, a commission. Just a silent soul, stilled by his own loneliness. Not the cold now, but the realization that crept into her thoughts, prompted the shiver that ran across her shoulder and up the back of her neck. When you were in the retail trade as long as she, there were certain skills that came with the territory. Intuition was one of them, though she mentally kicked herself for being so slow to piece together his situation. As with her female customer before him, she had been distracted. Now, in the peace that came with quitting time and the penetrating cold of the evening rain, everything was so much clearer.

"When did your wife pass away?" she inquired softly.

He brushed his cheeks clean of the tears that had blurred his eyes and made them burn. "Three years . . . this past Thanksgiving."

"And you've shopped for her every Christmas since?"

He nodded. Her shoulders crunched together in response to both cold and emotion.

"Do you mind if I ask your name?"

"Ed. Ed Eberhart."

Her warm breath imitated the smoke of the cigarette she had desired not moments before, now forgotten. "Look, Ed. How 'bout I buy you a cup of coffee?"

He shook his head, no. She interrupted.

"Ed, I'm not accepting 'no'. Besides, you owe it to me," she smiled through lips beginning to blue, "Consider it overtime pay. Now drive on over to the curb and give me a second while I run in and get my coat."

He hesitated, then noticing that she was shivering again, nodded. "Okay, thanks."

She ran back into the store, stopping long enough between the doors to shake out the umbrella.

"Problem, Shelley?" Mr. Shankar asked, repeating his refrain from moments before.

"Yeah," she smiled, "it's Christmas." She ran back to the time clock, grabbed her coat and purse and punched out.

"You know, as long as I've been in this country, I still don't understand this Christmas thing," he said. "Seems like a lot of trouble sometimes."

She smiled and he smiled in return. "Trouble, Manish?" she threw on her coat. "It could be a lot worse."

"Worse?" he held the first door open for her.

She looked into the hazy, yellowish darkness, rain still pouring down. Her customer was parked by the curb as she had directed. "Yeah," she laughed, the laugh of a woman who had served many customers in her time. "There could be no Christmas."

THE CHRISTMAS READING

Dr. Dexter Frank meticulously placed the next slide into the carriage of his microscope. His custom and practice never varied. He took one breath—no more—and held it, slowly lowering his eye to the instrument. When he was appropriately positioned—and only then—he exhaled.

"Dr. Frank, we're getting ready to leave," the voice of his lab nurse and primary assistant corrupted his concentration.

Frank withdrew from the scope. "Have a good evening. See you tomorrow." He began with another breath.

"Tomorrow's Saturday!"

"Of course it is. I'll see you Monday, then." Another breath.

"You're pretty funny, Dr. Frank. Monday is Christmas Eve. We're on half staff . . . and I got lucky this year."

"Of course," he sighed, only half attending to her comments, "see you Tuesday."

"Wednesday, Dr. Frank. I'll see you Wednesday. Merry Christmas!"

"That's right. Wednesday. See you then . . . and Merry Christmas. Give my best to Andy."

"Artie, Dr. Frank."

"Yes, Artie. And the kids."

"Thanks again for our Christmas bonus."

"You are welcome, welcome, welcome . . . now I'm back to work or I'll never get out of here."

The hospital personnel seemed only to think about vacation time. Not that there was anything wrong with that. They worked hard and they deserved their time off. On the other hand, patients were still sick, still underwent surgery—though nothing elective—and their pathology still needed to be read.

Dexter Frank, M.D. resettled himself on the metal and plastic, swivel chair that was his nest much of the day. Frank was a model of discipline and dedication. The past January, he had been honored for those attributes by the hospital administration and medical staff. Even during Christmas he made absolutely sure that the hospital pathology lab was well-staffed, including a physician on-site, from 7 AM to 7 PM, and that coverage for the evening and early morning could be called in for an emergency read. He had been chief of pathology for ten years and assistant chief for ten years before that. Even during residency and a two-year fellowship, he had forged habits that would serve as a template for all of the years that followed. And the respect of the medical staff, nurses, techs and hospital administration had been his biggest reward.

Now, back to work. Another breath and he lowered towards the eyepiece. He glanced at each cut and carefully removed it, replacing the just-reviewed slide with another. His preliminary diagnosis was fairly apparent, but Frank's protocol was to review each cut once and to review the complete series of cuts before he even contemplated formalizing his read in a dictated report.

There was obvious capsular and vascular invasion, though subtle, and while some of his colleagues might make the call on the side of a benign adenoma, Frank was fairly certain he would be interpreting what he saw as a malignant carcinoma. Once he had reviewed each slide the tech had presented in the holding tray, Frank began the process a second time, starting with the first slide. The read seemed obvious, but his protocol never varied. Every series of tissue samples received at least two reviews. If he was truly uncertain, he would have the tech prepare re-cuts from the available tissue block for review the following week. Then, if need be, he would have the tissue stained with any of a number of dyes and treatments, the purpose of which was to achieve greater clarity and accuracy.

"It is impossible to be absolutely, one hundred percent certain, Dexter . . . but that is the goal." This sentence, like a dozen others spoken by his primary attending and mentor over twenty years before, was etched—or better seared—into his mind's eye. He, in turn, had impressed those same phrases on his residents. Though his was a regional hospital, the University made a point of sending its pathology residents for four weeks at a time to suffer a stint of exactitude with Dr. Dexter Frank.

Some scoffed, but most understood the reasons for his almost anal fixation on perfection. While one hundred percent certainty was a one hundred percent impossibility, quite often it was nearly achieved.

After all, the public was not quite so understanding. Patients and their families wanted one hundred percent certainty, absolute and doubt-free. And, of course, they wanted good news. That was something he couldn't provide. Most of the news was bad. They wouldn't be under the knife or having their tissue or blood drawn by needle biopsy if their clinician didn't feel they were probably positive for something. It was the type of something that Dr. Dexter Frank typically delineated.

"Don't forget, you need to be at the school Christmas concert ten minutes before seven to get a seat. So you need to leave the lab early." Monique's advice was always short, clipped and direct. In twenty years of marriage she had learned that with Dexter, less was better. Never chit chat, unless they were on vacation or a long weekend. Chit chat only confused him. He would have made a good Sergeant Friday on the old *Dragnet* television program. "Give me the facts, ma'am, just the facts." That was Dexter Frank, M.D.

Actually, Frank was looking forward to the concert. Not simply because his son, Adam, was the school's pianist and soloist this Christmas. And not because the chorus would be superb, which was to be expected in light of their state champion status. He was looking forward to Christmas in general. Adam was sixteen and the events surrounding Adam's sixteenth Christmas reminded Frank of his own so many years before. Not that every Christmas wasn't worthy of celebration but, for some reason, this particular Christmas resonated on a deeper, more nostalgic level with Frank. Girls were in the picture, Adam was driving, and he was beginning to think about colleges. The first, embryonic inklings of a future, professional life were beginning to creep into his conversation. Moreover, Adam was coming into manhood. Whether he liked to admit it or not, Frank knew that Adam wouldn't always be at home for the Christmas season. Frank wouldn't be able to see Adam's every move, live vicariously his challenges and triumphs . . .

Frank's thoughts ended abruptly. Even before his brain articulated the realization of what was happening, his body reacted with a sudden chill. He had been drifting. His eye had scanned three slides even while his subconscious was playing through selections from Bach's *Christmas Oratorio* and a series of popular Christmas songs that would be on the program. In fact, he now realized he had been humming tunes from a Sarah McLachlan Christmas CD that had become his new favorite. Humming a tune, even as bits and pieces of lyrics jumped around in his brain. And all the while he was straying dangerously from his tried and true system. That sort of wandering was simply unacceptable.

Though the double-read protocol was the failsafe for just such mental lapses, Frank had never relied upon that failsafe. He had never needed to rely upon it. No matter what had been going on in his life over the past twenty years, he had never lost focus during a read.

Frank backed away from his lab station. Using his thumb and index finger he massaged the thin bridge of his narrow nose. Malpractice litigation. The bane of every physician's life suddenly rocked his very steady, very calm equilibrium and caused his thin, runner's frame—slumped from years of hunching over his microscope—to slump even further.

He had never been named in a malpractice action, never given a deposition where his care was being questioned, never even received a threatening letter from an attorney to the effect that an unhappy patient or his family or estate would be filing a case soon if a pre-suit settlement wasn't achieved. All doctors feared and loathed the National Practitioner's Data Bank—including Dr. Dexter Frank. While it meant little or nothing to one's practice to be listed once, twice or even three times over a lifetime's practice, it meant a great deal to one's self-image. And periodically someone in Washington would equate a listing in the Data Bank with a paperback book of "bad doctors." Settlement or loss of a trial required the listing, so every doctor assiduously avoided settlement and often went to trial simply because there was still a good chance to win. If they won, then they weren't listed in the dreaded Data Bank.

Frank found himself suddenly cold and clammy. This would never do. One wrong read or even one misinterpreted word in a report could spell disaster. A pathologist's interpretation of a specimen could mean the difference between predicting the malignant versus the benign, the positive versus the negative, a cancer versus a cyst. A subtle nuance, misunderstood by subsequent care providers, could end up in a court of law. Worse still, the effect on patients could be disastrous. To be incorrectly advised of their illness or to be falsely assured of their well-being would be equally unforgivable.

So there was nothing to do but start the second read again. Frank drew to an upright sitting position. A moment to clear his head, thankful for a mistake avoided. Thank goodness for Christmas miracles, he finally smiled.

For the first time since beginning this case, Frank picked up the cover slip that accompanied the slides. He seldom read cover slips. To do so was a temptation to be influenced by the predilections of the clinician. Frank never wanted to know in advance the impressions of the surgeon or interventional radiologist or whoever was rendering hands-on-care. That was the proverbial slippery slope. Awareness of another doctor's thoughts prejudiced his own reading. So he ignored those thoughts. Similarly he ignored the patient's sex, age and, above all, his name. The less he personalized the subject, the better.

But this time he erred. The age jumped out—62. The preliminary diagnosis—suspected kidney lesion. And then the name—Donald K. Ryan. As he read Ryan's name on the cover slip, that delicate, single sheet of paper floated from his fingers and descended, like a falling leaf, upon his lab table. This was not good, not good at all.

Don Ryan was a local defense lawyer who represented the hospital. He was also a trustee of the hospital, a philanthropist and a community leader. And Don Ryan was a man Dr. Dexter Frank considered a friend. Not only that, he was a friend who Frank had just seen the prior Sunday at church. The chit chat following the early service began to come back to him. It was chit chat that under ordinary circumstances would have melded with dozens of other passing conversations, lost after a week or two in the rush of life, like the identity of most of his fellow parishioners.

"So, how's the family, Dexter?"

"Fine. Just fine. Adam has a solo in the Christmas concert."

"That's great. I remember those concerts and the plays and the caroling."

"Well, you and Cynthia are probably glad you don't have those events to stress you out anymore."

"You've got a point there. A good point, but trust me, you come to miss all of the Christmas busy-ness when the kids are up and out of the nest. Makes you appreciate it more, Dexter."

"I suppose you're right. So are you and Cynthia going out of town for Christmas?"

"No, we're staying around this year. In fact, all the kids and grandkids are coming into town. I think they figure we might be selling the house—downsizing you know. And it would be a hoot to have everyone under one roof again for a few days."

"Sounds like a handful."

"Absolutely. But it's a good handful. Lots of laughter and talk and movies and games and even some singing. The girls and their brother were all pretty good when it came to music . . . ."

And so it had gone for another moment or two. Don grinning, looking healthy, never mentioning he was going in for tests. He was probably observing the same regard for privacy that ordinarily drove Frank to ignore the patient's name pasted above the description of the specimen he was about to read.

Frank wished with the zeal of a child anticipating Christmas that he could have maintained that privacy. That would have made his read fairly easy. Now, not simply self-chastised, but sobered by the twist taken on by too much information, Dexter Frank approached his second review from a different perspective.

He had been certain that the cut was positive for cancer. That's what he saw. That's what he would have reported. Now he wondered. Was the cellular make-up that distinct? Or might it simply be unusual—unusual, but benign. The tissue was clearly abnormal. It wouldn't have been removed as suspicious if it weren't. But was it really malignant?

Frank's slight frame went rigid. What was he doing? He threw his head back in a silent scream. Why was he sowing seeds of doubt where there was no doubt? This was insane. Frank was not given to headaches, but he could feel one instantly coming on. All because he didn't want to report what was there, plain and obvious to even a fledgling pathologist.

" . . . it's a good handful. Lots of laughter and talk and movies and games and even some singing . . . ." Don Ryan deserved a good Christmas. For the first time in years, his family would come together. And knowing Ryan as he did, Frank had no doubt that a diagnosis of renal cell carcinoma would throw them into chaos. Not that it wasn't treatable, especially at this stage. After all, he had another kidney.

The problems would flow, not from reality, but from the family's perception of reality. Cancer was still seen as a death sentence. Not that it wasn't at times. But in this case, given the cellular appearance, the limited invasion of tissue, the histology of the cell itself—Ryan should be okay. Should be . . . but one never knew. And if he wouldn't be okay, if Frank was underestimating the virulence of the cells under the microscope, then shouldn't Ryan and his family have their time to confront the disease now, directly and head-on?

Yes, confront it *ad nauseam*. Walk around treating Don as if he were the living dead. Whisper when they should be shouting, stilling grandchildren when they should let them run, offering excessive solicitation that would make Don feel as if he was already dead.

What was that old movie on Turner Classics just a few nights before? *The Bells of St. Mary's*. Frank loved it. Monique wouldn't even watch it. Hated Bing Crosby and the doctor for lying to Ingrid Bergman about her tuberculosis. How dare he, a priest, play God with the truth? For that reason alone Monique would slap Dexter Frank on the side of the head if she knew what was running through his thoughts.

Uncharacteristically bold and bordering on sacrilege to his creed as a pathologist, Frank found himself toying with a read that could be amended later, even completely reversed on further reflection. Such an option would never impede treatment. Frank could go back and re-read after the first of the year. But what if something happened to him in the interim? What if he was killed and his report was never amended? What if Don Ryan thought he was fine, until some moment a year or so away when the cancer emerged, clearly virulent and incurable?

Frank shook his head "no" to a person not present, in response to words not spoken. What had gone through his head wasn't simply malpractice, it was gross malfeasance. It was intentional deception and it was probably criminal. Yet it was what he wanted to do. Dr. Dexter Frank had never done anything like this before and, without warning signs or symptoms, he suddenly found himself extremely weary of simulating the functions of a machine. He wanted simply to be a man. One capable of erring, but also one capable of doing purposeful good. He could leave a note at his desk stating simply: "Open in the Event of My Death," explaining briefly the need for another read and reassessment. He could explain why he had misread Don Ryan's pathology, boldly, unapologetically and without remorse.

Frank looked into the eyepiece once more. Those damned cells were still affixed in frozen splendor, close enough to garden variety carcinoma to make the call a "no brainer." He ground his teeth and picked up his digital Dictaphone equipment.

He began with a brief history as presented, the date of the biopsy, the suspicion for renal cell disease, and the nature of the procedure. He turned off the dictation equipment. His choices were simple: he could make it a positive read, describing it as a carcinoma, or he could read it as negative for carcinoma and call it an adenoma. Maybe he could reference a vague plan to request further cuts.

His first call would be accurate and he would never be questioned. The second call would be malpractice and he wouldn't sleep well until he re-read the slides after the holidays. The first call would be simple, uninspired and to the point. If he ran into Don Ryan at the hospital, on the street or even at church, Frank could be his formal, clinical self. No apologies, simply polite sympathy. The second call would hurtle him towards potential disaster, but he could smile when he saw Ryan and his family together on Christmas Eve.

Dr. Dexter Frank swallowed hard. His tongue was thick, his mouth bone-dry. What little saliva he could muster seemed to fly to the roof of his mouth, where it hung like glue. "To hell with it," he heard himself mutter. And he finished the reading as calmly as he could, wondering with every syllable if he was doing right or wrong, acting with compassion or a sudden, pathologic God complex. He flipped the control button off and gave the "send" directive. By Christmas Eve, Don Ryan and his family would be assured that all was calm, all was bright—the world was a good place.

Seconds passed before he was consumed with guilt, overwhelmed with fear, and ready to expeditiously dictate a retraction accompanied by some lame excuse. Once or twice he started to do just that. But as the moments ticked away, a comforting and almost giddy sense of euphoria overcame him. Don Ryan's Christmas would be filled with laughter and lights and carols sung around the piano. Giggling children would cavort on Christmas morning. Good food, good wine and good feelings would flow. There would be nothing phony or strained or forced about it. His family's visit would be good. When it was all over, Frank would make amends and they would all move forward. Okay, Monique would be angrier at him than she was the priest, Father O'Malley, in the old movie, but he simply wouldn't tell her.

The lab was silent. No staff remained and he was the last pathologist to close out the day's readings. Dr. Dexter Frank slipped out of his lab coat and into his drab, brown sport jacket. He flipped off the lights, locked the door, and started down the outer hall to the hospital exit. The lab was in the basement and his car was parked two floors above. He could walk up the stairs or he could be lazy and take the elevator. Usually he walked—better cardiovascular exercise—but this was a different day. Today, or tonight as it was fast becoming, he would relax—savor the moment—and take the elevator.

Frank pushed the button, took three steps back and leaned against the far wall of the hall. He closed his eyes and smiled. "Just once," he thought. "Just this once. Take a deep breath. There's no rush." The elevator doors opened.

Don Ryan looked up, guarded concern on his face, and peered into Dr. Dexter Frank's obtunded eyes. Ryan was slightly out-of-breath and his smile seemed strained.

"Hello, Dexter. Looks like I just caught you in time!"

Instead of moving forward, Frank pressed his back hard against the wall. For a moment—a long moment—he said nothing.

"Dexter, you look as if you just saw a ghost."

"Uh, hello, Don. I was thinking about a case. I didn't expect to see anyone."

"I understand. I tried to beat the traffic out of downtown, but it was brutal. Rushed over as fast as I could. They told me upstairs that you hadn't checked out yet but I was afraid I might have missed you."

"You were looking for me?" Frank felt the same, instantly dry mouth he had experienced back in the lab.

"Yes, I was looking for you."

"You wanted something?" Frank tried not to be defensive, but his efforts were ineffectual.

"Well, yes, sort of. You see—well, can we step out of the hallway for a second?"

"Sure. Of course. We can go back to the lab if you'd like."

"I would. That would be fine."

The two men walked side-by-side, back down the hall to the lab. Frank slipped his keys from his jacket and unlocked the door.

"I hope everything is all right, Don. Any problems with the hospital, or whatever?"

"No, this is personal. Let's just sit down over here."

"All right. That would be fine."

The two men settled as comfortably as possible on two, rigid, plastic chairs. Don Ryan loosened his overcoat.

"Earlier today I had a biopsy performed."

"Yes. Yes, you did." Frank hadn't thought far enough ahead to decide whether he would acknowledge Don Ryan's medical problem. Now he was committed.

"So you remember reading my tissue samples?"

"Yes—I think so."

"A little slice of some kidney tissue."

"Yes, that's right, now that I think of it."

"You seem nervous, Dexter. I realize it's highly irregular for a patient to come directly to his pathologist."

"Well, it is, Don. Yes, it is. I can't say that it's ever happened in all of my years of practice."

"Of course, I am the patient. And you are my physician, after a fashion."

"That's right. I don't usually see it that way, but you're right."

"So, Dexter, I think we were talking last Sunday about my family coming into town for Christmas."

"Yes, I remember. Right after the service."

"That's right. Only I didn't mention that I was having these tests done."

"I don't think you did."

"And I didn't mention that two of my children are in the medical profession. My son's a CRNA and my oldest daughter's an internist."

"I didn't know that," Dr. Dexter Frank was telling the truth.

"And when they get here on Monday they'll interrogate me about my tests."

"I see."

"So?"

"So what?"

"So what are my results? I know that it's not official protocol. My urologist is supposed to tell me. I know all of that. But, Dexter, we're friends and I'd like a little forewarning."

Dr. Dexter Frank knew the question that had been coming. During the seconds before it was voiced, his mind raced through the words he might use, the explanation he might give. The warm and fuzzy feeling which had glowed within him just a few moments before was dissipating into remorse. He should never have altered his interpretation, never varied the pattern he had set for over twenty years.

"Well, Don, I read the slides as basically benign," Frank

gulped, "though I think I recommended a look at some re-cuts right after the holidays."

Don Ryan looked off across the lab, his look of concern dissolving into a smile, then growing into a slowly evolving toothy grin. Frank felt terrible. He was witnessing first-hand the product of his lie. He was experiencing the one-on-one, physician-to-patient bond that through twenty years of looking into microscopes he had avoided. He was learning rather late in the game the almost servile trust held by a patient for his doctor.

"So . . . I'll be able to focus on Christmas and my time with the kids and grandkids and all of the trappings!" Don Ryan was a large man. He slapped his knee and the sound reverberated through the empty lab. "I appreciate that, Dexter. I really do. You'll never know how much you helped me today. And I thought I was going to be too late to catch you."

Frank looked down at his hands. Though he, too, was heading off for a Christmas celebration, the supposed joy of the season was far from swelling within his chest. All he felt was the pathetic, rapid beat of his nervous heart.

"Dexter, you don't look well."

"I'm fine. It's just been a long day."

Don Ryan slowly extended his big, meaty hand and covered Frank's delicate, folded fingers. "You did a very brave thing, my friend. I'm not sure you should ever do it again. But I'm awfully glad you did it this one time and I'm proud of you."

Dexter Frank's eyes rose, meeting, then locking with Ryan's. "What do you mean?"

"Well," Ryan chuckled, "I have to confess, I lied to you just now."

"Lied?"

"I said I came down here to find out about my results. Truth be told I came down here to use my far-reaching influence," he winked, "to convince you to give me a clean read. That's why I was so damned concerned I'd missed you."

"But . . . " Frank began.

"And when I saw you standing at the elevator I knew I was too late. I didn't know what I was going to do because both of my medical kids are smart enough to keep pressing until I coughed up whatever report you rendered. I was in a real pickle."

"Look, Don," Frank began again, "there's something I've got to tell you."

"You don't have to tell me a thing. That biopsy was as positive as could be. I know that, and you know that, and my urologist knows that—but until January, when we decide how to treat the damned thing, the family doesn't need to know that!"

Dexter Frank bolted upright. "Don, you've got to believe me, I've never done anything like this in my life. And I promise—I swear to God—that I would have insisted on another read and a long conference with your urologist."

"Of course you would—and you will. You've always

been a great doctor. Everyone in the hospital knows that. And now, just between the two of us, I think you're a great guy as well."

"But I lied, Don. I might as well have put the malpractice carrier on notice. I did everything but put the noose around my neck and jump out the window!" Dexter Frank looked at the basement window well. "Well, maybe not my window."

Ryan guffawed. "Okay, you did something wrong. But you didn't do it to help yourself and hurt me. You did it to help me and possibly hurt yourself. That makes you a great guy in my book. And that's the only book that will ever record this little misdeed of ours. Come the new year, we'll forget that you misread a slide or that I came down here to convince you to lie for me or that we even crossed paths this Friday. And I'll start treatment and things will probably be okay," Ryan paused, "and if they're not, I won't have to regret giving into the system and having the biopsy made public before Christmas. You know I could have forestalled it all. If I was a braver, bolder soul, I should have. Then I wouldn't have dragged you into my sordid affairs!" Ryan nudged Frank on the shoulder. "But I would really like a normal Christmas—and Dexter my friend, you've helped me get my wish."

Dexter Frank suddenly felt the warmth of good feelings that had been so absent moments before. "You have taken such a load off my mind. This could have . . . "

"Life is full of 'could haves' and 'should haves,' Dexter.

Unfortunately, people judge history by results. That's how great people get written down as heels and big heels get written down as heroes and heroines. This one turned out all right. It's Christmas and we both got lucky. Now, I've kept you long enough. And I got what I came for. Thank you very much."

Dexter Frank finally smiled. "So, you say you've got a big Christmas planned?" Though physically overshadowed by Ryan, he stretched upwards as he rose from his chair, eliminating the prior slump in his shoulders, feeling taller by inches. They left the lab, Frank carefully re-locking the door.

"You bet we do," Ryan started expounding. "Weather permitting we'll take a long walk through the park, let the grandkids run out their anticipation, and then sit down for a Christmas Eve dinner of honey ham and sweet potatoes . . . " they were strolling briskly, nearing the elevators, " . . . and pecan pie and if I'm really good—before we go to the late service—the crew will deign to let me watch my favorite old Christmas movie."

"Let me guess," Dexter interrupted, "*It's A Wonderful Life*?"

"Close—very close—but I'm an oddball in that department, Dex . . . because I've always been partial to *Bells of St. Mary's*."

They had reached the stairs and the elevator. Dexter stopped abruptly at the mention of Monique's least favorite Christmas movie. "Why, Don, that's one of my favorites too. By the way, shall we take the stairs or the elevator?"

"Tonight I'm feeling peppy, Dex. I say the stairs."

Dexter laughed, reaching for the door. "I agree completely, Don." He paused. "They're better for you and usually quicker." And with that, the two, now fast friends, made their departure from the empty basement of the hospital.

LAW

THE APPEAL

Shawn Green's termination would be effective January first. There was no question in Adam Brittle's mind that his action was justified. He demanded perfection in his associates' work and their demeanor. Lawyers under his supervision dressed impeccably, spoke with deference to, about, and around the partners and performed their legal duties without fail. In Brittle's estimation Green met only two of these three crucial criteria. His dress and general good looks were unquestioned. And unfortunately for Brittle, he was dependent on Green's considerable legal talents as the days wound down towards Christmas. Green totally lacked humility.

It was also unfortunate that Green's dismissal, a fact previously known only to the management committee, was no longer confidential. The announcement was to come after Christmas, after the appellate brief was filed in the state Supreme Court and, most importantly, after Brittle had left for his two-week vacation in Scottsdale.

Everything had gone wrong. The detailed memorandum,

by the mis-click of his computer mouse, had been disseminated to every computer station in the firm. The analysis that had been intended for management committee eyes only, along with the letter of termination that Green was to receive by sealed envelope a few days after Christmas, was waiting for Green along with other "new messages" when he turned on his computer that morning.

Brittle was informed of his gaff by Julia Lyons who, being a good legal secretary, was willing to accept blame, even though they both knew it was Brittle who had mis-clicked. Brittle, in fact, wanted to blame her. She had been his secretary for some twenty years and was older than dirt, old enough to dump, without concern about an age discrimination suit, since her retirement was only months away. He had nothing to lose but those few months of compensation if she caused any trouble. Like Green, Julia Lyons was ultimately expendable. Worsening arthritis had slowed her down, she had not easily accustomed herself to word processing or voice mail or electronic mail or any of the other conveniences of modern practice, and her manner was insufficiently deferential. Unlike Green, however, Julia Lyons was no threat. She came to work on time, had no family commitments, did what she was told to do and seldom claimed overtime, even when she left a little late.

Shawn Green, associate posturing to become a partner, was a different matter. To begin with, he was black. That fact had nothing to do with his termination, but it made his termination much more problematic than if he had been white. He had been hired because of his talents, but his hiring had not been color-blind. The firm of Oldfield, Smith and Martin would be benefited by a black associate and by a black partner. Though no one would say it—publicly at least—the goodwill and political benefits of diversity were considerable.

Despite the advantages of his race, Green was a threat, a problem that had festered. As Brittle saw it, Green was too brash, too likely to speak as a lawyer of equal rank when they were together with clients, too successful in his representation without sufficient respect for Brittle, too independent in his thinking and his manners. None of this had to do with color, unless those traits went with the territory, but it was color that frightened Brittle and color that he carefully avoided when his lengthy list of Green's failings were composed. The composition that was now public. That was the embarrassment that might still justify firing Julia Lyons when the dust settled. That was the embarrassment that forced Brittle into hiding the rest of the morning and into the afternoon and evening. The last thing he wanted was an unpleasant confrontation with Green before the holidays.

He tried to change his itinerary to leave by early afternoon rather than that evening. No luck. Flights were full, with the holiday traffic. His wife had dropped him off at the office before leaving on an earlier flight that morning. He could have gone back home and caught a cab from there, rather than the office, but the final draft of the brief required his approval—particularly in light of Green's newly acquired knowledge. Brittle couldn't afford sabotage from a disgruntled associate. So for the better part of the day, he had sequestered himself in his corner office, sending Miss Lyons out for lunch, coffee and occasional forays to check on Green's progress. He had even sent the old lady out as an advance guard to see if the coast was clear to the men's room.

By five o'clock, all of the staff except Miss Lyons had left for home. Brittle sent her home at six. By seven o'clock the attorneys had left as well, and Oldfield, Smith and Martin was transformed from a nest of peripatetic ants into a cavern of soundless ghosts. Fluorescent ceiling lights were turned off throughout the offices and hallways, leaving only a few wall sconces or forgotten desk lamps burning. Phones rang, but were soon answered by machines. There was a calm about the place, but no peace.

While Brittle hid in his corner office, waiting for his cab, Shawn Green sat at his desk, staring at the same computer screen that had informed him of his demise earlier that morning. Instead of Brittle's memorandum, however, he was reviewing for the sixth time Brittle's revisions of the brief. It was due the day after Christmas. The fact that Brittle's sixth revision marked a return to Green's second draft was a fact that had not escaped Green's screen-weary eyes. Brittle was notorious for many things. One of them was running up billable hours and driving staff crazy with absurd revisions filled with minutiae in the name of legal perfection.

His eyes scrolled upwards from the computer screen to the vista of the city, sparkling with the additional lights of the Christmas season thirty-four stories below. Some of those distant lights on the hills beyond the downtown belonged to the Methodist church where his wife and daughter were just arriving to prepare for the fourth grade Christmas pageant. Green was the playwright. He smiled. No Tony awards, but it beat the wooden version someone had tortured into existence back in the fifties or sixties. The dress run had been the night before, the first and final performance tonight. He missed the dress and was typing through the performance. His daughter told him she understood. His wife was more direct that morning before he left for the office.

"The ogres own your body, now they want your soul," she paused, "and they're getting it."

Big surprise, he thought, they're giving both back. For a moment, musings about the Christmas pageant and the appellate brief were stayed. It was over. Green had never been fired, never failed. Failure wasn't a regular theme in his life's story. Other than a vague emptiness—like low blood sugar—he wasn't sure how he felt. Tears had begun to well up, like some virus deep in his being, but he had suppressed them. First he would have to finish the damned brief. Then he would have to figure out how to go on supporting his family. Before Alicia was born, his wife had taught school. She left for maternity leave and decided to stay at home. For years, she had volunteered her considerable talents to the old school, the church, some after-school programs down in the projects and a little here and there. Oldfield, Smith and Martin—or Oldfield S&M as the associates snickered over beer—had always paid top salaries to staff lawyers, probably so that partners like Adam Brittle could trumpet their salaries to law school recruits and use them as a marker for the firm's preeminent status. Shawn was convinced that compensation had little to do with recognition of the associate's work. When it came to even junior partnerships, Oldfield S&M was notoriously stingy.

Green bit his lower lip. It was easier than trying to kick himself. He should have seen it coming, felt it, like the early signs of a cold or flu. Others had fallen before him. The official statistic to recruits was that three out of four associates made partner. Shawn should know. He was senior associate on the hiring committee. He had quoted those numbers to attract new, raw meat, knowing deep down that another one out of four were practically driven away by demands on time, constant travel and assignments out of town, away from family. Many a six-month assignment sifting through and categorizing documents had effectively ended an associate's term at Oldfield S&M.

Green thought he was different, not because of his race, although he had privately thought that might be a failsafe. Somehow he thought he was indispensable within the office. His writing skills were matched only by his abilities before a jury. In nine years, he had won more cases than any other associate. That had given him the false sense of security that year after year prompted Anita's decision to stay at home. "Brilliant young attorney," he thought. Not smart enough, however, to figure that as he neared partnership he was more of a liability to Adam Brittle than an asset.

The obvious fallacy of his self-appraisal had become clear earlier that day. He should have seen it coming. Once clients started asking for him more than Brittle, once their letters of praise, addressed to Brittle but blind-copied to him, escaped Brittle's mention, Green should have known. Shawn Green was a threat. And then there were recent failures, recited in detail throughout Brittle's memorandum. Lost cases on which Green had urged settlement only to be second-guessed by Brittle who had advised the client that even a third year associate should prevail. Green was still recovering from the defeats eventually meted out by juries who later went out of their way to tell him how well he had done in spite of the facts. Brittle had been lukewarm in his condolences and Green suspected, heatedly direct in his off-the-cuff comments to partners and even clients. And Shawn Green was too naive to see it coming.

Now there was the issue of race. Factor or not, Green would have been the first black partner at Oldfield, S&M. His wife was Puerto Rican and very white. He wondered if that was considered by Brittle. Had their presence at social functions made some of the partners uncomfortable? He didn't know. He honestly didn't think so, but who would have told him? Maybe it was more subtle than even he could ever suspect. And he was never one to fall back on race paranoia. Besides, nothing about him or his situation fit a pattern. Brittle was a Democrat, Green a Republican. They were both Methodist. Brittle had once been an active member of the same church Green now attended. Green had readily joined the "open to all with money" eating club where most of Oldfield S&M's lawyers belonged. Brittle was a staunch supporter of affirmative action, where Green had his doubts about its long-term advantages. Nothing fit, and yet Green wondered whether he had been a big fool—another black sucker in a white man's world.

His eyes returned to the screen. Pride was the main force driving his fingers now. Pride, and the hope that if Brittle would ever talk to him, he might yet receive the courtesy of a strong recommendation for another position. He would gladly settle for a simple letter, combined with a promise that if Green listed Brittle as a reference he wouldn't purposely ruin his career.

An office door opened somewhere down the hall. Green's eyes jerked away from the screen. Probably Brittle emerging from his hiding place to leave for the airport. But Brittle's office was in the opposite direction of the opening door. Still, there wasn't anyone else in the office. Two days before Christmas, Oldfield S&M was dead. Green tried to work through an opening proposition that Brittle claimed was too wordy. He typed and then typed over, then typed again, and still the sound down the hall spooked him. He stood up and stretched. As long as he didn't disturb Brittle with one of his girlfriends, the worst that could happen would be a cold shoulder and a tart reprimand for Green's audacity in asking what the official line was on his termination.

He stepped into the gloomy corridor. The light near the end of the hall, like the sound of the door, was in the opposite direction from Brittle. There were twelve corner offices in the three-story kingdom of Oldfield, S&M and they were occupied by Brittle and eleven of his peers. Lords of the bar, movers in the community. Green passed one office after another, eliminating junior partners and fellow associates from the list of possible sources for the sound and the light. He was still new to the thirty-fourth floor, his office recently upgraded from thirty-two just a month before. The theory had been that he would be closer to his work with Brittle. Green now suspected that it was to make his interaction with clients easier to observe. Even as he approached the tiny, interior office to his right, Green was clueless. Maybe it was a paralegal's office. For the few weeks he'd been on thirty-four, the door was closed. He'd never seen anyone come in or go out. The possibility of some thief, there to rifle through secret files or steal valuable equipment, went through his mind. Christmas was peak season for stolen purses and loose change, disappearing televisions, cameras and VCR's. He softened his footsteps as he reached the door.

Green cleared his throat and a shrunken, old man looked up from behind an oversized desk.

"Good Lord, you startled me." The ancient caught his breath.

Green immediately realized this was no thief. "I'm sorry, but I saw a light. Except for Mr. Brittle, I thought I was the only one here."

The old man laughed. "Good old Adam. Working right up to Christmas."

"Yes, sir."

The awkward silence that followed gave Green a moment to take in the office. Eight feet by twelve at most, it was a clutter of antique furniture and mementoes, the walls covered with photographs and yellowed diplomas. Green was struck by the fact that everything except the wizened old man was out of scale and proportion to the room. The carved, leather inlaid desk seemed to span the room's width and the old, leather side chairs were squeezed up under the desk's overhang. The desk chair in which the old man perched gave almost no space to glide between desk and credenza. The brass desk lamp with its ruby-colored shade more than filled the room with light. The old man hadn't even bothered to turn on the overheads.

"Have a seat, young man . . . if you can . . . it's a bit of a squeeze," the old man chortled. "I can't say I've ever gotten too used to it myself."

Green still wondered where and with whom he was. As his eyes grew accustomed to the soft, incandescent light, he was able to make out figures in the photographs. This time it was Green's turn to be startled. Harry Truman, John Kennedy, Lyndon Johnson and, finally, Jimmy Carter all posed with various versions of the old gnome who sat across from him.

"I'm not sure we've ever met." The gnome extended his knobby hand. "My name's Oldfield. Wiley Oldfield."

"My God," Green murmured.

"Oh, I don't think so," Oldfield winked. "Even God in all of his humility would go for another couple of square feet and a window."

Green relaxed. "I thought you were . . . " he faltered.

"Dead?"

"Well, no, but . . . "

"Almost dead . . . close . . . soon?" Oldfield's wrinkled, bald head contorted in a grin this time.

"I was going to say retired."

"Ah, yes, retired. Twenty years retired. Smith and Martin had the good sense just to die. Do you know that one time the stationery print shop got it screwed up and listed all three of us as caput," he clapped his hands. "Just like that. Officially dead for about three days in 1999."

"What did you do?"

"Do? I didn't do anything. My old secretary caught it and called me out in Palm Desert. I petitioned for my life and the management committee—after due consideration—granted my request!"

"I'll bet that took some lobbying," Green cracked.

"So things haven't changed much!" Oldfield smiled. "They had twenty boxes of the stuff. I kept one sheet of the letterhead framed as a souvenir." He reached behind him, plucked an eight-and-a-half by eleven frame off the wall and tendered it to Green. As reported, Oldfield's death was duly recorded. "They eventually sent it back to the printer. Probably told them to hold on to it for future use." Oldfield winked.

"So . . . I'm sorry," Green started again, "but I didn't even know you still had an office here."

"You call this an office?" Oldfield raised his crooked arms and looked around. "It's really a storage room.

No place to put all of this stuff in California. But I can't complain. Wouldn't be any sense in keeping my old office. To tell you the truth, I only get by here once or twice a year at Christmas, and when no one's around. Funny how a place with your name on it can feel so damned foreign."

Green suddenly felt like crying again. The old man in front of him was obviously a victim on the other end of time, the down side of the legal bell curve. The very man who had founded the firm, retired and then been forgotten, as good as dead and maybe worse, so divorced from the partnership that he had been honored with a small storage room off of the library. This was his reward for creating a legal empire.

"Listen, Mr. Oldfield, anytime you need an office . . . " Green stopped in mid-sentence, his magnanimity running away with him. He had forgotten that in a short while he would no longer have an office.

"What's that?" Oldfield cupped his ear. "By the way, I didn't catch your name."

"Green. Shawn Green."

"Well, it's nice to meet you, Mr. Green."

"Please call me Shawn."

"Call me Wiley," the old man's eyes twinkled. "Even my great grandkids do."

Green saddened again, not for Oldfield's loss this time, but for the firm's. The whole idea of someone inhabiting the place who would ask a junior attorney to call him by his first name was refreshing. Green doubted that Brittle's own grown children had ever called him anything but "Father." Surely never "Daddy."

"Good enough . . . Wiley," Green nodded. "So what brings you in here tonight?"

Oldfield sighed, reaching for a document it was now obvious he had been reading before Green interrupted him. He turned it face down on the desk. "Just wrapping up some affairs. End of the year, you know."

Green acknowledged the year's-end duties, realizing the old man might as well have said "end of life".

"If I can be of any help, let me know," Green started to get up.

"Well," Oldfield's voice weakened and he cleared his throat, starting over, "I might need some help, but you must be pretty busy to be down here."

"An appeal. Due Christmas. Actually the day after. Mr. Brittle wants another draft done tonight before he leaves town."

"Adam has always demanded perfection."

"Yes."

"Demands a lot. Wins a lot. Usually gets what he deserves."

"Yes, sir," Green would like to punch Brittle in the nose just once before he walked out of the doors of Oldfield, S&M.

"Well, why don't you go back to the brief."

"I'm in no hurry. It doesn't look like I'm going to get out of here anytime too soon . . . " Green stumbled on his words, "tonight, that is."

"Okay then," Oldfield's focus seemed to wander, "did you have the Christmas party this year?"

"Yes, uh, Wiley. Had it out at the country club."

"I'll bet the staff had a good time out there."

"Well, actually the party was for attorneys and spouses or dates. No staff. The firm hasn't invited staff for as long as I can remember."

"Way back when," Oldfield's eyes seemed to water, their piercing blue irises blurring for an instant, "we put up a good-sized tree in the lobby. We closed early a day or two before Christmas. Then we partied. Attorneys. Staff. Kids. One year we even danced jigs. We had a great time," he paused. "No party, eh?"

"No."

"Oh well, bring back the Christmas party when you make partner!" Oldfield smiled serenely.

Green started to explain, then thought better of it. It was already past, his past. Instead, he mused on Oldfield's past. What a place the firm must have been when characters like Wiley Oldfield populated the bar. Eccentrics, oddballs, individuals. Whatever term best described Oldfield and his contemporaries. His generation had obviously been a lively bunch. In his prime, almost forty years before, Wiley Oldfield must have been a pistol. You didn't cross him, Green thought. Green looked around again at the stinky little space to which Oldfield was relegated. If Green ever got another job, he wouldn't stick around to be treated like this.

"So, anyway," Oldfield rose slowly from his chair, "could you walk with me down the hall. I'd like to see Adam one last time, but my eyes aren't good in dim light. And I get a little wobbly this high up . . . "

Green nodded. The end game. A great man, long forgotten, knowing that he probably wouldn't be back again. Cheery Christmas thought.

"Sure. I'd be glad to walk with you. Then I've got to get back to work."

"The brief . . . of course. Okay, well let me get my papers." Oldfield grabbed the papers from his desk and curled them into a cylinder, "and squeeze out of here." Oldfield's shoulders were hunched over so that his head stuck out like a turtle's. Balding as he was, his nose large and red with age, his old legs slightly bowed, he looked like a very old man imitating Groucho Marx. He stood barely five-and-a-half feet. "Can you believe," he muttered as they started down the hall, "that I once stood almost six feet tall. Getting old isn't what it's cracked up to be . . . it's worse," he laughed.

Green laughed too. This old elf was a hoot. He wondered what working under him would have been like. Demanding, no doubt. Not always pleasant with jokes and laughter. Green guessed he had mellowed with the passage of years, but he must have always been challenging, exciting and fair.

The corridor seemed interminable. Oldfield straightened up as they progressed, but his pace didn't quicken. Green had to pause between steps not to pass him.

"You know, Shawn, it takes my body a few minutes just

to change positions. Standing, sitting, walking. A real pain in the ass. But once I get warmed up, I'm fine." Oldfield began to look a little taller as his back stretched out and his head lost its forward lean.

"That's not a problem. We move a little too quickly around here anyway."

"Well, I appreciate your patience."

When they reached Brittle's door, Green turned to leave. He had as little desire to see Brittle as Brittle had shown towards seeing him the entire day.

"Stick around, Shawn. I'm sorry to say I might need some help back down the hall."

"Well, okay."

Oldfield knocked on the door. No response. He knocked again. Green could hear sounds within, like the scuttling of squirrels in an attic, then a voice, angered at the interruption.

"What is it?"

Oldfield turned the knob and pushed the door forward, then stepped back just enough for Green, but not himself, to be visible. Brittle sat behind his massive desk in a substantial room, a small conference table to his left, a settee, coffee table and chairs to his right. Two, floor-to-ceiling windows framed the city.

"What do you want?"

Green waited for Oldfield to speak, but the old man remained silent. Green began, "Nothing, uh, actually . . . "

"Hello, Adam," Oldfield slid from Green's shadow.

Brittle could barely see into the darkness of the hall, but

he recognized the voice. "Wiley? My God, what are you doing here?"

"Home for the holidays. Thought I'd piddle around my office."

"Well, it's great seeing you. Maybe if you stick around through the New Year we could have lunch."

Oldfield laughed. "I'm afraid I'll be gone again."

"Well, I'm on my way out of town, but it's great seeing you."

Oldfield nodded. "I guess you two gentlemen have something to talk about."

Brittle started. Green withdrew into the hallway's shadows.

"I don't think so . . . ," Brittle began.

"The brief? I thought you two were teamed up on some brief?"

"Brief?" Astoundingly Brittle had for an uncomfortable moment forgotten his personal instrument of torture.

"Yes, this," Oldfield held the curled-up document in his misshapen right hand.

"I don't understand." Brittle's face relaxed, dumbfounded.

"Well, you will, Adam." Oldfield's voice changed. Deeper perhaps, less phlegm-filled, the words punched with precision. Above all, there was a suggestion of hard metal that hadn't been present before, "Give us a moment, would you please, Shawn," Oldfield stepped inside the office and shut the door.

Green was too surprised to react. Seconds before, he had feared confrontation with Brittle. Now he was amazed that Oldfield had a copy of the brief. How had he gotten it? Why did he have it? What was there to discuss between Oldfield and Brittle that required a closed door? He wondered for a moment whether there was something more than termination that he had to fear. None of it made sense, and the fact that he was left on the other side of a private conference was more than disconcerting. On the other side of the door, he could hear voices, first Brittle, then Oldfield, but he couldn't distinguish a thing that was being said, only that it was being said with increasing emotion.

Five minutes passed. Green wanted to turn around and walk back to his office, hiding from whatever additional sanctions he might be on the verge of receiving. Instead, he froze in place. His palms grew cold and sweaty, the pits of his arms wet and clammy. He paced a step or two back, then to the side, still varying little from the spot where Oldfield had left him. Green thought of his wife and daughter, concluding preparations for the pageant, peeking behind a stage curtain to see how the church fellowship hall was filling. More than anything he wanted to be with them, putting professional crises behind him, immersing himself in Christmas.

The door opened abruptly. Brittle stood with his topcoat over his left arm and his brief case clutched in his right hand. He was flushed, red-faced and breathing hard.

"You can't do this."

"Please, Adam," Oldfield's voice was low, calm, but still edged with steel. "That's why I wanted to handle this one-on-one, in privacy."

"To hell with privacy," Brittle seethed, nodding towards Green, "you can't do this."

"Oh, but Adam, of course I can," Oldfield reached into his vest pocket and removed a document. Green could tell that it wasn't the brief, "and I have."

"I'll sue your shriveled old ass," Brittle retorted.

Oldfield chuckled, then seemed to lose control and laughed out loud. "That would be fun. I might enjoy that."

"I'll cut you off at the knees. I'll change the name of this firm and tell anyone who still remembers you that you're crazy . . . "

Brittle stuttered, " . . . nuts."

"You're welcome to try, but let's not call names, Adam."

"Bastard!"

"It takes one to know one. But I always knew how to deal with bastards. You, Adam, are something much worse. You're a bully. And I've always hated bullies."

Brittle started to respond, but had nothing to say, or couldn't say it. He brushed past Oldfield and half-shoved Green as he passed him, rushing down the hall. Green stood his ground, but didn't shove back. He watched Brittle for a second, until he rounded the corner out of sight, then turned back to Oldfield. Like Brittle, but for different reasons, Green was speechless.

"Don't worry about Adam, Shawn. He'll survive. He'll alight somewhere, reformed or, more likely, not."

"I . . . I . . . don't understand."

"It's not for you to understand, Shawn. Not tonight anyway. It's almost Christmas." Oldfield glanced at his pocket watch. "And if you don't leave soon, you'll miss that pageant," he paused, thinking of times past. "I'll bet you didn't know that I asked Adam to write the old one more than thirty years ago." He shook his head. "Terrible mistake. Terrible."

Green stared at the old man, his mouth open in awe and dumb surprise. When he found words they were thick and ill-flowing. "The pageant . . . the brief?"

"The brief's fine. I was going over it when you walked in on me. The pageant sounds like a winner."

"You knew?"

Oldfield smiled. "I have my moles around this place."

"Moles?"

"Long before Miss Lyons worked for Adam Brittle, she worked for me. We stay in touch. She keeps me up on things. You'd be surprised. We even have a date for a Christmas pageant tonight."

"I'm still not sure I understand."

Oldfield placed his gnarled hand on the young man's shoulder. "Twenty years ago this office was mine. I gave it to Adam. I didn't need it." His soft smile hardened. "But I wasn't stupid enough to give up my voting rights or my partnership share in this firm. Adam must have forgotten that, poor boy. So, Shawn, in a little while . . . after the new year . . . when the dust settles . . . this office will be yours."

"I . . . I . . . I . . . don't quite understand . . . " Green stammered.

"You do good work. Excellent work. Miss Lyons has kept

me well informed. Just don't forget . . . ashes to ashes . . . dust to dust . . . in between it's all a matter of who's naughty and who's nice. Now, why don't you be on your way. I'm going to stay around here for a moment . . . turn out the lights and so forth. I'll see you after the pageant."

Green thanked Oldfield, then thanked him again and tried to find other words, but couldn't. Oldfield slowly shook his head, then whisked his finger to send Green on his way. Green turned and ran, reached his office, shut down his computer, grabbed his overcoat and charged for the elevators. His mind was racing, his thoughts a jumble. The elevator doors opened and, as he started to get on, he could hear Oldfield whistling as he shuffled back down the hall. Green pushed the "lobby" button as he put words to the tune. "You better watch out . . . you better not cry . . . you better not pout, I'm telling you why . . . "

J
J

THE END OF THE RUSH

"Mom, we're ready to go." Tad was at the bottom of the stair, screaming over the din of voices, the television and Mary's hair dryer. "Mom . . . " a little louder. "Mom . . . " louder still. He took a deep breath and once more, "Mom . . . "

Mary flipped the switch. Her ears were still ringing from the whirling motor and swirling, hot air. She thought she'd heard a voice. As she flipped the dryer back on Tad bellowed, "Mother . . . let's go!"

This time she heard. She hit the off switch. "Tad," she refused to raise her voice, but it cracked slightly. For eighteen years, Tad had perfected yelling from the bottom of the stairs as an art form. For eighteen years, she had fought it. "If you want something, come and tell me in a normal voice." Her words were chosen precisely, spoken in a tone she hoped was civil, even if she was beginning to feel less than civil.

"Mom, I can't hear you," Tad cried out. "We're ready to go."

"I'll bet you are," she replied in a voice barely above a whisper.

"What?" Tad cried out.

"I'll be there when I'm ready."

"I can't hear you."

Of course, he couldn't hear her. No one had been hearing her for days. Caught in the Christmas rush, they were moving so fast and playing so hard no one was hearing or even speaking. They were just yelling a word or two, here or there, to signal that another activity was about to begin.

She sighed, ready to capitulate, then inhaled, ready to raise her voice. Then she heard the echo of Tad's boot heels clunking down the hard oak floors of the downstairs, front hall. Mary smiled. He didn't even have time for her surrender. She had won few battles as a mother, but her insistence on not screaming up the stairwell had been a losing proposition since Tad had a voice. Now he was a freshman in college. This was not a battle she could win on Christmas Eve.

Christmas. This year it had crashed on her like an unwelcome surprise party. One moment it was Thanksgiving, the next Christmas Eve. One moment her house was in order, the next total chaos. One moment it was just George, Molly, and herself; the next there was Tad, her mother and father, her brother and his wife, with her older sister on the way.

The Christmas rush was funneling into the season's climax: Christmas Eve, then the morning and stupefied

Christmas day which would follow. It would all be over in a final, fitful spurt of activity. Then kaput and done. The mild, bothersome depression would follow. Nothing life-altering. No all-encompassing black cloud. Nothing that wouldn't pass by the time New Year's rolled around. But not the joy of the holidays or some pleasant afterglow of their passing.

"We're ready to go-ohhh." This time Molly's soprano sing-song was followed by Tad's attempt from a distance to still his sister. Some things never changed.

"Molly . . . ." Mary was long suffering. "If you want to say something, come and tell me in a normal voice. Don't shout."

"Mom, I can't hear you," Molly sing-songed back. "But we're ready to go-ohhh."

"She heard you!" Tad's unquiet baritone.

"Please, both of you . . . ." She tried reason.

"What?" they cried out in unison.

Mary began to respond just loudly enough to be heard, then realized they were arguing again, distracted from their attempts to get old Mom in gear. Their voices faded away as they moved towards the kitchen. What was the use? If she called after them now, she'd be breaking her own rule again—for the umpteenth time.

Somehow the entire season had been out of sync. Usually George had all the decorations out in stacks around the living room the Friday after Thanksgiving. This year he had gone to the office that Friday and been out-of-town most of the next two weeks. Molly was in a school play that ate up more than a few evenings. Tad was away at college. Decorations sat dormant, dinners were eaten on the run, and with Tad away there just didn't seem to be the same impetus to trek into the country to cut down a tree.

Things had finally slowed long enough for George, Molly and her to race down to the Haymarket to pick out a pre-cut tree. It was beautiful, a fresh-smelling Blue Spruce. But they'd hurried through the usual Arab trader routine, thrown it on top of the van and rushed home to the next activity. The tree had gone a week on the back porch before they could even think of lights and decorations. Christmas was getting done, but that was all—getting done. No savoring the moment, no time to reminisce about past Christmases and their various adventures, no time to sit after the tree was trimmed and read even the shortest of Christmas stories. Maybe she was asking too much, but they'd enjoyed Christmas in the past and she wanted it back. Was there more to it than just the rush? She wondered.

"Come on, pumpkin, we'll be late!" Forty-five years and her mother still called her "pumpkin." And she was calling her that from the bottom of the stairs, like Tad and Molly. Her mother's voice resounded just as she was shutting the bathroom door. Not even a moment's respite for private matters.

Her mother and father had been the biggest surprise so far this Christmas. The plan had been to drive up to South Bend to see them late Christmas day. Sure, the house would seem empty on Christmas and the next morning, but by the evening when they arrived at her parents, it would be like having Christmas all over again—and at someone else's home. A small, quiet family Christmas with Molly, Tad and George on Christmas Eve—then an expanded affair with her mom and dad, sister and brother. Perfect.

Just two days before, her mother had called to announce they were on their way. Her parents had skipped the tree and outdoor decorations and now they missed them. Notre Dame had a less-than-perfect season and they didn't know the neighbors well enough anymore to party with them. The unspoken truth was that they were lonely. Long ago, she had told them there was an open-ended invitation to stay with her family forever if they liked. The guest room was theirs. There was plenty of room in their drafty old house. Except, of course, when the guest room was the repository for wrappings and gifts and any clutter that collected during the Christmas season. Now her mother had called in the offer.

Maybe it didn't sound like much, but it was. Everything in the guest room had to be transferred to the game room on the third floor. That meant that the game room had to be straightened up and her fabric put away from the last curtain-making venture. The sheets had to be washed and the carpets vacuumed and the furniture dusted. She wouldn't dream of letting her mother arrive at a messy house. The presents she'd planned on wrapping in a quiet moment before Christmas day now had to be prim and proper and under the tree by her parents' arrival. It was an unspoken rule, never recorded, but known and accepted between mother and daughter.

The guest room was only the beginning. Tad's and Molly's rooms were passable within the inner sanctum of the family foursome, but not when subjected to the scrutiny of her mother. If left as they were, the rooms would initiate an escalating series of subtle comments, then questions, then helpful suggestions, and finally outright criticism of their slovenliness. Her mother couldn't help it anymore than Tad and Molly.

Mary wondered whether she was contributing to it all by over-reacting. Probably, but if that was their way, she didn't have to feel guilty about her own neuroses. The worst part was that every time she got the bedrooms halfway neat and tidy, an unspoken conspiracy went into effect. Tad and Molly could undo in twenty minutes what it took her two hours to accomplish. George was an accessory by leaving his shoes, newspapers, coat, tie and even his drink glasses scattered around the house, diverting her attention long enough to permit Tad and Molly to do their damage. Over and over, hour after hour, day after day the pattern was repeated.

She had to smile in spite of herself. It would have been bearable if she and George had just been around the house during the past two weeks. Not this year. Ten years' worth of open houses, cocktail parties, church caroling, holiday concerts and Christmas plays and musicals had mysteriously appeared on the monthly calendar, transforming it and their lives into a chronology of disorder. The year before, she'd actually wondered out-loud whether they had become the Christmas pariahs. Their social dance card was empty.

Had they committed some subtle and barely-whispered-about faux pas?

"Do you think it was something I did?" George had asked innocently the year before. She had smiled. A fanciful thought had flitted through her mind and she had embellished it slightly.

"Not everyone remembers Bing Crosby, so your imitation . . . "

"That wasn't an imitation. That's how I sing *White Christmas*."

"I see. Well, you were the only one who slid your notes on 'bri . . . iiii . . . ght' and then added, 'buh, buh, buh, buh . . . ' after the beginning lyrics."

"That's how I learned it!"

"Well, truth is, you sing it pretty well, so it must be something else *you* did, 'cause I know it wasn't me." They had both laughed and enjoyed the time at home.

This year they had enjoyed the time away from home, but it had worn her out. Parties, plays and concerts were only the social part of it. Shopping and baking and Christmas cards kept her up every night until midnight or later, and she was notorious for needing her sleep. Now, just when all of the activity was supposed to be winding down, there was a Christmas Eve service.

"Honey, we'll be late." Now George was standing outside the bathroom door. She hadn't even heard his footsteps. At least he hadn't tested the echo chamber effect of the front hall.

The door opened slowly. George peeked inside. He was respectfully meek, but that irritated her even more.

"I'll be there," she said quietly, her lips set. "I'll be there."

George was right. If they waited on her they'd be late, even if they got there thirty minutes before the service began. If the family didn't leave now, they would never get seats for everyone. Years before, they had rediscovered the joy of church on Christmas Eve afternoon. They hadn't missed one since. That event, at least, had always been the one safe haven of the season. But this year was different. She simply wasn't ready to go and she wasn't even sure why.

"Go without me," she said more calmly than she felt. She was no longer wavering. Things were coming into focus. She didn't have to go. No rules dictated her attendance. They probably wouldn't miss her once they got settled and the music began. They could tell her all about it when they got back home. She could make some hot cider and tea, maybe sip on a glass of wine. It would be just fine.

"We wouldn't go without you," George laughed. His laughter died once he sensed she was serious.

"You could, you should, and you will." She went back to brushing her hair and spraying it. "I think I'm going to stay home and get things together for dinner."

"Darling. . . ." First "Honey," now "Darling." He was in fine pleading form. "We're all together this Christmas. Maybe we won't be next year."

"We've all been together for two days—and its beginning to seem like two weeks," she whispered. "I just need a little time alone. Quiet time."

Anger, guilt and relief washed over her simultaneously. She had said it. Selfish perhaps, but necessary for her own peace on earth. It felt good. Interestingly enough, instead of arguing with her, George was nodding in agreement.

She tried to read his thoughts from the look in his eyes. He wasn't upset. His eyes were open, gleaming. He wore the unbroken smile of understanding. Not lost, not smug, but understanding. How could he understand? He wasn't in charge of house functions. He didn't have to make the pieces fit. The meals, the clothes, the division of labor. If the table wasn't set or the extra groceries stocked, or the neighbors' presents wrapped, would George know what to do? She doubted it.

"You don't have to get angry," he finally said, "but I wish you'd go."

She spoke deliberately, to underscore her seriousness. This wasn't going to be another exchange in the endless exchanges of prodding and surrender. This time, she wouldn't surrender.

"I am angry. And I'm not going to say I'm sorry, and I'm not giving in again."

"Well, I don't know what you're angry about."

"You wouldn't. You wouldn't understand. You've never understood." In the deepest corner of her soul, she knew she was sweeping too broadly, cutting deeper than the moment justified, but she didn't care. Just once she was going to resist. Christmas was not going to be some cheery excuse to justify drudgery.

"Mary, you're not being reasonable."

"Don't talk to me about reasonable. I've been doing everything for everyone around here for the past month."

"Now hold on. I've been swamped with work." Now, at last, George was showing his defensive colors.

"I've been swamped too. I work too. But it's gotten done. And right now, I'm sick of it. I've cooked the meals, done the dishes, washed the clothes—then folded them. No thanks to you. And I've been damned busy."

"You shouldn't have stressed yourself out like this."

"And let it pile up instead? Not likely."

Another chorus of cries arose from downstairs. They were ready: coats on, front door open, the church service only half an hour away.

"You should have told me," his voice controlled, but strained.

"You weren't here to listen."

"I'm sorry. I had work out-of-town, but that was over two weeks ago."

"Leave without me. Go. Go before I raise my voice and let everyone know how horrible I'm being."

George smiled. She interpreted it as a smirk. Mr. Christmas refusing to be a Scrooge. "I understand." He added words to his smile. "We'll see you a little later." Then George turned and left.

For a moment she sat staring at herself in the mirror.

Christmas should be a time of peace and love, insight and contemplation. It should be religious throughout the season and not just on Christmas Eve. Instead, endless activities and mindless shopping merged to make the season a hectic nightmare. They paraded from one scheduled stop to the next. They shopped for hour after hour for the perfect gift, harder to find each succeeding Christmas.

It transformed the most symbolically perfect day into the most dreaded. Everyone already had everything: clothes, CD's, electronic gadgets, toys for little and big kids. George usually bought things for himself. Molly and Tad were impossible since they were so particular, the peculiarity of being teenagers. Santa Claus had always had it so much simpler—in most cases. Things had been better when Molly and Tad were young.

Mary put on her lipstick and applied blush to her cheeks as if she were going out. A touch of perfume and she was ready. But ready for what? The door slammed, then silence. They were all gone. George, Tad, Molly, her parents, her brother and his wife. The house was filled with quiet.

Mary turned off the bathroom light and walked downstairs. If that's how it was going to be, she'd make the best of it. Time for a glass of wine, time to sip and enjoy the opportunity for quiet. They would be back soon enough and she'd be immersed in the noise once more. The long stairway creaked as she made her way deliberately down the steps. She paused halfway down, delayed by an image from another Christmas.

When Tad was small and Molly a toddler she caught

them together on that very step and snapped their picture, both in Santa Claus pajamas. Tad was seated behind Molly. Molly had leaned backwards, her head resting in Tad's lap. They were both laughing. Mary had grabbed her camera and caught the moment. Now it was framed, sitting on a small table in the front hallway.

How could it seem so long ago? Ten years, or was it eleven? Nothing compared to the decades that marked high school reunions or wedding anniversaries or birthdays. Yet it was most of Tad's and Molly's lives. Tad and Molly thought of that picture as ancient history. They couldn't even remember when they had looked like that, let alone the evening it was taken or the Santa Claus pajamas Mary had carefully packed away for her theoretical grandchildren. How was it, when she could remember her own childhood almost forty years ago, that ten years back seemed so irretrievable for Tad and Molly?

Mary shook her head and went on to the kitchen. The wine was from a little vineyard in the Sonoma Valley, brought back by Puck Carver from a recent tour and presented to them as a Christmas gift. She picked out a piece of her best crystal and poured the light, oak-colored Chardonnay until the glass was three-quarters filled. A sniff and a quick sip. The aroma alone was relaxing. She re-corked the bottle, put it back in the fridge and meandered towards their front parlor. George had built a fire earlier in the day and it would be exquisite just to sit by the open flame and savor the peace.

The parlor glowed in the amber light of late afternoon.

Solstice had come days before. Early darkness bothered her. She loved light and its warmth. For a few moments, at least, the front room would be washed by the western exposure. Mary eased into the oversized wing chair by the fireplace. The last log added to the grate was still spitting up flames.

The tree—her tree, with all white lights and papier mâché turtle doves—began to dominate the room as the dusk grayed. In the distance, bells sounded from St. Stephen's Catholic Church. A Mass was about to begin. Down the street, the Episcopalians would be recreating a service as old as the church's English roots. Up the street, her family would be listening to the brass ensemble beginning its preliminary medley of carols.

Across the room, on a table display of her creation, the wooden nutcrackers stood guard. Mary smiled. Tad and Molly probably had no idea that their names were recorded with magic marker on the bottoms of the wooden carvings. She and George had bought one for each of them every Christmas. They splurged, buying the ones from Germany and Switzerland, avoiding the knock-offs from Asia even if they were good imitations. They were given well in advance of the day when Tad, and then Molly, would have their own homes, their own families, their own reasons for passing along remembrances to children of a future generation.

Mary allowed her eyes the luxury of wandering. She stared at every corner of the front parlor as if she hadn't seen it a thousand times. In some ways, she hadn't. It had been years since she really took the time to examine the minutiae she had collected during her marriage. On the mantelpiece was a photo of the family as it had been years before. George's father was seated in front, Paterfamilias. George's mother had died years before. Tad was on his grandfather's lap, his namesake. Molly wasn't born. George and Mary stood with Mary's brother and sister. Her brother wasn't married yet and her sister was married to Marty. Mary's parents flanked the group. All were smiling.

Things changed. George's father was dead. Molly was alive. George's hair had thinned one night right after his fortieth birthday. Mary's had turned gray, hidden with increasing frequency by the girls who did her hair. Marty and her sister had been divorced for almost eight years. Strange how at Christmas these passages were so painstakingly documented, the sadder passages more prominently, the happier one's sliding by little-noticed.

At Christmastime, the past seemed reborn. George's father's cigar smoke seemed to pervade the parlor, Marty's habit of belching after dinner recurred to her for the first time since the Christmas before. It seemed as if Tad should run squealing into the room and jump into her arms. Lives that had passed were remembered. Past times were embellished and relived. Memories were permanent and continuing, cumulative rather than exclusive.

Across the room was George's folly—the piano he'd found at a bargain price in a used furniture store downtown. It played. The sound board wasn't cracked. Once tuned, it stayed in tune, at least for awhile. There was only one problem—no one could play it. George couldn't play any instrument. He'd thought she could, but her best efforts to revive the skills she'd had at age twelve were doomed. She squeezed a chord or two out of it and nothing more. Tad and Molly refused to take lessons. George had tried to buy them both off at one time or another with no success. Christmas carols materialized around the piano only on the one or two occasions when Puck Carver came in for their Christmas open house. Puck had played weekends at a local bar and restaurant and he could perform on any piano known to man, including the one George had bought. But Puck's opportunity to make magic on George's folly were all too few.

Mary's eye emitted a tear. She wiped it away, but it returned. Playing the piano wasn't really the point, though they'd all told George it was the point several hundred times. The point was the sentiment that George had tried to convey with his folly. He wanted a point of focus, an effort they could all share at Christmas or any other time of the year. More important than his failure to make it happen was that he'd tried. Maybe she was caught in the same dilemma. Maybe her desire for peace on the earth of their household and good will between the members of her family was a similarly well-intended sentiment. Well-intended but not assured of success.

The room seemed to come alive as she noticed one detail after another. The cheap glass figurine Tad had given her when he was six. Each year she took it from its box and displayed it on the mantel. But when had she last recalled the embarrassed smile on Tad's lips when, at George's urging, he placed it in her hands on Christmas morning. "I picked it out, Mommy," he said, George behind him grinning.

And there was Molly's self-portrait from Mother's Day Out pre-school. Her stick figure arms outstretched, a smile from ear-to-ear on the round, slightly disproportionate face. "I love you, Mom," written in the mangled grammar of a four year old.

Where were these precious angels? Where had they gone? Where were the fleeting, delicate, delicious moments when their small kindnesses had transcended all other expressions of love? Why did it move so irrevocably forward? Couldn't just a little slice be frozen, never to change?

Realization suddenly invaded her ennui, understanding dissipated her anger. She wasn't upset with the present, she was irritated that it didn't sufficiently mirror the past. No one could replace George's father, no amount of maturity the exuberance of youth, no amount of family the magical dependence of small children. The Christmas rush was a spoiler, but hadn't it always been? Trudging around buying children's toys in the rain hadn't always been a picnic, but Tad and Molly's faces on Christmas morning had made up for it. Christmases past and seemingly lost were what had her down.

Mary closed her eyes and took a breath. Not the smell of cigars, but things even better. The smell of fresh-baked cookies her mother had finished not an hour before, the scented candle made in school, Tad's Old Spice—passed along from father to son. Why hadn't she noticed these before, as she was getting ready?

The same went for the church bells as they continued to play. Everything had been a constant, dull drone of voices and television and competing radio stations. Now there was George's antique clock ticking and the occasional creak of the house as the wind blew, the faint sound of someone in the neighborhood playing Christmas carols and the rustling of the last leaves left on the oak trees outside the front window. The bells sounded again from the church. The service would be beginning soon. She wondered if her friends would ask about her, question whether she was sick.

The wine just poured seemed to cleanse away her sense of being bloated with responsibility. Crunched time had nearly crushed her. There was no sense to crunching time anymore. It was almost Christmas. Anything she hadn't done, she wasn't going to do. Christmases past were just that. Why hadn't this been as obvious twenty minutes before, her house filled with present lives?

The phone rang. Like a bullet fired in the middle of the night. Her hand nearly toppled her wine glass. She caught its stem and steadied it. A second ring. Her daydreaming ended. She headed for the family room. Tad had moved the portable phone and she could hear it ringing but couldn't find it. Something was wrong. Her mother had been complaining of a headache. Mary thought stroke. Her father's eyes weren't good in the dark. He could have tripped going into the candlelight of the sanctuary. Molly was never careful at intersections. Traffic was heavy around the church before the Christmas Eve service. Mary ran to the kitchen for the other phone.

The answering machine clicked on after the second ring. Another message must have been on the phone from earlier in the afternoon. From the back hallway she heard Molly's brief, recorded directions to leave a message, then the person calling. It was George.

"Guess we missed you. Which is good. Means you're on the way down to the church." Mary started to pick up, then stopped. The strange, almost voyeur-like desire to listen in on George's conversation with the other Mary—the one not at home—overcame her, "Whatever you needed to get done at home," George paused, "hope you got it done. We love you. Every one of us. See you soon." Then the click of George hanging up. The machine turned off. The red light started blinking again to signal their recorded calls.

Mary stood in the kitchen, feeling for the first time that season the anxious, almost aching, yearning for Christmas not to pass. The rush and confusion and mindless activity were gone, but so was another year together with her ever-evolving family. How had George concluded his message: "We love you. Every one of us. See you soon." They were out of contact for the first time in weeks. That's what she had needed so urgently not a half-hour before. Now, with a single, brief monologue from her husband, a sense of separation overwhelmed her.

Her family were demanding, difficult, drawing out her demons and dismissing her own desires. But they were family. Memories of family had just provided calm and perspective on the most hectic and emotional of seasons.

They weren't perfect, but they were her family. Her mother and father were impossible at times. They were aging, no longer independent or free in their travels. They asked a lot and received a lot, but did they ask or receive any more than they had given her or that she was now willing to give to Tad and Molly? There was no way she would not be indulgent of them now. They deserved that indulgence.

Mary smiled. How noble of her to think that she was the indulgent one. The fact of the matter was that she wanted them to visit her, to stay as long as they liked, to spend time while they could with Tad and Molly, her and George. Where else would she have her parents on Christmas Eve than in her home sharing these days with the rest of her family. Not in South Bend, not off on vacation somewhere. Opening her home to them was no grand gesture, it was subtle self-interest at work. They were her fondest memories in process.

George. Other than an inconvenient work schedule, what had he really done to get her so upset? She hadn't borne the brunt of preparing for Christmas by herself. He had helped. They had both gotten rushed. Neither had the time they would have liked to celebrate the Christmas season with more contemplation and less sound and fury. But that didn't make him a bad guy. His salary paid the mortgage, provided food, clothes, school tuition, the material things they could pare away and do without, but which made life more comfortable. Work couldn't stop for the month between Thanksgiving and Christmas. And he was a good father, a good husband and a good lover. They weren't brittle and embittered with each other, living empty lives under one roof the way she knew some couples existed.

Tad and Molly weren't perfect, but in a mother's eye they were close to it. Good students, creative kids, engaging company as they passed from childhood into adulthood. They had wit and intelligence, sensitivity and grace—even if it was sometimes obscured by their bad habits. If they hadn't been born, her memories would be completely different and she had no desire for memories other than her own.

Now they were gone. No one screaming up the stairs. No one messing up wherever and whenever she straightened up. No one fussing after whatever she did—second guessing how she made the bed, cooked the meals, cleaned the house, even how she guided her high school students towards college admissions. No one to second-guess her every spousal decision. The solitude cleared her head and focused her thoughts. And it produced a longing for the good times that were happening that very moment. Good times every bit as fragile as any others she had ever enjoyed. Good times ready to disintegrate in an instant at a misspoken word or a compliment not given.

Freed of the day's expectations, rejuvenated by the twenty minutes she had allowed herself to collect the past, she was now overwhelmed by the feeling of separation from her present. Good times hadn't ended at some vague moment in the past, everyone then alive included, those dead or not yet alive, excluded. Good times weren't defined by the degree of Molly's likeness to her four-year-old fairy princess, as opposed to her present incarnation as a pre-teen pain in the neck. And they weren't dependent on Tad's willingness to be three again, cuddling in her arms as opposed to cuddling some other female in his arms. And good times had nothing to do with her youth or lack of it. Good times were what each moment allowed, if she received it.

The parlor clock struck the hour. The service was beginning. If she just sat down she could really enjoy the fire, pour a second glass of wine, turn on a Christmas CD or read one of their ten million Christmas stories. For that matter, she could take a nap. The Christmas rush was over. No more frenetic activity, no more juggling work and play, as if they were one and the same. There was no place she had to be, but now there was one place she wanted to be.

The bells were ringing again. The brass ensemble would be taking their spots in the front of the church. The pews would be filling up. That's where she wanted to be. She wanted to be with her family. She wanted to hear Tad and Molly whispering inappropriate comments about their friends from school. She wanted to see her parents fumbling through their hymnal. She wanted to feel George squirming beside her, anxious to sing another carol. She wanted to smell the greenery and the candles and her mother's perfume. She wanted to poke her brother on the shoulder, remembering when she carried him down the aisle as the baby Jesus and she, the Virgin Mary, so many Christmases before. The present was where she wanted to be, its blemishes included. Future Christmases were unknown, but the immediate future seemed terribly clear: if she was going to church, she'd better do it, knowing that she'd probably stand rather than sit through the service.

She arrived late. The congregation was already singing. Every pew seemed full to overflow. That was okay. She could watch and enjoy from a distance. She was among friends. The ushers practically embraced her. Other stragglers at the back patted her on the hand and laughed. She knew everyone and they whispered, "Merry Christmas". She looked for her family. Her eyes roved from left to right, then back again. They weren't there. Maybe something *had* happened. Then it caught her eye—the crystal on George's watch, reflecting candle light from the tapers lit at the end of every pew. She hesitated. If there wasn't a seat she didn't want to walk down the aisle. It would embarrass her and the people who realized that only by giving her their seats would she be able to sit with her family. She looked again. George was motioning to her. She shook her head. George smiled. He motioned again. She pointed and pantomimed "no seat."

Then, like a magician tapping his wand, George touched Tad and whispered something. Tad passed it along to Molly and then Molly to Mary's parents and Mary's parents to her brother and his wife. Everyone in her family, as if choreographed, shifted slightly away from the aisle. Three inches each, no more, but a place suddenly appeared where there hadn't been one seconds before. George motioned a third time and Mary hurried down the aisle and took the newly-created spot next to him.

"How did you know I'd make it?" she whispered as the congregation sang the second verse of "O Come All Ye Faithful".

"We didn't," he started to say.

"But you saved a spot for me."

"We were pretty sure you'd be here once the phone went unanswered."

"You thought I'd left?"

"No. I figured you were still at home. But if all of the hassles of Christmas still had you down, you'd have answered. We're all compulsive that way. But if you took the time to listen to the recording, then I knew you were over it."

Mary laughed at George's contorted logic, but realized he was right. Everyone was belting out the third verse. She looked down the row. Her family's eyes were trained on her, bearing an unspoken apology for their role as conspirators in the Christmas rush. It was over now, part of the past. The future was ahead and for awhile, at least, they would be together as a family. And that, Mary knew, was what mattered.

FOR THE GOOD

Rusty Warren and Carter Pitt were the two most influential lawyers in the substantially influential congregation of the First Presbyterian Church. The church itself was an influential force for good in the modestly influential city. As their position in the community dictated, they shared the common goal of the public good. Pro Bono Publico. And for years they had quietly competed for preeminence in the cause of justice. In recent years, their competition had grown to fever pitch. One and only one of them would be named Humanitarian of the Year and there would be no first runner-up.

The two counselors actually complemented each other. Rusty was short and muscular, younger appearing than a man of fifty. Carter was tall and beefy, his thinning hair giving him another decade on his forty-five years. Rusty moved quickly, darting from one spot to the next like a rabbit. Carter was a shuffler, plowing forward like a battleship. Rusty spoke in clipped, short sentences. Carter slightly slurred his words in a southern drawl. They were both bright beyond their peers, law review students who had matured, somewhat, into icons of their profession.

Their competition wasn't in the court room or the board room and certainly not in the social clubs to which they belonged. In fact, they were unabashed allies in the battle for the city's welfare. In the local bar publications, they were often recognized for their achievements. Rusty's firm was the first to dedicate two hundred hours of their associates' otherwise billable hours to community service. The article, with substantial input from the firm's Director of Marketing and Public Relations, noted that, as senior partner in charge of pro bono affairs, Rusty had thereby contributed the equivalent of forty thousand dollars to worthy efforts.

Then Carter's firm followed with the creation of a unique corporation to provide "meals on wheels" for the city's homeless. The daily newspaper ran a half-page story on the front page of the Metro section. Accompanying it were photos of Carter, standing in his firm's massive reception area with the firm's name clearly legible in foot-high brass letters in the background. Next to that photo was one of three young associates, carefully pre-selected for their racial, gender and ethnic diversity, administering a hot meal of pork tenderloin, snow peas, fresh asparagus, and a twice-baked potato to one of the downtown's most renowned panhandlers.

The next day Rusty was incensed. "What they didn't report was that the old bum wouldn't let them take his picture until they slipped him a twenty," Rusty confided to one of his partners over lunch at the club. "One of my paralegals was there and heard the whole deal come down."

"Why, Rusty," his partner patted his lips with his napkin and replaced it on his lap, "you sound a little peevish."

"Peevish!" Several fellow club members looked up. Rusty lowered his voice. "You should be peevish too. Pitt's firm gets free advertising for some half-cocked program of keeping those guys on the streets where they can hit workers up for change, while we're the first firm to start a program to pick those guys up and bring them back to the shelter where they can sober up and not freeze to death!" Again, stares.

"I see your point, Rusty. Absolutely." His partner took a sip of Perrier. "But what can we do about it?"

Rusty thought hard. Then his brow arched and his eyes intensified. "I've got it! Hot meals on wheels *and* a ride to the shelter. We underwrite a van that not only serves them, but takes them back to the shelter, out of the cold!"

"Brilliant . . . another coup, Rusty. Well done."

The plan was announced before Thanksgiving and "Meals and a Ride to the Shelter" immediately eclipsed "Meals on Wheels."

The following Sunday, after church, Carter graciously congratulated Rusty for "stepping up to the plate in a major way," then with a warm and ostentatious handshake introduced Rusty to his new friend, George Tanner, a resident of the downtown shelter. Carter went on to point out that his firm had committed to bringing a minimum of twenty-five homeless men and women to church with them each Sunday during Advent.

Inwardly, Rusty reeled, trumped again, but he kept his game face, jingling the change in his pocket. Compose, he told himself. But with the simultaneity that crashes in during the rushed but heartfelt exchange of greetings during the half-hour between church services, Rusty was suddenly pelted with words. First, his wife. "Rusty, I've got to get my robes on. Choir sings at eleven. Remember, potluck for the choir members is two weeks from Wednesday."

"Okay, darling." During the holidays their conversations took on the cadence of Morse code. She rushed off and he started to say something . . . anything, to show that Carter hadn't stunned him.

But before Rusty could catch his breath, his son was on the other side. "Dad."

"Can I catch you in a second, Buddy?"

"Gotta know now. We're doing caroling for shut-ins and nursing homes. We need drivers."

"You can take the car." Rusty turned back to Carter.

"We need drivers, Dad. We need you."

"Okay. You got me. Sign me up." His son disappeared as quickly as he had appeared.

"So . . . " Rusty groped for words, "are you from around here, George?" Not good, he immediately thought. Dumb question. Ask this poor guy something more substantive. Are the streets tough? No, that won't do. Of course, the streets are tough.

In the meantime, George was answering. Rusty's ears

seemed to tune out. The older he got, the more often words escaped him when things started happening at once. " . . . here . . . " George flapping his arm to indicate something nearby, " . . . sure looks like . . . ."

Rusty's mind instantly cavorted in a thousand directions. Damn Carter Pitt. No. That's not right. Can't damn him in church. But it's still not fair. Just once I'd like to checkmate him. Corral him and keep him there. And all the while, George kept talking. " . . . my mom . . . I wish . . . ." Then George was tearing up and Carter was patting him on the back. Rusty reached for a clean handkerchief he kept in his back pants pocket for emergencies. Carter hadn't been listening any more closely than Rusty, his own mind wandering through layers of self-congratulation at seeing his old nemesis so obviously flummoxed.

Into this chaos stepped the Reverend Ron Smithers, bringing the entire exchange to a crystal clear end with one, carefully chosen sentence. Like a wise pastor, Reverend Smithers knew his flock, their strengths, their weaknesses, and how to turn both to the common good. And so through the years he made sure that Rusty and Carter and their considerable, competitive zeal were well channeled. If Rusty was tapped to sponsor the church's efforts to find apartments for Bulgarian political refugees, then he made sure Carter was told about it, along with a careful mention of their need for jobs. If Carter chaired the committee for fairness and diversity, then Rusty soon learned that the conservative right's challenge of a new anti-discrimination ordinance called for legal representation in a counter-challenge. If Rusty was to organize a commemorative civil rights march, then Carter soon learned of its funding requirements. To each challenge, Rusty and Carter had responded beneficently. In reaching for new heights of light and glory, however, like Icarus, the Reverend Smithers was about to set things on fire.

"Gentlemen," he nodded at George Tanner. George nodded back as if they knew each other, "I wanted to make sure that you knew that First Presbyterian is one of the sponsors of the new Humanitarian of the Year award this Christmas."

"I'm gonna grab a smoke," George eased gently towards the side door of the fellowship hall. Rusty and Carter didn't notice his exit. A significant event was in the making. Like the movement of continental plates, their fates were shifting. The prize was so obvious it was everything they could do, inwardly and outwardly, to suppress their covetous thoughts.

"Well, uh," Rusty began, "that sounds like a great idea." Then realizing that his voice had cracked with eagerness, he quickly added, "And I've got to say that Carter here would have to be the first nominee." What an idiotic thing to say. But that was the only way to appear selfless. What if Ron took it to heart? His fears immediately melted as he registered what Carter was saying.

"Are you kidding? If anyone deserved an award like that it would be Rusty." Carter didn't mean it. Rusty knew that. But he had to say that to counter what Rusty had said. Call it a draw.

"Well, I think both of you are obvious choices, but the committee will have a lot of good works and good workers to consider in the next few weeks. It should be interesting." Ron smiled, then glanced at his watch, "I've got to get ready for the next service. I'm glad I caught you both together."

The moment of in-between service fellowship ended. Carter went to find George Tanner, and Rusty started looking around for his family. Rusty was still trying to digest it all, halfway to his car parked a half-block away, when he remembered that Gloria was singing in the choir and Buddy was presenting a minute for mission to urge caroling in two weeks. He turned and raced back in time to find a spot near the back of the church. A good place to meditate on what had transpired and what it would take to become the year's humanitarian.

Rusty settled into the pew, studied his program and, before the opening hymn, found himself listening to Buddy at the podium. He was delivering the pitch for remembering older members of the congregation during the shut-in caroling evening more than two weeks away. It would take more than two weeks of announcements and harping to generate much interest for that project, Rusty thought. While the church had a solid shut-in ministry, Rusty knew that Buddy's cause was lackluster and more than a little unpleasant. All of those smelly, smoky nursing homes with zoned-out-looking attendants and residents. Rusty knew. He had been head of a committee to study the Presbytery's vote to impose non-smoking rules and procedures in all affiliated nursing homes. Unpleasant places, no matter what you did. Just the same, he was proud of his son, and remembering his request for a driver, resolved that this was one grunt job he wouldn't dodge.

The Reverend Smithers stood up next. "I want to remind everyone that our own, unique Angel Tree is right outside the door to the sanctuary, in the fellowship hall." Rusty unslumped, attendant now to every word. Somehow he had missed the Angel Tree during his harried time with Carter, his homeless guest, Buddy, Gloria and the Reverend Smithers. "Our church has agreed to take on more wishes from the needy than any other congregation in the city. Maybe we've taken on more than we can handle." He looked down at Carter Pitt who sat on the front row with his guest, George. His eyes roved the sea of faces. Rusty realized he was looking for *him*. "Here . . . " he wanted to cry out, "I'm back here and ready for the challenge!" But Rusty was obscure near the back, in a wing of the vestibule where the visitors and less social types hung. Smithers continued. "But I believe that if the humanitarian spirit that drives this season prevails, we'll answer every wish on that tree."

That was it. Like a secret handshake or an encrypted passage in some ancient tome, Smithers had laid down the gauntlet. He'd even used the word "humanitarian." It was as clear as could be. The person who fulfilled the most angel wishes would be the inevitable front-runner for Humanitarian of the Year.

Rusty forced himself to remain in place rather than bolt for the back door and immediately circle back to the fellowship hall. There was a time to cough and a time to stifle it, a time to scribble notes and a time to refrain from scribbling, a time to depart the service and earn nasty stares and a time to quietly slip out while diversionary activities were taking place. It wasn't like he hadn't sat through the service once already, but Rusty knew he would have to pick the right moment.

The fidgeting began. He knew that Carter was sitting near the doors that led to the fellowship hall. He would have some key opportunities to slip out, especially when the four-year-olds-and-under were released to play before the sermon. Before that, however, was the scripture reading. Rusty studied the program. Evelyn Lovejoy was the reader. He craned his neck to see where she was. Aha! All two hundred and sixty-one pounds of Evelyn was squinched into the third row from the front. It would take at least thirty seconds for her to get up, straighten her dress, go to the microphone and clear her throat. That was the window of opportunity.

When the time came, Rusty was ready. He smiled at the person next to him, lowered his head and slid up the aisle unnoticed. The game was afoot. During moments like this Rusty felt like some green beret in the name of good . . . Special Forces for peace and justice, a true Christian soldier. His fantasies dissolved when he reached the fellowship hall. Carter Pitt was already there.

In the silence of the hall, they slowly approached the tree, like two gunslingers from the Old West. "I've got a meeting at noon. Thought I'd go ahead and pick up a card or two," Carter said slowly.

"Right. I get it. My family has plans, right after church," Rusty rejoined. "Better pick one up now before another work week gets under way."

They went about their work without further small talk. Rusty picked the first card off the tree. "A new man's winter coat. Size 44 or XL." At the foot of the tree was a sign-in sheet. Rusty scribbled his name and the number that assured anonymity of the donor on the first sheet and reached for the next card. To his right, Carter was doing the same, taking advantage of his height to snatch cards higher on the tree. Rusty opened the next card. "Woman's blouse, preferably silk, size ten." Rusty started wondering how he was going to accomplish the task of shopping, wrapping, then returning the gifts for distribution. The next two weeks at work were a bear, not to mention getting accounts receivables paid and money distributed. Those details he could address later.

They worked with feverish professionalism. Rusty felt he was ahead, but he was too busy attending to his own list to keep an accurate count of Carter's. Time raced by in what seemed like seconds, the doors leading to the sanctuary opened and a new flood of competitors entered. Fully half of them made a beeline for the tree. Rusty and Carter held their ground, pressed against the branches filled with wish cards. But as unlikely teammates in the onslaught of the amateurs, they were outnumbered. Cards disappeared from the tree quicker than Rusty could possibly count. He grabbed one after another, sometimes before another member's fingers could clamp down on it, never stopping to read the wish, knowing that Carter was doing the same somewhere off to his right. In ten minutes it was over. The tree was plucked bare. All that was left was the recording of who had claimed which number. The pages of the log disappeared as soon as they were filled, whisked eagerly away by none other than Evelyn Lovejoy, chairwoman of the project.

Rusty and Carter filled their names in for the last time and, with the crowd dispersing, faced each other down.

"You get a few cards?" Carter murmured nonchalantly.

"Oh, half a dozen or so," Rusty lied, slipping his stack of more than fifty cards in his suit pocket. "Say, where's your friend, George?"

"Oh my God, George!" Carter had left his new charge in the sanctuary. He started looking around, then saw George through the window, out on the sidewalk smoking. "Well, got to go. Have a good week."

"You too. See you around."

They departed and Rusty started looking for his family. The building was empty. He knew they wouldn't leave without him. They must have gone to the car to wait.

Rusty's guess was correct. "Where did you go right before the sermon?" his wife asked.

"Go? Oh, I remembered something I had to do, uh, leave a memo for Ron on his desk."

"Memo?"

"Yeah, nothing important. Say, do you want to go out for brunch?"

"I saw you over by the Giving Tree," his wife continued, unswayed. "You looked busy."

"Yeah," Buddy added, "you must have had a million cards in your hand . . . "

"Oh, not really, just a few . . . "

"How are you going to have time to shop for all of those gifts?" His wife bored in.

"Oh, I'll find a way. I'll find a way."

By the next morning, Rusty had found a way. There was a reason why law firms with two hundred or more lawyers could amass the troops on short notice. Orders from the top. The e-mail Rusty sent was simple, but direct, to all associates. "I have volunteered our firm's assistance in making Christmas wishes come true for the needy. Anyone in the office this morning may pick up a wish card from my secretary. I'll look forward to seeing you before noon."

In the way of a well-oiled fighting machine, the troops responded. Rusty signed out the last of the cards before eleven. The nature of the gift, the name of the lawyer and the number of the recipient had been registered by Rusty's secretary. The only disturbing part of the entire morning came as one of the second-year associates claimed one of the last cards.

"Thank you, Eva, I'm sure our firm's efforts will have a singular, positive impact on the indigent community this year."

"Well, maybe not 'singular', Mr. Warren." At five-foot-eleven, Eva towered over Rusty. Rusty found himself rising on tiptoes.

"Have a seat, Eva. Tell me what you mean."

Eva sat down and Rusty did the same, immediately leveling their eyes. "Well, I mean, my husband works over at Witt and Cummings."

"Yes?" Rusty's voice became pinched. Witt and Cummings was Carter Pitt's firm. "And?"

"Well, he called this morning to find out the best place to buy a new pair of women's Nike joggers."

Carter Pitt. His nemesis had done it again. Copied his idea and had the nerve to distribute cards without regard to matching the gender of the respective shopper and recipient. He was tempted to bring Eva into the inner circle. Maybe she could offer to take her husband's card off of his hands, then turn in the gift to Rusty. No. Bad idea. He might get caught and an accusation of gift fraud would ruin him. The Humanitarian of the Year had to be beyond reproach in every respect.

"What did you tell him?"

"The Jogger Shop, of course."

"Of course. Well, keep me posted on anything you hear." Rusty started to arise, Eva following his lead. "And keep our conversation under your hat, so to speak."

"Absolutely, Mr. Warren. I know this is sort of a contest . . . or whatever between you and Mr. Pitt."

"Well, not exactly," Rusty chortled. How could she know? Was it that obvious? "Old Carter and I like to keep up with each other's Christmas traditions. That's all."

"Right. Well, I'll let you know if I hear anything."

"Good. Good."

* * *

The next two weeks were worse than preparing a major case for mediation. He knew there was no way he could collect all of the gifts from his little helpers and deliver them to the church at one time. So four days after "Operation Wish Tree" was implemented, he issued the first of what would later be known as Warren's Words of Warning, or WWW. Get the gift. Get it right. Get it soon. And get it to Rusty's office wrapped and ready to go. The first memo worked wonders. By the end of the week, there was a steady stream of beautifully wrapped boxes which Rusty collected by his desk. At the end of every day, Rusty had one of the firm's runners transport the gifts to the church, where a dozen charities were making regular pick-ups.

"You don't think an everyday run is a bit of overkill?" his partner queried over lunch at the Club.

"Absolutely not." Rusty raised his finger for emphasis. "The first night we had a good stack going. I almost left them overnight. Luckily, I was working a little late and I noticed the night cleaning crew working outside of my office."

"And? I'm not sure I'm following you . . . "

"And I saw them getting ready to empty my trash can and do some dusting."

"And?"

"Don't you see? If I left those presents overnight, they might not all be there the next morning. And then where would we be?"

Tempted to point out that Rusty was not only unfairly

suspicious, but ironically undermining the very principle of charity which the gifts represented, his partner refrained. After all, he was Rusty's junior partner by four years and Rusty chaired the year-end compensation committee. "Good point, Rusty," he said instead. "Good point."

So day after day the gifts mounted, and for the next two Sundays Rusty and Carter outdid themselves in handshakes and smiles. The campaign was in full swing. The members of the Humanitarian of the Year selection committee were anonymous, but insider sources suggested that at least two members of the committee were also members of First Presbyterian. That meant anyone who was seen and greeted before, between or after church services could be crucial. The old war horses worked the congregation like ward healers, neither Rusty nor Carter missing an opportunity for cordiality. They knew the margin between victory and defeat was infinitesimal, capable of turning on an inflection of a word or the wink of an eye. The Christmas spirit was flowing and the season was in high gear.

"You'll be at the dinner this Wednesday?" Ron Smithers asked Rusty in the line at the back of the church after the eleven o'clock service. Rusty's smile erupted into a grin. This was the clue. Ron was letting him know the decision was made. The fix was in. "I've already checked with Carter. He offered to give me a ride. So I'll be going with him." Rusty's grin froze, then slowly drooped. "Don't forget to dust off your tuxedo and shine up those patent leathers." Ron laughed. Go ahead, Rusty thought. You can laugh. You're not on the hot spot.

The week before Christmas was always slow. Monday and Tuesday were no exception, and the waiting was agony. Rusty wished some crisis would strike. Perhaps a dispute over a trademark, thus calling for an injunction. A major suit against one of their drug company clients. One of their corporate client's CEO caught in a sexual harassment scam. Anything to take his mind off of Wednesday night. But nothing happened. People walked around the office wishing each other "Merry Christmas." Secretaries and staff wandered by to chit chat, thanking Rusty for their Christmas bonus. Partners took long lunches with old friends and associates left before six to be with their families. It was awful. Just awful. Finally Wednesday came.

Rusty was carefully laying out his tuxedo and selecting his most colorful, Christmas cummerbund when his wife dropped the first bombshell. She was hurrying around the bedroom, getting dressed. No dress shoes, no jewelry, no evening gown. Rusty knew something wasn't quite right.

"I think your black knit dress with the beaded front would look nice."

She looked up, surprised by his comment. "To go to the choir potluck?"

Rusty's usually rigid shoulders slumped. "You're not going to the Humanitarian Awards Dinner?"

"Honey, I told you weeks ago this was the annual choir potluck. Besides, once you get to the banquet and start working the crowd, you'll never miss me." She smiled and went about selecting a plaid jumper.

Rusty solemnly went about selecting his shirt studs and cuff links. Well, he thought, maybe it will be for the best. I wish she could come, but it might be a little nerve-racking for her, what with all of the tension and expectation, other wives speculating on the awards and exchanging anecdotes on how the candidates were handling the pressure. Rusty wiped a bead of sweat from his upper lip. No, it would definitely be best for her to avoid that stress.

Studs and cuff links in place, Rusty had just tied his bow when Buddy ran up the stairs and into their bedroom.

"I can't believe it!"

"Believe what?" Rusty continued the task of working the knot on his tie so that it wasn't crooked.

"Half of my people bailed. They all made excuses. So now they're not going!"

Rusty lowered his hands to his side. The tie was perfect. "Aren't going where?"

It was Buddy's turn to register surprise. "Going to visit the shut-in seniors, of course. One of the guys actually had the nerve to say it wasn't important." Buddy paused. "Say, aren't you getting sort of dressed up?"

Rusty felt a slight wave of nausea. His mouth turned to tack cloth. "Why shouldn't I be getting dressed up?"

"Well, I mean, no reason I guess. It's just that you look sorta like a professional singer or waiter or something with the tux and all."

Rusty slowly rubbed his hands together. "Tonight's your visit and caroling with shut-ins." It was a statement, but more like a question that Rusty hoped Buddy would answer in the negative. Rusty's usual baritone had reverted to puberty.

"And you're one of my last drivers."

"Gloria!" Rusty called out. "I guess you're driving?"

Gloria was just putting on her shoes. "You know I can't." She had listened to every word of their exchange.

Rusty stared at his watch as if doing so with sufficient intensity would cause the hands to freeze, or better, fly backwards. It was almost six. Cocktails were at seven. Rusty's plan had been to watch the news, read the paper, maybe have a glass of wine, and get there early. Dinner was at eight, awards around nine. Then he stared at Buddy and Buddy stared back. Buddy wasn't sure what other plans were about to prompt his father's desertion, but he could sense it coming. Rusty swallowed hard, more than a little short on saliva. His mind raced to find a solution. There was only one.

"Where are your drivers and teams meeting?"

"Here," Buddy answered.

"When?" Rusty was shifting from relaxed humanitarian into Def Com Alert.

"In about five minutes."

"Do you have the list of where you're going?"

"Well, yeah."

"And what's the plan?"

"The plan?"

"What are you going to do at the nursing homes?"

"Well, visit our church members, give them a candy cane and sing a carol or two."

"May I see the list?"

"Well, sure," Buddy handed his father the list of stops. Rusty tore down the front stairs to his desk in the downstairs study. "Say, where are you going?" Buddy cried after him.

"I'm getting a map," Rusty called back. "We can't afford to get lost."

"We won't get lost."

"Trust me," Rusty held his county map upwards, "tonight . . . we could get lost. Time is of the essence. We can't take any chances."

Before Buddy could protest, the door bell rang. The troops were amassing. Red with imminent embarrassment, he led them into the dining room. Rusty had the county map spread across the table. Within moments they had all arrived, noticed how strangely Rusty was dressed and eased into the patronizing smiles Buddy had dreaded.

"All right," Rusty began, "you have twelve stops to make, thirty or so senior citizens to visit, and let's see . . . " Rusty did a quick head count, "eight, nine including myself, volunteers." He walked to the head of the dining room table. Smirks and scoffs were transforming into guarded respect. The mere recitation of statistics suggested a mastery of the situation lacking amongst the teenagers. "We'll divide the county into three sectors. Here," Rusty stabbed the map, "here . . . and here."

"Three of us in each group?" Buddy found himself surprisingly engaged in his father's rendition of Eisenhower before D-Day.

"Exactly."

"Which is good, because we only have three drivers and cars," Buddy added.

"Buddy, you take two of your friends and cover the north and east. Kyle," Buddy's best friend looked up with the shock of any foot soldier singled out by the high command, "you take the west with your two and I'll take my crew east and south."

He checked his watch. It was now six. Plan A—cocktails at seven—was history. Plan B was in full swing: complete the visits by seven forty-five, go straight downtown from the final stop and make dinner shortly after eight.

"Okay . . . does each group have a cell phone?" The little army looked at each other with a lost sheep shyness and Rusty finally received an acknowledgment from each group that they had at least one cell phone between them. "Exchange numbers on a sheet of paper. Each group needs a number for the other two groups."

As they wrote down phone numbers or swore to Rusty that they were already stored in "memory" Rusty divided up the nursing homes. His command of locale and geography was impressive, even to Buddy's friends. By now, they were all following his lead. After all, he was wearing the tuxedo.

"Now, Buddy, when it gets to be around seven-thirty, I want you to call me on your cell, confirm that I'm at Spring Hope Nursing Home on Beauregard Lane and meet me there. You'll need to take over my two charges here and get them home. I'll head on down to my dinner."

"I understand, Dad," Buddy smiled. Rusty paused.

There was something about how Buddy said "Dad" that sounded different, better than it had for a long time.

In a matter of minutes, they had dispersed. Rusty checked his watch. Six ten. Eighteen ten, military. Each group would have to cover four stops in a little less than an hour and a half. It could be done, but not with any time to spare.

Rusty took to the expressway, immediately breaking the speed limit and producing fearful silence and awe from the fifteen year olds who knew him only as a short man in a tuxedo. Rusty's mind was all business, clicking off coordinates, exits, main streets, secondary streets and, most importantly, short-cuts. His passengers' first audible breath was heard as they turned down an obscure lane and slowly approached the Manor House. In the dark, the dimly-lit nursing home could have been a terrorist installation or a recycling center. It wasn't very welcoming, but a sign on a post confirmed that it was the right place. He pulled the car over and parked. Rusty checked his watch. Six twenty. Not bad.

"Yes, who is it?" Rusty had pushed the front door intercom button three times in rapid succession. Calm down, he told himself. Haste makes waste.

"A group," Rusty almost corrected himself. Three was hardly a group. Oh well, he thought, "from First Presbyterian Church. I think you were expecting us."

Silence. After a few seconds, the door opened. A tall, older woman calmly assessed her night visitors. She looked at Rusty's suit. "I don't think the magic show is until tomorrow night."

Rusty held his tongue. "I have a banquet after this. We're here to visit . . . " and he read off the names of his church members.

"Oh, yes, I do remember now. I think they're expecting you. Please follow me."

Suddenly Rusty and company were following rather than leading. Down one hall, turn right, down another, turn left, past the back sliding doors that led to the backyard. The sheen of fluorescent lighting on polished linoleum was making him woozy. But the threesome held ranks and, after passing through one more set of swinging doors, their hostess stopped.

"There we are . . . all waiting for you."

Three ancient ladies and a man somewhat younger were sitting around a television set watching *Wheel of Fortune*. They looked up. Rusty suddenly realized that Plan B didn't include what he was going to say.

"Hi, everybody." One of the girls broke the silence. "We miss you guys a lot at First Presbyterian and thought it would be fun to drop by and wish you a Merry Christmas."

"Yes, we'd sure like to see you at church . . . " Rusty mimicked.

"I know you," the youngest of the ladies interrupted him. "You're Russell Warren . . . Robert's little boy. I'm Mary Ward. I taught you in fifth grade Sunday school."

"Mrs. Ward!" Rusty neared her and grabbed her by the hand. "It has been so long. I can't believe it."

"Thought she was dead, didn't you?" the old man barked.

"Well, I, uh," Rusty fumbled, having thought exactly that.

"And if you'd really like to see us at church you'd pick us up and take us once in awhile," the old man continued.

"Oh, Fred, just forget it." Mary Ward shook her head. "If he doesn't get his medication at night, he's a real bear."

"I'll say," the oldest of the ladies perked up.

"Now you're ganging up on me," Fred grumbled.

"We're not ganging up on you," one of Rusty's girls giggled. "You remind me of my boyfriend." Fred's frown immediately melted into a buttery smile.

"And you remind me of my granddaughter . . . who graduated from Virginia, *summa cum laude* . . . "

"Oh, Lord, not again," the third lady moaned.

For another ten minutes the chatter continued, Pat and Vanna forgotten in the stimulation of laughter and teasing. Then, without the need for prompting or inching away, it was time to leave. They all knew it.

"Well," Rusty said, "we want you all to have a candy cane to remember our visit, and we'll leave you with a little song."

There had been no pre-arranged song book or sheet music. Buddy had made his plans and sought help from friends without the church's formal assistance. Ron Smithers had been caught up with the Giving Tree and the banquet and there was only so much one person could negotiate. The committee in charge of shut-ins had met last in October.

The lack of printed words wasn't going to stop Rusty Warren. "Let's all sing O *Come All Ye Faithful*," he said, and they did exactly that, including the four residents who knew the words at least as well as the fifteen-year-old girls. Then the girls recommended *Jingle Bells*, which seemed like a nice upbeat choice, and Mary Ward herself suggested they wrap it up with one verse of *Silent Night*.

Once the front door closed behind them, Rusty checked his watch again. Six thirty-five. On schedule. The next stop was only a few miles away. Rusty jumped in the car and turned on the radio. *Run, Run, Rudolph*. Now, he thought with a smile, Chuck Berry could have really livened up the nursing home. The girls were giggling in the back seat, obviously relieved not to be speeding down the expressway in the left-hand lane. All was looking up in the world.

The next two stops were as different from the Manor House as they were from each other. The second home had only one church member and she was very old. She held their hands and accepted their candy, but it wasn't clear whether she knew exactly who they were or why they were there. The third stop, in keeping with Rusty's timetable, began at seven ten.

Not only was it the liveliest, it presented Rusty and his two-girl team with the greatest challenge. The Cherokee Road Baptists had arrived five minutes before them . . . in a bus. Rusty took the scene in and nearly turned around and left. There must have been twenty or more carolers, men, women, and a few children, all dressed in matching red sweaters and Santa Claus hats. They had song books and Christmas stockings for all of the ladies and men at the nursing home and their leader even had a pitch pipe.

"Disgusting," Rusty mumbled.

"What did you say, Mr. Warren?" one of the girls asked.

"It's gusty in here . . . brrrrh . . . I wished they'd close that front door."

But they were there to visit shut-ins and Rusty persisted. They located the three Presbyterians they were supposed to visit, happily seated amongst the Baptists, Methodists, Episcopalians and heathens, enjoying the program. Rusty's plan was simple. Introduce himself and the girls, let them know they were from First Presbyterian, then join in the caroling with the Cherokee Baptists and try to meld into the crowd. Invisibility was the key. If you couldn't beat 'em, and that was obviously the case, thoroughly join them. Being of good cheer, and thinking by his dress Rusty was the minister of music, the Baptists didn't complain, though a few were seen to snicker.

Downtown, Carter Pitt continued to make small talk, though given his girth, nothing was small about Carter when holding forth in a crowd. Even while he chatted about an endless list of worthy projects, his eyes slowly roamed the reception room where the cocktail hour was proceeding. The crystal chandeliers overhead created pockets of intense brightness where anyone standing within was visible with exacting detail. Yet they also allowed for dark corners where no features could be distinguished. Rusty Warren must be in one of those pockets of darkness, he thought. Hiding away with some scheme to achieve one-upmanship. The glitter of the lights, the sparkle of the ladies' jewelry and the sheen from a sea of black tuxedos made the evening more memorable than Carter could have imagined. But where was Warren? He was up to something and Carter couldn't truly relax until he knew. One thing was certain—when Carter's associates left the office and swung by the Mission, picked up his homeless friend, George, and brought him back for the awards presentation, Rusty Warren would be crestfallen. The ultimate coup!

Rusty checked his watch. Seven thirty. He was running behind schedule, but not so much that the evening was in jeopardy. He almost missed the Spring Hope Nursing Home turn-off as he found himself speeding down Beauregard Lane. The sign appeared on the other side of a sharp bend. He braked hard, turned sharply and, with wheels squealing, pulled up under the portico front entrance. His cell phone rang. Rusty flipped it open and pushed "send."

"Talk to me," he said.

"We're on our way, Dad."

"Made all of your stops?"

"All done." Buddy paused. For a moment, Rusty thought they'd lost connection.

"Dad."

"Yeah."

"Thanks a lot for helping tonight."

"Thanks a lot for including me, Buddy. Best two hours I've spent in a long time."

"We're on our way."

Rusty pushed "end" and slipped the phone into his pocket. This was it. The last visit. In, out, and on their way.

The door opened. Rusty had the routine down pat. By now he had entrusted his list to the girls. He looked around while they handled the formalities of the "who we are and why we're here." The pleasant lady with a tight perm hesitated for a moment, then remembered their appointment.

"Ginny's back in the smoking area waiting for you."

Rusty smiled politely. Could they never break these people of the habit. Oh well, he thought, plenty of time to clear my lungs when we get outside again. But what about my tux? It will reek. The lady was escorting them through a set of doors and Rusty had no choice. Follow. Every military operation had its dirty side.

The room was not only smoky, but hot. And even through the smoke, the familiar odor of nursing home antiseptic was pervasive. For an instant he couldn't decide which odor was worse.

"Ginny, your visitors are here."

The woman sitting by herself at the table looked up from a book she was reading, removed her reading glasses and stubbed out her cigarette.

"Well . . . " she caught a breath, "come on in and have a seat." Her gravelly voice was nevertheless friendly. "You all are from the church. Glad you could drop by," she sucked in air. "I've been looking forward to this."

"Well, we're glad to be here," Rusty made quick introductions.

"I remember your face. I haven't been back at the church for more than fifteen years. Wasn't the best attendee when I went. But I remember you were always active. Happy to see you're still at it."

"Well, thanks." Rusty tried to place her face. It wasn't an immense congregation, just influential, but one couldn't remember everyone. The odd thing was that Ginny wasn't that old. Seventy or so, give or take a few years, he thought. Not your average nursing home resident. "We're just here to wish you a Merry Christmas, bring a little candy and cheer . . . " The girls presented their candy cane.

"Thanks, I love peppermint."

" . . . and to sing a carol or two."

"Well," Ginny laughed, "I'm not much of an audience." She looked at Rusty and winked. "But the three of you aren't exactly the Mormon Tabernacle Choir," she started chuckling and broke into a coughing spell.

"You okay?" One of the girls asked.

"Just a cold. Just a cold."

Rusty wondered. It sounded more like emphysema. Probably was, the miracle being that she was still breathing at all.

"*The First Noel*," Rusty suggested. The girls took their cue and they started singing. Since their first, unrehearsed performance more than an hour before, the trio had improved. Rusty had even begun to push the envelope with a few Bing Crosby-like dips and croons. Out of the corner of his eye, he saw Buddy and his two male team members walking through the door. It was all coming together. Their timing was perfect, their execution exquisite, and they had joined them before the carol was finished. The three boys joined Rusty and the girls and the choir became impressive.

"Ginny, this is my son, Buddy, and two of his friends. They've been out visiting other church members."

Ginny's eyes grew teary. Her breath seemed to catch and Rusty felt sudden panic. Three years before he had chaired a program to train his firm in CPR. Given time constraints and scheduling problems, he had never been able to make the classes himself. What would he do if this was a heart attack of some sort? Mouth-to-mouth resuscitation wasn't an attractive prospect.

"Are you okay?" Rusty looked around for an attendant.

"I'm fine . . . " gulping air, "I'm fine. Really. Sing another carol. I was just thinking about my son. He used to sing in the church choir. I'm fine."

"Okay. Good. Well then," Rusty wanted something upbeat, "*Rudolph the Red-Nosed Reindeer*," he blurted. Not a choice from the Presbyterian hymnal, but then, as church emissaries, they were as unorthodox as any committee Rusty had ever served upon.

They started up, sang with gusto and given the simplicity of the lyrics, made it through without a hitch. Towards "Then one frosty Christmas Eve . . . " Rusty snuck a peek at his watch. Seven fifty-five. The evening was slipping away and they were off schedule. Time to move along.

"Well, Ginny, it was great getting to know you. But we need to get along."

"I understand. You're a lot like my late husband," Ginny shook her head, laughing, "Always had somewhere to go. Well, thanks for coming. It was great. Come back sometime. I'm not going anywhere," she laughed again.

"Bye." Rusty grinned.

"Bye, ma'am." Everyone wished her well and the two teams, minus Rusty and Buddy, started shuffling for the exit.

"Well, have a Merry Christmas, Ginny. We'll come back and visit again sometime." Rusty nodded and started to turn.

Buddy paused. He had been thinking about her comment a few moments before.

"So does your son, uh, live around here?"

Rusty halted, pushing his sleeve back to scrutinize his watch. Eight o'clock. Hardly the time for Buddy to pursue Ginny's family tree.

Ginny hesitated, then answered. "He lives somewhere around here. I'm not sure where. We sort of fell out a few years back, after his father died. I wasn't easy to live with back then and Georgie started drinking. But anyway . . . it was good seeing you, Buddy."

"Gee, I'm sorry. But I hope you have a Merry Christmas anyway." Buddy turned, colliding with Rusty who had also turned, now staring back at Ginny, still sitting at her table.

"I'm not sure I ever formally introduced myself," Rusty said. "I'm Rusty Warren . . . "

"Oh, that's okay," she lowered the cigarette she had started to light, "my name's Virginia Tanner. Ginny. It was nice meeting you. Give my best to everyone at the church."

"Yes. Yes, I'll be sure to do that," Rusty started to back slowly away, "I will for sure." Then he walked with Buddy back to the front door. The cold air hit them and together now, father and son, they took a deep breath.

"That name sure sounds familiar," Buddy said. Rusty was silent. Since they had left Ginny Tanner with her book and cigarette, he also remembered where he had heard her name before. The fellowship hall. Noise everywhere. His wife, his son, images of Carter Pitt and his latest *pro bono* efforts. And the guy from the shelter Carter had randomly dragged to church—George Tanner.

"Say, Dad, is something wrong?"

Rusty looked at his watch. Eight ten. Dinner had begun. He could practically taste the Waldorf salad the hotel always served. Downtown was fifteen or twenty minutes away. He could register all of this Tanner information away, talk to the director at the Mission Shelter, find out more about George and his story. Maybe he was schizophrenic, or even psychotic. One never knew with those guys. There was plenty of time another day.

"Wrong? No. Nothing's wrong. If you can give the kids a ride, I'll see you later, back home."

"Okay, great," Buddy started towards his four fellow visitors standing in the parking lot.

"Damn it," Rusty said. Buddy spun around. "Damn it," Rusty repeated.

Buddy smiled. "You can't help yourself, can you, Dad?"

"What?"

"You're not going to wait are you?"

Rusty looked at his son out of the corner of his eye. Buddy had put two and two together as well. And then son had read father's mind.

Rusty shook his head. "Get the kids back. Then, if you have a little time this evening, meet me back here in about an hour. I might need some help."

Rusty entered the Mission Shelter just as Carter's associates were leaving their office. For possibly the first time in his life, he had the jump on Carter Pitt, but he didn't even know it. There were several residents milling around the front lobby area and for a moment Rusty wondered if he was better off just coming back another day.

"George Tanner live here?" he asked one of the more clear-eyed men who was watching the television.

"You looking for George?" A slight, balding man with glasses emerged from the next room.

"Well, yes, I am."

"I'm sorry. We haven't met. I'm the night director on

duty. You must be the lawyer who's taking George over to the banquet tonight?"

"Banquet . . . right," Rusty barely missed a beat. He could sense Carter Pitt's handiwork.

"He's over there waiting for you," the director nodded.

Rusty looked over his shoulder. George Tanner sat quietly with his hands folded on his lap, clean-shaven, hair trimmed, nicely dressed, and all ready for the banquet, or the awards portion of it to which he had been invited. He had on a decent blue blazer and a pair of khakis with a crease, a blue shirt and red-striped tie. This will do, Rusty thought. This will be just fine.

"You ready to go?" Rusty asked.

George shrugged.

"That's good enough for me," Rusty grinned. "My car's right outside the door."

Driving away from the Mission, Rusty could see the headlights of another car in his rearview mirror. The car merely took the spot Rusty had left. It wasn't following him. Carter Pitt's lackeys, he thought. Too late this time!

"What are you smiling at, mister?" George asked.

"Nothing. Nothing at all." Rusty turned the next corner, started up the ramp for the expressway and accelerated.

"I don't really want to go to any awards," George mumbled.

Rusty chuckled. "Then you won't," he said.

George turned, unsure of whether this vaguely familiar man in a tuxedo was pulling his leg.

"Can I smoke?" he finally asked.

Rusty started to lecture him, then reconsidered. "What the hell," Rusty answered, cracking the passenger's window of his Lexus. "Go for it."

Rusty checked his watch. Almost nine. Now the concern was that he'd be too late for visitor's hours at the Spring Hope. Surely they wouldn't close their doors at nine. That couldn't be. It just couldn't. Rusty gunned the Lexus to eighty, weaving in and out of traffic. Just past nine, he pulled his car in front of his spot under the portico.

"Let's get out, George. We have someone we have to see inside."

"I don't know . . . I don't know if I want to go in there."

Rusty turned to him. The clock was running and his patience was wearing. "I'm going to say this once. Get out of the car and follow me. If you don't, I'm leaving you here. Someone inside wants to see you."

Reluctant, but driven by the no-nonsense tone of Rusty's imperative, George followed him to the door. He rang it once, then twice, then a third time. Finally a voice.

"Visiting hours are over."

"No, they're not."

"Oh, yes, they are."

"Please open the door."

"We can't. The rules are we close at nine."

Rusty took a deep breath. "I have a check here for five hundred dollars to be used for employee Christmas bonuses at Spring Hope."

The door swung open. "I'm sorry," said the familiar lady in the tight perm, "I must have misunderstood. Now I remember. You were here earlier. Well, of course, you can come in."

Rusty grabbed George by the arm and pulled him across the threshold. "Is Ginny still out there?"

"I'm sure she is. She usually reads until ten or later."

"Excellent," Rusty said. "I'll be back with my contribution in a second."

With George still in tow, Rusty walked up to the doors and glanced through the crack between them. Ginny was still there. "Okay, George, I'm going to be straight with you. Your mother is waiting for you in there. I know you haven't seen each other for a long time. I know you had issues. I don't care about them and, after all of these years, you shouldn't either. Just do your best and tell her the truth . . . but for God's sake, tell her you've missed her."

"Do I have to go to the awards after this?" George asked.

Rusty wiped his hand across his mouth. "Not if you're good and go in there right now."

Rusty opened the door and George gazed through the smoky fluorescence. Ginny looked up and took her glasses off. George turned back to Rusty. Tears had formed in the crusty corners of his eyes. "Thanks, mister."

"My pleasure," Rusty said. "I'll be out here when you're ready to go."

Rusty let the door slowly close. Whatever happened during the next few minutes might be his fault, but it certainly wasn't any of his business. His last fleeting vision was of mother and son exploding into each others' arms.

"So you made it?" The voice was Buddy's.

"Well, yes, sort of."

"But not the banquet and awards."

"No." Rusty looked down at his patent leathers. "I'm sure Carter's a happy man. But you know, son," he threw his arm around Buddy's shoulders, "so am I."

Not until Rusty and Buddy arrived home just before midnight did they receive confirmation of the night's awards. Waiting up for her soldiers in bathrobe, curled up on the couch, Gloria delivered the story which had already made the eleven o'clock news: for her remarkable success with the Christmas Giving Tree, the honor of Humanitarian of the Year had been bestowed upon Evelyn Lovejoy. Rusty Warren smiled, his mind distant in thought from Carter Pitt and Evelyn Lovejoy, focused instead on the Spring Hope Nursing Home and what already seemed like a memory long past. For the Christmas good, he thought. Most definitely, for the Christmas good.

ACKNOWLEDGMENTS

Many thanks to the friends who have invited me to read these stories to various groups over the years. Particularly my lawyer buddies, Larry Ethridge and Dan Goyette, who have actually invited me for encore seasons before some tough audiences: fellow church members early on Sunday morning and convivial lawyers after an otherwise satisfying cocktail and dinner hour. Only a few from either group dozed—you know who you are!

I am indebted to Charles Bracelen Flood, one of my oldest and dearest friends, whose literary accomplishments continue to astound and whose author's eye is ever perceptive. Small volume books like this one would not be possible were it not for my colleague in the law and pioneer in a new wave of memorable publications, Carol Butler. Thanks, Carol. And for my long-time and sad-to-say long distance friends, Anne Blackford and Steve Vinsavich, who always ask what's new from my pen and are always eager to support the cause.

Many of us have enjoyed the acquaintance of an older

mentor, by whose guidance we have been inspired, though we may not have known them intimately. Two men who served in that capacity for me were Barry Bingham, Sr., who generally supported my writing and once helped produce a play I had written; and Frank Capra, the director, who once corresponded with me: " . . . writing does not happen instantaneously, like a bulb that lights over your head. Writing is to practice like a marathon runner, he must run and run and run—which means write and write and write . . . The will to write comes from within, and only the writer himself knows when he has satisfied that hunger for good writing."

Finally, love and thanks to my family, for putting up with the many hours when I was distracted in my study. To my daughter, Jennie, whose lipstick like Lindsay's will always be remembered and through many Christmases since has further inspired her father by her often heroic efforts to return home for the Holidays from all around the world; and to my son, John—fictionalized in a number of stories—whose understanding of my quirks and eccentricities is exceeded only by his sensitivity to the human condition and his own love of the Christmas season, my never-ending love. (Both of my children's talents as writers far exceed their father's.) And, of course, to my wife of over 27 years, Carol, whose criticism is always direct and on the money, whose editing is always precise and appropriate and whose loving support is never failing, more love than I can ever adequately express.

ABOUT THE ILLUSTRATOR

PASCALLE BALLARD grew up in the woods of southern Indiana, drawing pictures and making costumes that she imagined in the stories she read. Not a lot has changed, except now she has a BFA from Indiana University and a fierce case of wanderlust.

ABOUT THE AUTHOR

GERALD R. TONER has practiced law for 35 years, specializing in the defense of Kentucky's medical community. He is a graduate of Harvard College and Vanderbilt School of Law. His short fiction has appeared in *The Saturday Evening Post*, *Redbook*, *Ladies Home Journal*, and Louisville's *Courier-Journal*. He is the author of three Christmas volumes: *Lipstick Like Lindsay's and Other Christmas Stories*, *Whittlesworth Comes to Christmas*, and *Holly Day's Café and Other Christmas Stories*, as well as a radio adaptation of *The Christmas Visitation*. He spearheaded the Kentucky Bar Association's Oral History Project, culminating in the publication of *Kentucky Lawyers Speak*, co-edited with Professor Les Abramson of the University of Louisville School of Law. His stories have been included in the collections *Savory Memories* and *Christmas in My Heart*. He lives in Louisville with his wife, Carol, where they have raised Jennie and John—now experienced world travelers.